The Order of Time

Scott P. Southall

ISBN: 978-0-6486954-0-0

Any references to historical events, real people, or real places are used fictitiously. Names, characters, and places are the product of the author's imagination.

Printed by Ingram Lightning Source in the United States of America

First printing edition 2020.

Seaview Press Holdings

www.scottpsouthall.com

Thank you to my beautiful and amazing wife Kylie for inspiring, encouraging, and loving me in equal parts. I couldn't have made this journey without you.

Chapter 1

Anastasia and Edward watched as the afternoon sunlight reflected brilliantly off the building's golden dome. In centuries past it could have served as a beacon, calling out to those seeking knowledge or answers to mysteries unsolved. While they had been here more than a hundred times, the beauty of this magnificent neoclassical building always took Anastasia's breath away. Edward said it reminded him of a temple from ancient Greece. Inside the Smithsonian Museum of Natural History lay some of the greatest treasures in the history of the world. Those treasures were waiting, just for them, to be discovered.

They walked up the sandstone steps, dodging a family of tourists wearing T-shirts that said "Don't blame me. I voted for the other guy!", and in through the front entrance of the Smithsonian. Anastasia paused as she undid her hair tie and shook out her dark brown ponytail. Her long, naturally curly hair was like a shiny mane outlining her olive complexion. She was the complete opposite of Edward's straight, blond hair and pale skin. Most people couldn't believe they were twins as they were actually nothing alike in looks or almost anything else. She was dark where he was light. She loved math and science and he loved history and art. She was athletic and he was the opposite of athletic. Despite this, they were inseparable.

Edward turned to Anastasia and smiled as they entered the museum. "Where do you think we'll find Dr. G. today?"

Anastasia hesitated for a moment in front of Henry, the enormous African elephant that dominated the inside of the soaring rotunda. He was fourteen feet tall and reminded her that elephants were the largest animals that walked the earth today by a long shot.

Before she could answer her eleven-year-old twin's question, Anastasia's train of thought was hijacked by the scene unfolding in slow motion right in front of them. Out of the corner of her eye Anastasia saw a man burst from the recesses of the left stairwell at the back of the rotunda. As her focus shifted, she noticed that there was something strange about the man. He was dressed

1

from head to foot in gleaming black. He wore a shiny, black shirt made of silk with sleeves that billowed below the cuff. His tight, black pants were tucked into his polished, knee-high, black boots and his black cape fluttered through the air behind him as he ran. His dark hair was long and slicked back. His skin was deeply tanned with a raised purple scar that started at the corner of his right eye and disappeared into his long beard. He moved athletically like someone used to action. It struck Anastasia that the man looked like a pirate from the past, like Blackbeard. He even had a sword attached to his wide, brass-buckled belt. *Has the Smithsonian started a Pirates of the Caribbean exhibit?* she wondered in that split second.

A fraction of a second later, it dawned on Anastasia that he was running straight toward them, his eyes filled with malice and lips curled in a snarl. The hair on the back of her neck stood on end as her brain registered the danger. Her alarm deepened further as the man reached across his body for the golden hilt of the sword on his belt. She turned her head and realized that Edward hadn't even seen Blackbeard yet. Her twin was off in Edward world, whistling to himself. Just as her lips parted to tell Edward to run, a large blur of blue and white crashed into the man like a Mack Truck, making a loud crunching noise before the man in black toppled to the marble floor.

"What the heck was that?" Edward asked his eyes wide, clearly startled.

"I think that man was running toward us," Anastasia said as her heart thumped wildly within her chest. She turned her attention back to the tangle of arms and legs on the ground, uncertain of what had just happened.

A familiar face looked up from the ground. The blur of blue and white had been DJ, a former linebacker at the University of Maryland and now a security guard at the Smithsonian. He was 250 pounds of muscle. Not surprisingly, the other man didn't appear to be moving.

The noise in the rotunda stopped as all eyes turned to investigate the commotion. Anastasia felt a hand on her shoulder, which caused her to jump. "Don't worry, kids, the police are on their way. We have been watching this fruitcake Zorro look-alike for the last hour," a calm voice reassured them. It was James, another one of the security guards at the Smithsonian. He was an older man, older than their parents. His gray hair and mustache were evidence that his own children were fully grown. His kind, green eyes were focused on the two of them.

"But who is he and why was he running toward us?" Anastasia asked with her heart still racing and her mind trying to process what was going on.

"He's been skulking back in that staircase for the last hour or so watching everyone as they come through the entrance. DJ's just been waiting to put a hurt on that loser. We didn't realize he had a sword though," James said shaking his head angrily.

"He had a what?" Edward squeaked as what little color he had drained from his face.

"Don't worry, Edward, I am sure it's a fake. He's probably just a pirate version of those renaissance festival freaks," James said reassuringly.

Anastasia watched as DJ roughly flipped the man facedown on the floor and pinned his hands together behind his back with a plastic zip tie. Another member of the security team spoke loudly and calmly as he addressed the crowd. "Nothing to worry about folks. Everything is under control. Please keep moving and enjoy your day here at the Smithsonian Museum of Natural History."

"Don't worry kids. We'll take it from here," James said, gently nudging the two of them toward the staircase on the right side of the rotunda. "I imagine Dr. Gregorian will be waiting for you kids anyway."

"Yeah. We texted him when we got off the bus. We're supposed to meet him upstairs." Edward said anxiously while eyeing the man DJ had pinned to the ground.

James joined his security team as they hustled the man toward the discreet door to the security office. Just as they passed in front of Edward and Anastasia, Blackbeard's head turned to the right and his eyes locked on them. The malevolence in his dark eyes and his ugly purple scar were even more frightening up close. "This isn't over. We will find you wherever and whenever." It sent a chill right through Anastasia's heart.

"Save your big talk for the judge. You won't be going anywhere but a US penitentiary for the next seven to ten years." James said as DJ shoved their detainee toward the door.

"I am so freaking out here. That guy was totally crazy!" Edward said, shaking his head like he was trying to shake the bad memory out.

In a city as big as Washington, DC, you always ran into your share of crazy people, but this didn't seem like a random crazy person.

"Edward, I think he was looking for us. I mean for us specifically!" Anastasia said, thinking about the man and his evil eyes staring back at her.

"James said he'd been checking out everyone. He wasn't just after us. I know that was really freaky, but you have to chill out. If anyone's supposed to get all paranoid, it's me. You're supposed to be the calm one." Edward shrugged his shoulders in acknowledgment of his own faults.

Anastasia wasn't convinced that she was overreacting. *I know what Edward is saying makes sense. Why would anyone be after us? Then again, Edward didn't really see what happened. The way Blackbeard looked at us was definitely more evil than crazy.* She took a deep breath and gazed up at the three levels of gray and white marble pillars that led to the soaring ceiling of the rotunda. There were sixteen pillars on each floor laid out in a symmetrical pattern. Four groups of four pillars aligned to the four points of the compass. Anastasia exhaled, letting the air stream out of her lungs. "Alright, let's go see Dr. G." She nodded to Edward, paused for a second, and then added, "It's probably best if we don't mention the crazy guy to Mom and Dad. They'll never let us come back to see Dr. G. if they think we're not safe at the Smithsonian."

They walked up the staircase on the right at the back of the rotunda to climb to the second level. Dr. G. came into view, standing in front of the Hope Diamond, the forty-five-carat, blue diamond that had once belonged to King Louis XIV of France.

Dr. Alfred Gregorian, the curator of the Smithsonian Museum of Natural History, was impeccably dressed in a three-piece tweed suit. The gold chain from his pocket watch was visible on the front of his vest jacket. His white hair always looked like he had just walked out of a wind tunnel, and his wire-rimmed glasses framed his clear, blue eyes. He was a bit wrinkly but radiated kindness. Anastasia didn't know exactly how old Dr. G. was. Most people she knew who looked like him were retired and residents of an assisted living center like the one where she visited her Nan. That's not how Dr. G. acted though. He was always buzzing like a kid with an endless supply of curiosity and energy.

Dr. G. saw them coming and waved them over with a smile. "Thanks for texting me to let me know that you and Edward were on your way, Anastasia."

"No problem, Dr. G.," Anastasia replied, slightly more somber than her usual cheerful self. She was still trying to shake off the aftereffects of the incident downstairs. "Sorry if we're late. We kinda had a run-in with a weird and freaky guy downstairs, but James and DJ took care of it."

Dr. G.'s eyes narrowed and his forehead creased. "What kind of run-in?" he asked in a wary tone.

"This nut job dressed up as Zorro was watching people down in the rotunda. He came running at us, and DJ flattened him like a pancake! It was totally freaky. I'm so glad that DJ uses his powers for good," Edward said in a rush of words while gesturing wildly with his arms.

"A man dressed as Zorro you say?" Dr. G. asked with a hint of alarm in his voice.

"Yeah, he had the whole shiny, black Zorro outfit including a sword and a cape! He was totally nuts!" Edward said, shaking his head and twirling his finger around his ear for emphasis.

"He told us that they would find us wherever and whenever. It was really weird and scary," Anastasia said, feeling the same unease that she had felt downstairs. "He looked totally evil, Dr. G.

It's like Edward said—thank goodness DJ was there," Anastasia said as she shook her head and then bit her lip.

Dr. G. seemed frozen for a moment, his jaw clenched, before he nodded in agreement. "Thank goodness for our very large and muscular friend DJ. As you know, most of the world is comprised of good people; however, bad people have existed since the beginning of time. Please do be mindful, Anastasia and Edward, of your surroundings at all times. Also know that I will always be here to help," he said seriously with his eyes radiating concern.

"Thanks, Dr. G.," Anastasia said, feeling a little better. It always helped talking to Dr. G.

"Speaking of weird and scary stuff, did the new artifacts you were telling us about last week come in?" Edward asked hopefully.

Anastasia felt the corners of her mouth curling up. Nothing could get between Edward and history, even a crazy pirate dude. She looked at Dr. G. and saw that his face had lightened and he was also fighting off traces of a smile.

"What? You know how excited I get about these things," Edward said, nodding his head toward the security door that separated the public part of the museum from the private research wing that included Dr. G.'s office. Dr. G. smiled as he led them to the door and used the ID badge on his lanyard to buzz them through to discover the treasures that were waiting for them.

Chapter 2

The twins had first met Dr. G. almost three years ago when they were eight. They had taken a school field trip to the museum and had loved it. Edward had been taken in by the historical facts associated with each display, while Anastasia had loved how the different displays had been arranged and the sense of being taken to another time and place. After that field trip, they had gotten in the habit of going to the museum on the way home from school—luckily, admission was free. They would spend an hour wandering in a single exhibition hall and then get a soda and pretzel for a snack before they caught another bus back home to Georgetown. It was always a good day when they visited the museum; it was the twins' special place.

Anastasia would always remember their first meeting with Dr. G. very clearly. She and Edward had thought they had gotten themselves into big trouble. They had been in the *Last American Dinosaur* exhibition. Edward had been reading the information plaque next to the stegosaurus model when he'd exclaimed, "Wait a minute! That's not right at all. There were no stegosaurs in the Cretaceous period; they lived in the Jurassic period. This plaque is wrong by ninety million years!"

Anastasia had looked at her brother with raised eyebrows. "The museum is not going to be wrong. It's the Smithsonian Museum of Natural History. I'm sure they know more than a kid like you."

This had been exactly the wrong thing to say to Edward as he'd turned red with indignation and had practically shouted, "I'm telling you this exhibit is wrong, Anastasia! Stegosaurs were extinct for ninety million years before the date on this exhibit! So, as it turns out, they do not know more than a kid like me."

People had turned around to stare. Anastasia had felt the flush creeping up her neck and spreading through her cheeks. She didn't like being the center of attention.

"Be quiet, Edward. People are looking. This is not a big deal."

"It is, too, a big deal!" Edward had continued, still speaking too loudly. "Just because you're two minutes older than me doesn't mean you know more than me. I'm telling you this dinosaur display is wrong and so are you!"

Anastasia could never believe how hung up Edward was on being born second. He brought it up all the time. *It was two minutes. Get over it.*

"Is this wrong in the same way you said it was wrong for them not to call Pluto a planet anymore—like everyone else thinks it's okay except for you and a few of the geeks from the Star Wars Club?"

Just then an older man in a three-piece suit had appeared right in front of them. He had addressed them confidently with the air of someone who was used to being in charge. "What's this about an exhibit being incorrect?" the man had asked with bushy, gray eyebrows raised. He had worn a Smithsonian badge pinned to his breast pocket. "Come now, what exactly is all this fuss about? We can't have you disturbing the patrons of our fine museum."

Edward had stopped yelling. As a matter of fact, Anastasia had barely been able to hear him as he'd looked down at his shoes and said, "Well, sir, it appears that information regarding the stegosaurus might be slightly incorrect."

The man had looked Edward up and down while Edward had continued to examine his shoes with great interest. The man had then turned and looked directly at Anastasia. When she'd tried to speak, it seemed that her throat had closed over and all she had been able to manage was a squeak. She'd tucked her hair anxiously behind her ears and had started examining her own shoes, hoping that the floor might open and swallow them both before this went any further. All she had been able to think was that they were going to be arrested for disturbing the peace or they were going to be kicked out and never allowed back.

The man had then examined the display plaque. He hadn't said anything, but his wrinkled forehead had creased with concern. He had nodded and said, "Please come with me."

He'd led them to the museum café. Not only had they not gotten kicked out, they had been treated to chocolate chip cookies and milkshakes. The man had introduced himself as Dr. Gregorian, the curator of the museum. When Anastasia had asked what that meant, he'd said he was the one in charge of all the displays and making sure they were all historically correct. He had said he was incredibly thankful for them noticing the error in the stegosaurus exhibit. It had clearly been an oversight by the staff, but he had assured them that it would be corrected in the next twenty-four hours. He had given them his business card and had asked Anastasia and Edward to please keep their eyes open and make sure they let him know if they ever spotted another error. He'd said it would be very useful to have two additional pairs of sharp eyes around the place. After that day, they had seemed to keep running into Dr. G. almost every time they'd visited the Smithsonian. He was always full of amazing facts and stories. He had a way of bringing history to life that was more exciting than any movie or book you could ever read.

After passing through the door with the security reader, Dr. G. led them down a long corridor toward his office. The paint on the wall was a bland shade like cookie dough ice cream. The carpets were an uninspiring dull gray and the hallway was lit dimly by old-fashioned, phosphorescent lights attached to the ceiling. The first time Dr. G. had brought them into the drab offices, Anastasia had come to the realization that the Smithsonian spent all its money on acquiring and displaying artifacts. Dr. G. had told them that the museum hadn't been renovated since the 1980s.

They continued down the corridor, passing several other doors and several of Dr. G.'s colleagues as they walked. The men wore things like tweed jackets, bow ties, or suspenders, and the women wore outdated suits or long dresses. To be honest, most of them looked kind of pasty like they didn't spend enough time in the sun. There were more than a few pocket protectors among them. Anastasia had the distinct feeling that most of them had probably been picked on at school when they were her age. She loved science,

9

but these people seemed to radiate, "I'm a geek. Feel free to steal my lunch money." The kids at Anastasia and Edward's school, the Blake Academy, definitely weren't following these people on Instagram. It was a good thing she did mixed martial arts, because nobody was taking her lunch money.

"Excuse me, Dr. Gregorian, but there has been a terrible accident!" The words came tumbling out of the mouth of a distressed young man in a beige tweed jacket and bow tie. "The heads and tusks of the mammoth and the mastodon skeletons have been mixed up by the maintenance crew. Now I'm afraid they can't tell the difference between the two. It's a disaster!"

Dr. G. placed his hand reassuringly on the young man's shoulder. "Please take a deep breath Jeffrey. Now consider what we know about these two species. You will remember the skull of the mastodon is flatter than the mammoth, and its tusks are typically longer and less curved."

Relief spread across the young man's face. "Yes, of course. Of course. Thank you, Dr. Gregorian. I will see to it that this is resolved straight away," the young man said before happily rushing off.

At the end of the corridor, Dr. G. opened the door and they entered his office and workshop. His massive French antique desk and chair sat squarely in the center of the room. There were several wooden trunks scattered around the room and piled high with books and various artifacts from centuries past. The hardwood parquetry floors were covered in silk rugs that looked like they came directly from a Persian bazaar. The walls were covered in framed, black-and-white photographs and all sorts of old maps of countries that no longer existed. The largest trunk was made of dark brown leather with brass caps on the corners and sat between two worn, brown, leather wingback chairs and a chaise lounge. This was often where the three of them sat when Dr. G. told his stories about important items or events from history. Anastasia always felt like she had traveled to another world whenever she visited Dr. G.'s office. It was one of her favorite places.

Dr. G. strode across the office to his desk. The lamps shone brightly, illuminating a microscope, a series of magnifying glasses, journals full of notes, an old-fashioned fountain pen, and assorted knickknacks. A brown wooden crate sat open on top of the desk with straw and other packing materials peeking over the top edges. The lid of the crate and the crowbar that was used to pry it open sat next to the crate on the desk. Anastasia could feel a sense of excitement and anticipation building. While it wasn't quite like opening birthday or Christmas presents, she always felt her heart beat faster when Dr. G. had a new treasure to share with them. Dr. G. smiled and beckoned them over to the desk. "Come," he said. "This is what I wanted to show you."

Anastasia and Edward hurried over to his desk, eager to discover the contents of the crate. Dr. G. slid on a pair of white cotton gloves and reached inside the crate with both hands. He slowly withdrew a small, golden statue of a serpent with eyes made from green stones. The serpent's body was coiled and etched with feathers and small wings. It looked kind of like a dragon but not the ones in movies or fairy tales. It was more similar to the Chinese dragons you saw in parades with its reptilian head, long body, and lack of wings. It was both fierce and beautiful. Anastasia was wondering where in the world this awesome statue came from when Edward blurted out, "Quetzalcoatl! Cool!"

"Quetzalwhotal?" Anastasia asked.

Edward's face was full of wonder and joy. Wherever this thing was from, the faraway look in his eyes told her that he was already there. "He's the Serpent God of the Aztecs," Edward said without removing his gaze from the statue.

"You are correct, Edward," said Dr. G. "It is a statue of Quetzalcoatl. A very fine specimen as well."

Anastasia jumped to what she thought was the most important part. "Is that made of pure gold?"

"Yes, it is," said Dr. G. "What's more the eyes are made of jade. In ancient Mexico, jade was even rarer—and more precious—than gold."

"What did Quetzalwhositsbutt do that was so special that they made a statue for him out of gold and jade?" asked Anastasia.

"There are a few different theories as to the deity's role in Aztec life," began Dr. G. "The most notable ones are that he was the God of Wind, Knowledge, and Renewal. I was fortunate enough to spend some time at the Temple of the Feathered Serpent in Teotihuacán in central Mexico. My personal opinion is that Quetzalcoatl was actually the God of the Hurricane, which obviously included incredibly powerful winds."

Edward was slightly confused and asked, "But don't hurricanes only happen on the East Coast along the Gulf of Mexico, Dr. G.?"

"You are right that most hurricanes in Mexico do emanate from the Gulf region. However, I can assure you that there was a powerful Category 5 hurricane around 150 BC that began off the Pacific coast of Mexico. It traveled all the way inland to central Mexico."

Anastasia gasped. "Category 5 means winds of more than 156 miles per hour." She definitely watched too much of the Weather Channel.

"Exactly," said Dr. G. "It is scary, and we have meteorological warnings and news channels to provide us with updates every fifteen minutes. Think how scary that would be to a more primitive people who had no idea what was happening. The people naturally assumed this was the work of a very angry and frightening god. They built the Temple of the Feathered Serpent and sacrificed many innocent people in an attempt to appease Quetzalcoatl."

"Can I hold it?" asked Edward.

"You can both hold it, just please be very careful and put on a pair of protective cotton gloves. It is a priceless artifact."

The next forty-five minutes passed in a snap as their earlier concerns faded into the background. They were enthralled as they examined the golden god and discussed its origins and meaning. Anastasia playfully punched Edward on the shoulder and pointed at the miniature grandfather clock sitting on the mantel. It was definitely time to head home for dinner.

Edward quickly handed the small, golden statue back to Dr. G. In his rush, Edward inadvertently impaled Dr. G.'s index finger on one of Quetzalcoatl's razor-sharp, golden teeth. A red drop of blood welled on Dr. G.'s fingertip as he placed the little statue back on his desk.

"Oh no!" Edward exclaimed. "I'm really sorry, Dr. G. I didn't mean to hurt you."

"Nonsense, Edward. It is only a pinprick," Dr. G. said reassuringly. "It won't even require a Band-Aid."

Anastasia looked back at Quetzalcoatl and saw a drop of blood dangling from one of his golden fangs. The elongated base of the drop separated from the tooth and fell into the recess of the statue's open mouth. Suddenly, Anastasia saw the jade eyes of the statue change. The hard surface of the gems opened momentarily, revealing small, red pupils deep within orbs, before closing just as quickly. Anastasia gasped and looked at Dr. G. and Edward.

"What is it, Anastasia?" Dr. G. asked, his eyes searching for the cause of the concern.

"I could have sworn the statue just opened its eyes!" Anastasia said, knowing that what she was saying must sound crazy.

"Opened its eyes?" Dr. G. repeated back to her, as if confirming what she had actually said.

"It sounds even crazier when you say it back to me." Anastasia cringed, both alarmed and embarrassed. "It's just when the drop of blood fell off the tooth into the statue's mouth, I could have sworn its eyes opened just for a second."

"It swallowed the blood?" Edward's voice quavered before he quickly took a large step back from the desk.

Dr. G.'s brow furrowed speculatively for a moment as he pursed his lips. "I am quite certain it is nothing, Anastasia. It is just the events of today catching up with you. It has been fairly traumatic, and I am sure you will feel much better after a good sleep tonight," Dr. G. said and smiled reassuringly.

Anastasia nodded in agreement. That had to be it. It had been a big day. She would definitely feel better tomorrow. Although she couldn't help but notice how quickly Dr. G. put Quetzalcoatl back in his crate.

"Thanks for dropping by again to see this old man. Please come back soon, as I am going to have something really exciting to show you."

With the promise of something incredibly exciting on their next visit, Anastasia did her best to put the strange incidents of the day behind her. She said, "We promise we will, Dr. G.!"

"Thanks for having us," Edward said as they ran out the door for the bus.

Chapter 3

When they arrived home from the museum, Edward instantly knew that his day was about to get better. From the smell of it, Dad had made lamb shanks and they were just about ready. Edward pretty much loved all meats, but lamb shanks were his favorite. It was the perfect meal for Dad to cook because it was incredibly tasty and essentially required no skills whatsoever to make. The hardest part was actually getting the mashed potatoes that the lamb shanks were served on top of right. They had to be firm but soft. You also had to add the right amount of butter and milk to make it perfectly creamy. Edward hoped that Mom was doing that part tonight. He scampered down the hardwood hallway to the kitchen, for once leaving Anastasia eating his dust.

Edward entered the kitchen at top speed to see his mother, whisk in hand, stirring the mashed potatoes. *Yes!* He applied the brakes as he crossed the kitchen and managed to slow to a stop directly in front of his mother before wrapping his arms around her. "Thanks for making the mashed potatoes, Mom. You're the master of the mash!"

She hugged him back with a slightly bemused look on her face. Her long, blond hair was twirled up in a cool bun with a big, silver hair spike holding it in place. She was wearing a black jacket, black skirt, and black stiletto heels. Her work clothes were almost always black and were set off by her white gold jewelry. She wasn't a yellow gold person. Edward definitely looked like his Mom. Blond hair—check. Blue eyes—check. Fair skin—check.

"What are you saying about your dad's mashed potato skills?" his father asked while attempting to look crestfallen.

Anastasia rounded into the kitchen and said "I love you for more than mashed potatoes" as she wrapped her arms around her father.

Dad smiled and hugged her back. "Thanks, sweetie. But you do have to admit that your dad can make some mashed potatoes." He smiled and nodded his own positive affirmation. His dark, floppy bangs fell down over his eyes, forcing him to let her go with one hand to brush them back.

"Well, Dad," Anastasia said slowly, "you can definitely make mashed potatoes. I'm just not sure that anyone here likes eating them."

Now he was crestfallen. His eyes darted to Edward, looking for some type of support or male solidarity. Edward quickly looked away. He was not going anywhere near eye contact. He was a terrible liar. Dad would see through him in a heartbeat. Dad looked at Mom next.

Mom said, "Let me put this in a language you can understand, darling. You may have the supply, but there's just no demand." Tilting her head slightly to the left while explaining it to him slowly like he was slightly simple. "If you were a cook instead of an economics professor, we would be broke. Luckily you're not. So it's all okay."

Edward and Anastasia were both trying not to laugh and were failing. Edward was fighting so hard to control himself that he actually snorted. It wasn't a little snort either. It was the full-bodied kind of snort normally associated with wild pigs. It made his Mom and sister laugh even harder.

"That's just cold," his father said, shaking his head with his hands on his hips. His tall, lean frame was draped in his university professor uniform of tweed sports coat, button-down dress shirt, and khaki slacks. His skin was olive and his dark hair framed his youthful face. He was proud of the fact that he was still often mistaken for a South American graduate student.

"Okay. Now that that's out of the way," Mom said as she released him and gave Anastasia a hug as well. "Hi, darling. It's good to see you." Mom turned and looked back to include Edward as she said, "Now remember, kids, to be nice to Dad for the rest of the evening. He's got a big presentation to the dean of the business school tomorrow so we don't want to dent his self-confidence."

Having gotten control of his snorting, Edward said, "Yes, Mom. I promise I'll be extra nice." He turned around and hugged his dad and said, "You make the lamb bit of the dish really well, Dad. I'm not just saying that because Mom said to be nice."

"I know," Dad nodded ruefully. "It's because it's the one dish I make that you actually like."

Anastasia grabbed Edward and said "Let's set the table" to help change the subject.

They were soon settled down around the table, sharing the day's events with one another. They were following the tradition that their father had started a number of years ago by each sharing the best thing and the worst thing that had happened that day. As always, Dad went first in his attempt to break the ice and ensure that everyone in the family was engaged with everyone else's life.

"The best thing that happened today," Dad began, "was catching up with Father Simpson for lunch at the Tombs. He told me this amazing story about the legend of the Minotaur. It comes from Crete, which is a Greek island in the Mediterranean Sea. It's just so much more fun than some of the political machinations in the Economics Department."

"That and Father Simpson also enjoys having a beer or two with lunch. It's not like the Tombs is renowned for great food," smirked Mom.

Dad ignored the comment and kept going. "The worst part of my day was discovering that there was an anomaly in the Fed data that I am using for my latest research paper. It's unbelievable. I am going to have to fundamentally rebuild my models," he said, shaking his head.

Given Dad's focus on economics and international trade, Edward had learned by the age of nine that the Fed was the Federal Reserve Bank. The discovery that it was not the Federal Bureau of Investigation destroyed his misplaced image of his father as some sort of international crime fighter.

Unbelievably, the best part about Anastasia's day was the fact that she had decided what she was going to do for her science project. She'd already started building her radiometer, which would measure radio magnetic energy, today in class. "If I get an A on the project, I'll definitely get an A for the class. That means straight As for the quarter again," Anastasia said excitedly.

As they'd discussed earlier, Anastasia and Edward both steered clear of mentioning the crazy guy from the rotunda. They agreed that there's only so much parents can take before they completely lose it.

The worst part of Anastasia's day was that her math teacher, Mr. Brown, had let her know there weren't enough people interested to form a math club. Only one other person besides Anastasia had signed up. Mr. Brown had said that she would have to settle for having a study buddy instead of an actual club. "I can't believe how under-appreciated math has become. What if the next Einstein only needs the support of a math club to change the world?" Anastasia said without a hint of sarcasm.

Edward's best part of the day was getting to see the Quetzalcoatl statue. Nothing else was really close. The worst part of the day was a disgustingly smelly man on the bus ride home from the museum. Well aware of Edward's aversion to public transport, his parents both rolled their eyes. "Honestly, Mom and Dad," he said. "You would have been proud of us. Less resilient children would have taken the easy way out and died right there on the bus. We toughed through it and lived to tell the tale."

"You're right, son," said his dad. "Now that I think about it, wasn't surviving the bus ride with a smelly guy one of the twelve labors the gods assigned to Hercules? I am pretty sure it was."

Edward just smiled back serenely at his dad. He knew what he had survived. It was like *Man vs. Wild*. Their sarcasm just couldn't touch him. Mom shook her head and told them it was time to stack the dishes in the dishwasher and get on to their homework before bed.

Chapter 4

It was the last class of the day. Anastasia struggled to pay attention in Mr. Elderton's Biblical Studies class. She resorted to pinching herself to stay awake. Most of the class seemed to be having the same problem. The only one who wasn't on the verge of hibernation was her brother, Edward. He sat right at the front of the class and kept raising his hand to ask Mr. Elderton questions about the Old Testament as he lectured. Part of the reason he sat in the front row was because he was a little bit nearsighted; the other part was just because he was Edward. She loved her brother, but at times like this, she was amazed they came from the same gene pool. The only thing that enabled her to keep a steely grip on consciousness was the prospect of getting to see whatever Dr. G. had in store for them at the museum.

The bell rang like a defibrillator jolting them all back to life. Suddenly, the classroom was full of the happy noises of eleven-year-old chatter. Anastasia packed her backpack and looked around for Edward. He was still jabbering away with Mr. Elderton. He looked up and saw her. When they established eye contact, she nodded her head toward the door. She could actually see the imaginary light bulb turn on over his head as he realized that it was time to go to the museum. Now he was moving.

She quickly said goodbye to her friends and darted for the door. Edward was hot on her heels but had them make a quick stop at his locker to unload a voice recorder, two small glass bottles, and a spray bottle.

"What are those for?"

"Just a special project I'm working on," Edward said coyly.

"Is it your science project?"

"Something like that," Edward said with a wink but offered nothing more.

Why is everything a covert operation with him? Such a boy, she thought to herself. Then they were off again as they trotted across the school lawn. Mom always said they looked like two preppy little Sherpas toting their Blake Academy backpacks that were as big as they were. They waved to their friends as they crossed the grounds and made it to the front gates.

Soon they were on the bus. The air conditioning was working and the sun was shining. Anastasia loved the fact that the days were still warm even though the nights were starting to cool off. Soon the leaves would start to change colors. Green would turn to yellow, red, or brown. Her favorite trees were the maples, which had leaves that turned a deep red. In her mind, fall was even more beautiful than spring despite the daffodils and cherry blossoms.

They got off the bus at 10th and Constitution Avenue and hurried around to the front entrance of the museum. There were two large banners attached to the pillars on either side of the front door that advertised the political fundraising gala "A Night to Make History" later that evening. Excited to see what Dr. G. had in store for them today, they hustled through the entrance and crossed the rotunda as fast as they could without running. You could get in trouble with James and DJ for running, so Anastasia settled for a power walk and waved to them from across the room. Edward was so excited that he ran every few steps before stuttering back into a walk. He looked completely uncoordinated. Anastasia couldn't help but laugh. He looked like he was going to hurt himself. They took the stairs two at a time and headed for the restricted staff security door that led to Dr. G.'s office.

When they arrived at the door, Dr. G. wasn't there yet. Anastasia knew that Dr. G. was a busy man, so she wasn't surprised but she still felt a little impatient. Seeing whatever Dr. G. had in store for them had become Anastasia's sole, conscious focus during Biblical Studies. Edward swung his backpack off his shoulders and around to the front and pulled something out of the zipper pocket. Anastasia looked closer and saw that it was his museum security badge. Dr. G. had let them keep their badges as souvenirs from the two weeks they had spent helping him catalog a new collection a couple of summers ago. The badge had a big red *V* on one side and no picture. She looked at Edward questioningly. *Surely they don't still work. Surely he's not going to try to go in without permission from Dr. G. or another museum employee.*

Edward shrugged his shoulders and held his badge up to the black security reader on the wall. It beeped and the light flashed green. It worked. Edward turned the handle on the door and pulled it open with an impish smile.

Anastasia felt her heart race. *What is he doing?* "Don't be an idiot!" she scolded him. "Shut that door. You'll get us kicked out of here forever!"

"I wasn't . . ." Edward began, then stopped. He shut the door and looked at her sheepishly. "Okay. I just didn't want to wait any longer. I'm excited."

"I don't want to wait either, but that's not a good enough reason to destroy Dr. G.'s trust in us. Honestly, I know you're supposed to be smart, but sometimes I don't think you have a brain."

"Alright. Alright. I was wrong," her brother said. "You are such a goody two-shoes. Is there a rule that you don't follow?" Now Edward was starting to imitate a girl's voice, using a higher-pitched tone than his own speaking voice, if that was possible. "I am miss perfect pants. I love all rules and follow them all! Fun is not allowed."

Anastasia felt her temperature rising. Just because she tried to make good choices, it didn't mean she didn't know how to have fun. "Be careful, Edward. If there's a rule about not killing your brother, I'm about to break that one."

Instead of listening to her, Edward sashayed around, pretending to be a girl and saying over and over, "I just love rules!"

Just then the security door opened. Edward was so busy doing his "I just love rules" routine that he didn't see Dr. G. right away. When he did see him, he froze.

"Edward, if you have some sort of secret you want to tell me, you can. I won't judge," said Dr. G. while giving Edward a concerned look and raising his eyebrows.

Edward started to splutter, trying to explain himself, and Anastasia just cracked up. "On second thought," Dr. G. hesitated, "maybe it's better for me not to know. Everyone has their secrets."

"I don't have a secret. I was just pretending to be a girl," Edward said, his cheeks bright pink with embarrassment.

Dr. G. looked at Anastasia and said, "He just keeps digging the hole deeper, doesn't he?"

"Halfway to China by now, Dr. G.," said Anastasia, laughing, her anger long gone.

"Come on, you two. Let's get going." Dr. G. beckoned them through the door and led them down to his office. Dr. G. opened his office door, and Anastasia and Edward scooted through. They dropped their backpacks by the wingback chairs as their heads swiveled around, looking for whatever it was that Dr. G. was going to share with them. Anastasia couldn't spot anything unusual. She looked at Edward and he shook his head. She looked questioningly back at Dr. G., who was now standing behind his desk and laughed. "You two are about to burst! Don't worry, I won't keep you in suspense any longer."

Just then his cell phone rang with some sort of weird pipe organ ringtone. It was a bit creepy sounding. Dr. G. seemed startled.

"What gives with the medieval ringtone?" asked Edward.

Dr. G. pulled his cell phone out of the breast pocket of his jacket and looked at the screen. "I am going to have to take this call," he said apologetically. He wandered toward the back of his office, speaking in hushed tones.

Anastasia couldn't hear everything that was being said, just a few words here and there like "No," "Are you certain?" and "1863." Dr. G. shook his head, and his forehead was furrowed in concentration. She could tell he was worried. He finished his phone call by saying, "Give me five minutes. I will call you right back."

Then he turned to Anastasia and Edward and said, "I am really sorry. I am afraid there is a bit of an emergency and I am going to have to postpone our time today."

Anastasia was puzzled. She had never seen Dr. G. worried about anything. She wanted to fix whatever was wrong. "What can we do to help, Dr. G.?"

Dr. G.'s expression changed as the worry and tension seemed to melt away from his face. "Thank you, my dear, but please know there is nothing to worry about. Everything will be back in order by this time tomorrow. Now I must ask you and Edward to excuse me."

"Oh. Okay. Of course, Dr. G.," Anastasia said slowly.

She was confused. Dr. G. was normally one of the most easygoing people she knew. However, a minute ago he was Mr. Gloom. His forehead had been so wrinkled that he had looked like a pug. When she asked if she could help, he had changed back again. Now he seemed completely fine. Something funny was going on.

Edward grabbed Anastasia's hand and led her to the door. "Good luck, Dr. G. I hope your emergency gets fixed," Edward said. "Let us know when we should come by to visit next time." Edward practically dragged her down the hallway.

"Wait a minute," said Anastasia, pulling her hand from her brother's. "We can't just leave. There's something wrong with Dr. G."

"What are you talking about?" Edward asked. "He said everything was going to be fine by tomorrow, Anastasia. There's nothing to worry about."

Anastasia shook her head. "Sometimes you are so blind, Edward. He told us that so we wouldn't worry, not because we shouldn't be worried. I'm telling you something is really wrong." She spoke more loudly than she intended.

"He told us he needed us to leave. We're eleven years old, Anastasia. What exactly is it that we're supposed to do?"

Anastasia had no answer for that. She had been so excited when she had arrived at the museum, wondering what Dr. G. might have in store for them. Now her heart raced for a different reason. She had never seen Dr. G. worried, so that made her worried as well. This was not how today was supposed to have gone. She wished she had a punching bag to pound on until her frustration disappeared. Unfortunately, there was nothing to kick here but Edward and that would not go down well with the parental units. *He doesn't really deserve to be kicked either. He's just being a boy.*

She sighed in exasperation, and they headed for the bus stop.

23

Chapter 5

Edward and Anastasia trudged glumly through the front door like two-day-old balloons. Edward dropped his backpack in the usual spot next to the coat stand and headed for the kitchen to find a snack. A chocolate brownie might not fix his day but it certainly wasn't going to hurt it either. Halfway down the hall, he heard Anastasia exclaim, "Oh no!" He turned around to find his sister with a panicked look on her face.

"What's wrong, sis?" he asked.

"I left my backpack in Dr. G.'s office. I was so worried about him when we left, I just forgot it. My science project is in it and I need to finish it tonight. It's due tomorrow!" She looked decidedly pale as she bit her lip. Anastasia always did her homework and turned things in on time.

"What are you going to do? The museum will be closed by the time you get back. That big fundraiser thing is happening tonight," he said.

"I'll call Dr. G. I'm sure he can leave it with security," Anastasia said confidently as she pulled out her cell phone and called Dr. G.'s number.

Edward saw the confidence ebb away the longer she waited for Dr. G.'s phone to pick up. She left him a voice mail, telling him to please call her because she had left her backpack with her important science project in it in his office.

Anastasia stared at the floor, looking decidedly unhappy. "Dr. G. is probably busy working on his emergency. What if he doesn't get my message? Mr. Phipps doesn't give extensions, and that project is 25 percent of our grade. I'm going to get a C in science for the term!"

"Why don't we just ask Mom and Dad for help? They won't want you to blemish your perfect academic record," Edward said, trying to be logical.

"I can't ask Mom and Dad. They're always telling us how we have to be responsible for our things. They'll be so disappointed in me."

Edward decided to use humor to lighten the tension. "I've got it! It's not too late for us to go to the pound and get a dog."

"What does a dog have to do with anything we're talking about?" asked Anastasia incredulously.

"Well," said Edward, breaking into a smile, "then you call and tell Mr. Phipps that the dog ate your science project. Isn't that what they say in all those old TV shows?"

Anastasia gave him a look of cold fury that confirmed humor was not the right choice in this situation. He slowly backed out of striking range and apologized. "Sorry. I was just trying to lighten things up," he said, holding the palms of his hands out defensively.

Anastasia's fury seemed to harden into some sort of resolve. "I'm going to get my backpack tonight and you're going to help me. Is that clear?"

After dinner, Mom and Dad reminded them that they needed to clear the table and put the dishes in the dishwasher. It was part of their chores, which included making their beds, keeping their rooms tidy, and taking out the trash. Their parents had plans to watch a BBC special on Queen Elizabeth I and were settling in with a bottle of wine, two glasses, and popcorn. Sadly, this was excitement for Mom and Dad.

After they cleared the plates from the table, Edward and Anastasia kissed their parents and told them that they were going to go upstairs to do homework before going to bed. This of course was all a big lie. Anastasia had gone completely insane and hatched her craziest plan yet. She was making them climb out of the upstairs window and catch an Uber to the museum. They were going to sneak into the fundraiser and then break into Dr. G.'s office with Edward's security badge. Then they were probably going to jail. Edward would never last in juvenile detention. Anastasia knew mixed martial arts and would probably end up running the whole juvie gang. He, on the other hand, was an intellectual and would suffer. The pen was supposed to be mightier than the sword. Unfortunately, that was only true until they took the pen and shoved it up your nose. He was going to hyperventilate. He just knew it.

On the way upstairs from the kitchen, Anastasia unlocked their Dad's iPhone that was charging on the computer in the office. She opened up the Uber app and ordered a black car to take them to the museum and, covering her tracks, she then turned off the alerts on the phone so Dad would be none the wiser. She turned to Edward and said, "We have about three minutes until the car gets here so we'd better hurry."

Edward swallowed hard and nodded at his sister as they started up the stairs. Edward turned on the desk lamp in his bedroom and laid a couple of his textbooks out on his desk to look like he was studying and maybe just in the bathroom. It was pretty lame in terms of cover, but he was probably going to jail anyway so it really didn't matter.

He shut his door behind him as he went into Anastasia's room. She already had her window open and beckoned him over. "Alright, I'll go first. I'm going to climb down the downspout. Follow what I do. Make sure you put your weight on the metal brackets that have been hammered into the brick. If you just hold onto the pipe it could bend or break because it's only aluminum."

It was bad enough that he was going to break every one of Mom and Dad's rules to salvage his sister's science grade, but now he was just as likely to die before he even made it to their illegally-ordered Uber. Anastasia seemed to glide down the pipe in about three seconds. Edward braced himself and started to climb out of Anastasia's bedroom window. He tried to make sure that he put his feet on the metal brackets, but he couldn't see in the dark. He got nervous and gripped the pipe tighter than he was supposed to and felt it begin to bend under his hands. Fearing that he would pull the pipe off the wall and fall to his death, he lightened his grip and slid down the pipe like a rocket. He squealed as he hit the ground a lot harder than he had intended. His legs buckled and he ended up landing on his butt on the sidewalk. He lay still for a minute, making sure that everything was still in one piece. Thankfully, the drainpipe on the front corner of the house was far away from where Mom and Dad were watching television. Anastasia grabbed his hand and hauled him to his feet as the Uber approached. So far so good.

As they got near the museum, they were surprised to find a traffic jam of really nice cars and limousines. This fundraiser must be a pretty big deal. Their driver dropped them off a little way from the front of the museum. As the front entrance came into view, they saw a stream of people in ball gowns and tuxedos filing in on the red carpet. There were photographers and television cameras everywhere. Edward thought that they might be a little under-dressed.

Anastasia put her head in her hands and said, "How are we going to get my backpack? There are people everywhere. James and DJ don't work these events. We'll never get inside!"

Edward noticed a white trailer about fifty yards away. He smiled at his sister and said, "Misdirection. We'll use misdirection."

Edward felt pretty good about his plan. Sure, Anastasia was complaining. But this would work. The white trailer he'd spotted was for the entertainers and reminded him of the ones they used on movie locations. He'd watched enough Entertainment Tonight to know that.

They snuck into the trailer and found that it was full of costumes. They quickly dressed in ancient Roman outfits from head to toe to ensure that they didn't stand out. Now all they needed was the misdirection.

"I feel ridiculous," said Anastasia, looking down at her toga.

Edward looked at his sister. "You feel ridiculous? I'm wearing exactly the same dress and I'm a boy. Get over it!" Sacrifices had to be made for undercover work. He'd watched James Bond movies. "Come on. Follow my lead, Moneypenny," Edward said, putting on his best English accent. He was digging this secret agent stuff.

Edward led Anastasia toward the red carpet where the photographers were stopping glamorous couples to take pictures.

"Okay, just do what I do." Edward took Anastasia's arm and they ran up to the paparazzi and he screamed, "Oh my gawd! Kim Kardashian is in the white trailer!"

The whole place went crazy as the paparazzi and the crowd moved like a tidal wave toward the trailer. It was complete mayhem.

Edward and Anastasia made their way to the museum entrance and walked through the front door completely unnoticed.

"How do you even know who Kim Kardashian is?" Anastasia asked her brother.

"I know all about pop culture, sis. They had a special on BBC about the impact of social media on teenage buying habits, and it said that Kim Kardashian is big. Apparently, her butt broke the internet," he said earnestly.

Nobody even took notice of them as they crossed the rotunda. It was full of actors dressed in clothes from all different time periods as well as formally dressed patrons. They left the crowds as they slipped up the stairs and headed for the second floor. It was dark and a little bit scary without anyone else around as they walked through the exhibitions on the way to the staff security door. Edward reached inside his toga and pulled out the security badge. He placed it up against the security reader and the light went green. Anastasia eagerly opened the door. The backpack and an A in science class were just down the hall. Anastasia didn't waste any time heading down the long, dark, silent hallway. Edward was glad she was here. It was good to have a sister who could kick some serious butt.

"Wait up!" Edward whispered loudly after his sister as he pulled out his phone and turned the iLight on. *Why am I whispering? No one's here.* He ran down the hallway after Anastasia to Dr. G.'s office door.

Anastasia put her hand on the knob and turned it. She couldn't believe it was unlocked. Dr. G. was usually a stickler for locking his door. As the door opened, Edward shined the flashlight on the ground by the wingback chairs. Anastasia had dropped her backpack there earlier that day. There it was—right where she had left it. She ran across the office and scooped it up and hugged it like a baby.

"Thank god! I'm saved! I'm still going to Harvard."

Edward interrupted her perfect moment and said, "Remember we have to get home before Mom and Dad know we're gone."

"Right. Sorry. I was just excited to find my backpack," she said, composing herself. They started to leave when the room suddenly lit up with a strange purple light coming from under a closet door.

"Why is the closet glowing?" asked Edward, his voice trailing up an octave. "Maybe we should get out of here."

"What if Dr. G.'s in there? You know he always locks his door, but it was open tonight. Maybe he's still here. He might need our help," Anastasia said emphatically.

The light was getting brighter by the second. Now Edward could also hear a low humming noise.

"Stop being crazy, Anastasia! This is the part in the movies where you yell at the screen for the characters not to open the door. We are not going to open that door."

"I'm not being crazy. If Dr. G. is in there and needs help, we'll never forgive ourselves."

Edward looked at her pleadingly, but she wasn't giving in. His shoulders slumped in defeat. *Oh god, please don't let there be a monster or anything really scary in there.* Anastasia dragged him over to the closet door. The light pouring out around the cracks was incredibly bright and the humming was getting louder. She gripped the large, brass doorknob, took a breath, and opened the door.

For a minute, Edward was completely blinded. The purple light was so bright that he couldn't see anything. As his eyes adjusted, he saw that it wasn't a closet at all. It was a circular room without any furniture. There was a beam of white light shining straight down from the ceiling onto a large, purple gemstone. The gem was oval and set upright in a golden stand in the middle of the room.

The stand was attached to a series of gears and what looked like a mechanical clock face outlined on the floor. It wasn't a normal clock face though. It had seven or eight different hands instead of just two. The clock face was also covered in symbols that weren't numbers or Roman numerals. Edward couldn't identify them.

The purple light that had blinded him was pouring out of the gem like a purple sun. The aura that radiated out from the gem stretched seven or eight feet in all directions as it lit up the room like it was daytime. The humming noise also came from the gem. Except now it wasn't a quiet humming; it was like the noise you heard when someone turned on a giant power generator. You could actually feel the vibrations pulsating through the air. Edward wasn't sure if this contraption was space-age or medieval. He looked at Anastasia and she was looking back at him, shaking her head in wonder.

Suddenly, a black crack appeared in the middle of the purple aura. It started as a sliver but spread quickly. In a few seconds, it had expanded three feet long and a foot wide. The crack itself was the color of midnight, like a black hole. The edges of the crack continued to stretch until they were seven feet high and three feet wide. Then the edges of the crack stopped expanding and stabilized. It looked like the entrance to a cave had been carved out of the purple light. As he stared at the cave mouth, a hand holding a straight sword emerged from the darkness. He felt a scream starting to rise in his throat. He knew it. He had been right—they never should have opened the door. He was never going to make it to twelve.

The hand and sword were followed by an arm in a blue coat sleeve. Within a second, a man wearing an old-fashioned army uniform emerged. Through his rising terror, Edward recognized the blue jacket lined with brass buttons and the matching blue pants as a uniform of the Union army in the Civil War. It didn't make any sense. He was actually screaming now and backing away. The man sheathed the sword and looked up. He had glasses and gray hair. Just as Edward realized the man in the uniform was Dr. G., his heel caught on something on the floor and he tripped over backward. His arms flailed as he tried to catch himself, his mind trying to grasp what was happening. *Where did Dr. G. just come from? Why was he dressed up like that in a Civil War uniform? Was he a psycho murderer?* Then he hit his head and everything went black.

Chapter 6

When Edward finally opened his eyes, they were glassy and unfocused.

"Edward, can you hear me? Are you hurt?" Anastasia asked, bent over him.

Slowly, his eyes started to focus. Anastasia was so happy that Edward was waking up. She still didn't understand what had happened in the other room with Dr. G. She had been petrified; however, Dr. G. had said that he would explain everything later and that they needed to worry about Edward first. That made sense to Anastasia. Dr. G. had quickly retrieved an ice pack for Edward's head and had helped to gently lay him on the floor of his office.

Edward opened his mouth and groggily said, "There were two of you a minute ago. My head really hurts. Where am I?"

"You hit your head, Edward," Anastasia said. "You've been unconscious for a little while. We're still at the museum."

Suddenly, Edward's eyes shot open and he became completely alert. "Was that real? Did we get away? I was hoping that was a dream."

"Calm down, Edward. Everything's okay. We're safe." Anastasia tried to use her most soothing voice. This seemed to help put Edward at ease.

"What happened in there, Anastasia? I was so scared."

For a moment, Anastasia didn't know where to start. "I want you to stay calm, Edward. Dr. G. is here and he can explain everything."

Panic struck her brother. He sat up unsteadily and realized where they were. "Why are we still in Dr. G.'s office? He's crazy and he might be from another planet! He had a sword and he was going to kill us!"

Then he heard Dr. G.'s voice from right behind him.

"I can assure you, Edward, I have no intention of killing either you or your sister. As a matter of fact, I think I was more surprised than you were when I stepped through the portal and found you two there."

Edward turned around and saw Dr. G. sitting in a chair and smiling at him. He was still in the Civil War uniform. Edward looked like he was going to make a break for the door.

"Edward, if he was planning on killing us, we'd already be dead. Just listen to what he has to say. Trust me," said Anastasia.

"I am so sorry that I surprised you, Edward. I feel terrible for giving you both such a fright. Even worse that you hurt your head as a result. You are both very dear to me," Dr. G. said earnestly.

Edward nodded but remained silent. Anastasia decided it was time for them to understand everything now that Edward was okay.

"Dr. G., what exactly happened tonight? What was your emergency? What was the glowing gem all about, and how did you appear out of nowhere?"

Dr. G. sighed and said, "I owe you an explanation. What you saw would have been both scary and confusing." He got up from his seat and began to slowly pace around his office and then turned to face Anastasia and Edward. "What I am about to tell you is my most guarded secret. I have been sworn to secrecy. Now that you've seen, however, I am afraid that telling you two is unavoidable at this juncture." He paused as he ran his hands through his gray hair. "Telling you is no small thing. It could put the lives of many people at risk, including yourselves. While you may not be sworn to secrecy, it is a secret that must travel no further." Dr. G.'s eyes were drawn and his forehead furrowed with deep lines as Edward watched in suspense. "I am part of a secret society called the Order of Time."

"A secret what? Are you in some kind of cult?" Anastasia couldn't help but interrupt.

"No, my dear, the Order of Time is not a cult." He smiled. "It is a secret society focused on preserving the natural order of time across the history of mankind. You see, time is not fixed. It is a fluid continuum where changes to the past can create ripples of change all the way through to the present. We seek to ensure that the integrity of human history is not corrupted through unnatural changes in history."

"Are you saying that history can be changed? That someone can change the past?" Edward asked.

"Yes, Edward, the past can be changed. Even more to the point, changing the past can also change the present. The path of history is full of interdependencies. What would have happened if Columbus hadn't convinced King Ferdinand and Queen Isabella of Spain to fund an effort to find a western passage to India? What if the Roman Empire hadn't fallen? What if the Allies hadn't won World War II? All of these events had a profound effect on shaping our present."

Anastasia tried to process what Dr. G. was saying. "Do you mean that if Columbus hadn't set sail, there would be no America?"

"Well, the land that we call the United States of America would undoubtedly exist, but the construct that currently governs that land and people who live within it could be very different. Perhaps the Portuguese would have ended up discovering the Americas and, as a result, there may not have been a George Washington. If we were to follow that thread all the way to the present, none of us might exist either. Although we like to think our study of history enables us to fully understand the past, it's very hard to predict exactly what will happen in the future when the past is changed. History is a very complex system."

"So history can be rewritten? Awesome! That is totally mind-blowing!" Edward said, smiling, his eyes dancing with excitement.

"You are essentially correct, Edward. History can be rewritten by those who know how," said Dr. G. gravely.

Anastasia could feel herself slowly shaking her head. Part of her just wasn't sure she had heard him right. "What do you mean by 'know how'?" asked Anastasia. "And why would anyone want to rewrite history?"

"Allow me to start with the second part of your question first. History is written in terms of winners and losers. Wars and kingdoms lost that could have been won. Fortunes that slipped away instead of being accumulated. Power and control that faded instead of grew. There are those who would corrupt the past to change these outcomes for their own selfish reasons. Those who think only that they have been chosen to have the means and insight to rewrite time and human history. Those who do not believe in the natural order of time and the associated ebbs and flows of humanity within it. They are the sworn enemies of the Order of Time. It is our fundamental belief that their attempts to corrupt the natural order of time must be stopped. The ramifications of their actions if left unchecked could destroy both humanity and our world. They call themselves the Corsairs—the pirates of time." At that point, Dr. G. walked to Anastasia and Edward, who were both still sitting on the floor. He held his hands out to help them both to their feet. "For the first part of your question, and a number of others you have already posed, I will ask you to follow me back to the Crystal Chamber," he said as he led them back to the door they had previously mistaken for a closet and into the room that had previously glowed with purple light.

Dr. G. removed a heavy iron key from his vest pocket and inserted it into the keyhole. He turned the key and Anastasia could hear the mechanism inside moving as it unlocked the door. "As a rule, I always lock the door both when I enter the Crystal Chamber and when I exit. I forgot earlier this evening." He smiled ruefully.

The first thing Anastasia noticed when they walked through the door was that neither the room nor the large oval gemstone were glowing brightly anymore. The room was lit by four normal, wall-mounted light fixtures spaced evenly around the circular room. The floor was made of marble and the purple gemstone sat mounted in the very middle. The oval gem itself was the color of a lilac and was roughly the size of a football but less pointy on the ends. It wasn't glowing, but it seemed to be pulsing softly. The mounting mechanism was made of silvery metal with four evenly positioned prongs securing the gem. The base of the mount was surrounded by a number of stacked gears, which each had long clock-like hands attached. There were eight different levers that seemed designed to manipulate the gears. A circular band of metal about two inches wide and twelve feet in diameter was attached to the floor and surrounded the mounting mechanism. There were rings of strange metal symbols inside the metal circle that were placed in various patterns that Anastasia's mind couldn't grasp. It looked like the most complicated clock she had ever seen.

Dr. G. led them right across the marble floor full of strange metal symbols right up to the gem. "I told you that history can be rewritten by those who know how. This crystal is a Refractium Crystal. They are extremely rare. There are only twelve of them on the entire planet. The term refractium refers to the bending of light as it passes from one surface to another. The Refractium Crystal not only bends light—it also bends time."

"It bends what?" Edward asked, shaking his head as if trying to dislodge something that was blocking his ears.

"I know what I am telling you will sound incredible. Bear with me for a moment. I think I will be able to answer all your questions. If you notice the hole in the ceiling of the room, it is the end of a mirrored pipe that goes right to the roof of the museum. It is closed right now, but the pipe gathers the sun's rays either directly from the sun or as they reflect off the surface of the moon. That light is funneled into the Refractium Crystal, which bends the light to create a source of energy unlike any other source you will find on earth. That energy is what creates the intense purple light you saw earlier this evening. This energy can be focused across a number of specific vectors by these eight levers," Dr. G. said, reaching out and grasping the handles of two of the levers.

"Um, what are vectors, Dr. G.?" Anastasia asked, visually following the path from the levers to the gears and then to the hands pointing to different spots across the floor.

"A vector is essentially a direction but also a magnitude. The eight specific vectors are latitude, longitude, year, month, day, hour, minute, and second. In other words, an exact time and place within history. When the energy of the crystal is focused in this manner, it disrupts the space-time continuum and creates a portal or passage that can allow someone to travel through time."

"Come again, Dr. G.?" Anastasia just couldn't get her head around what she had just heard. "This thing does what?"

Dr. G.'s eyebrows quirked upward as he looked at her and shrugged his shoulders. "Essentially it's a time machine."

"So that's how the bad guys change history?" her brother asked with wide, questioning eyes. "They pick a point in history and use the crystal to travel back in time to change what happened?"

"Yes and no, Edward. They do use a Refractium Crystal to travel through time. Just not this Refractium Crystal. Do you remember how I said there were only twelve of these crystals on earth?" Both Edward and his sister nodded yes. "Eleven of the Refractium Crystals are in the possession of the Order of Time. The other crystal is in the hands of the Corsairs. The Corsairs use the twelfth crystal to enact their plans to defile the course of history in order to gather power and wealth." Dr. G. looked up at the mirrored pipe that funneled the sun's rays into the Refractium Crystal and ran his hands through his hair. "They have been doing so for more than a thousand years."

"So these Corsairs stole a Refractium Crystal a thousand years ago and have been causing trouble ever since?" asked Anastasia in amazement.

"Yes, Anastasia, the Order managed to lose possession of the crystal to the man who started the Corsairs. His name was Rafael Augustino and he used to be a member of the Order. He was incredibly bright and ambitious. He was admired and well-liked by everyone. Unfortunately, we didn't fully comprehend his character or his intentions. We have spent the last thousand years trying to put that genie back in the bottle. It has become the primary focus of the Order to prevent the Corsairs from achieving their ultimate goal of domination. The destruction they have tried to wreak is unspeakable."

"How exactly does the Order stop the Corsairs?" asked Anastasia as she tried to piece the puzzle together. "Do you travel back in time to stop them?"

Dr. G. patted the front of his Union military jacket. "It is the only way, Anastasia. When changes are made to the past, there is only a finite amount of time for those changes to be rectified before the ripples from those changes become reality and history is truly rewritten. Tonight I had to travel back to 1863 in Gettysburg, Pennsylvania. I had to undo some of the work of Augustino's agents to ensure that General Lee didn't successfully invade the North. The implications if the general had been successful could have been catastrophic."

"Wait a minute," said Edward. "If these guys can travel anywhere in time, how do you even know when there's something wrong? How could you have possibly known you needed to go back to 1863 and that exact moment?"

"That is a very good question, young Edward. How does the Order know where and when the Corsairs have enacted their nefarious plans?"

Anastasia saw Edward light up at the compliment. *He is such a teacher's pet.*

"Please take a look at the Refractium Crystal." Dr. G. continued. "The crystal works in two directions. When sunlight is funneled directly into the crystal, it creates a portal to the past like the one I used earlier tonight to go back to the battle of Gettysburg. In its resting state, the crystal draws and projects energy from the past and brings it to the current day. This drawing of energy is why the stone is pulsing. Through this energy, the crystal reflects the actual images from the past. This could be the actual image of George Washington crossing the Delaware River or of Napoleon's surrender or even dinosaurs walking the earth before the end of the Cretaceous period."

"You can actually see the past? The real past? So you know what Cleopatra or Jesus actually looked like?" Edward said, his eyes narrowing in disbelief.

"Yes. We know what they looked like and we also know exactly what happened at those specific points in time. If we see something from the past change, we know this is undoubtedly the work of the Corsairs."

"That sounds like a completely impossible job. How can you monitor all of history?" Anastasia said in her own state of disbelief.

"You are correct that this is a monumental job. That is the reason why many of the senior members of the Order of Time act as curators at the greatest museums around the world. Much the same as I do here at the Smithsonian. Each one of these museums also houses a Refractium Crystal. The orientation of the crystal is changed every fifteen minutes to capture different pivotal moments in history. We project these moments as actual displays within the museum. While it doesn't allow us to view every moment in time, it does allow us to sample more than a thousand key benchmarks in time each day. It provides the means to identify the ripples from an illicit change in the past. The ability to spot these changes quickly is critically important. When the Order spots a ripple, we only have twenty-four hours in current time to correct the changes in history wrought by the Corsairs before they become permanent."

"You really can't miss anything, can you? Talk about job stress," Anastasia said.

"It's not so much that it is stressful, it's just that the stakes are high for mankind and our planet. Further, even when we do identify when a change in history has occurred, it doesn't mean that we can always repair that change perfectly. Even the smallest of errors can have consequences. Like the reappearance of an extinct species such as the coelacanth you see stuffed on my office wall. In this specific case, I was lucky that my error led to the reappearance of a relatively benign species instead of a Mosasaurus or a Tyrannosaurus Rex."

Anastasia tried to process it all. All she had wanted to do was to get her backpack and science project so she could still get an A in class. This was a whole lot more than she had bargained for this evening. Dr. G. wasn't just a friendly museum curator; he was some sort of time-traveling policeman. This was what you got when you lied to your parents and snuck out of the house. *I am never going to do that again.*

"Oh my god! What time is it?" Anastasia asked, realizing that they had been at the museum for a while. They had only planned to be gone from home for a thirty-minute round trip. Now it was almost nine thirty, and they had climbed down the downspout around eight o'clock. Their parents would undoubtedly have discovered they were gone. *They are going to be so worried—and they're also going to kill us!*

Edward gulped and looked at his watch after realizing what Anastasia was thinking. "I thought we were going to get caught sneaking into the museum and would get sent to juvenile detention. I hadn't even thought about Mom and Dad catching us sneaking back in. This is going to be really bad."

Anastasia got an idea. There might be hope. "Dr. G., can we use the crystal to travel back in time to get home before Mom and Dad we're gone?" she asked.

"Anastasia, that is pure genius!" Edward shouted at the prospect of not getting killed by Mom and Dad.

But Dr. G. shook his head and looked her in the eye and said, "Anastasia, I would love to help, but the crystal is not a toy. There are serious implications associated with using the crystal to travel through time. There is also a more technical issue with being in two different places that are so close together at the same time during your own lifetime. I am afraid I cannot allow you to use the crystal in that fashion."

Anastasia felt her heart sink. She and Edward were going to be in so much trouble. All further thoughts about the Order and time travel were going to have to wait.

Dr. G. drove them home. He had offered to come in if that would help the situation with their parents. Both Anastasia and Edward knew that it wouldn't be right for Dr. G. to get blamed for their mistake.

They stood at the front door, knowing that the end of their lives as they knew them was waiting for them on the other side of the door. They had never pulled a stunt like this. They might be grounded forever or, even worse, banned from their phones.

Anastasia gritted her teeth and opened the door. It was quiet. She had half expected to find their parents pacing in the hallway on the phone with the police.

"Where do you think they are?" Edward whispered as they walked quietly down the hallway to the kitchen.

She could hear the sound of the TV in the lounge room as she entered the kitchen. She looked at Edward. He put his finger to his lips with the universal sign for being quiet. He tiptoed over to the lounge room entrance. He looked back at Anastasia and waved her over. As she peered around the corner, she spied Mom and Dad on the couch—asleep! Her Mom's head resting on Dad's shoulder. It looked liked she had done some serious drooling. Dad's head was laid back, resting on a pillow and pointing toward the ceiling. His glasses were on the armrest of the couch and two half-full glasses of wine sat on the coffee table. The credits for the BBC special on Queen Elizabeth I were scrolling down the screen.

Anastasia pumped her fist in relief and then turned and silently high-fived Edward. Either there was a benevolent and all-powerful being controlling the course of events on earth or it was time to buy a lottery ticket.

They quietly crept out of the room and then stopped in the office to delete the Uber email receipt from their father's iPhone. With their tracks covered, they headed upstairs to their bedrooms. About thirty minutes later, Mom and Dad sleepily popped their heads through Anastasia's door to say good night. They were completely unaware of her and Edward's escapades. Anastasia crawled into bed after finishing her science project near midnight. She yawned and smiled to herself as she snuggled under her blankets. The neighborhood outside was quiet and peaceful, but Anastasia knew that nothing would ever be quite the same after tonight.

Chapter 7

Edward's shock of learning that Dr. G. was part of a secret organization called the Order of Time had slowly faded over the last week. Technically, he had completely freaked out when he'd woken up the next morning and remembered what had happened. He hadn't wanted to believe that their friend Dr. G. was more than the curator of the Smithsonian Museum of Natural History and that he was a time-traveling special agent tasked with protecting the integrity of time. He had tried to convince both himself and Anastasia that it had just been a nightmare.

"You know as well as I do that last night wasn't a bad dream." Anastasia had rolled her eyes.

"Maybe we both had the same crazy dream. You know we're twins after all." Edward had shrugged speculatively.

"Do you still have a bump on the back of your head?" Anastasia had asked with her hands on her hips.

He'd reached up and felt the lump on the back of his head. It had still been tender from where his head had struck the floor. He hadn't been able to bring himself to speak and had only managed to gulp as he nodded back affirmatively.

"You got that when you passed out after Dr. G. came through the portal. You know, dressed in a Civil War uniform and holding a sword. Now stop being an idiot!" Anastasia had barked at him impatiently.

"Maybe we should tell Mom and Dad?" Edward had squeaked. He had felt his chest heaving like there wasn't enough air in the room to breathe.

"We can't tell anyone. We're sworn to secrecy," Anastasia had reminded him. "We're just going to have to figure out how to deal with it."

That was when Edward had started hyperventilating and the room had started spinning. With Anastasia's help, he'd eventually stopped and had been able to breathe again without a paper bag. It turned out that time had a way of taking the edge off things. Once they had gotten used to the idea of time travel and the Refractium Crystal, life had pretty much gone back to normal.

Today was good. Edward hadn't stopped happy dancing all morning. It was his birthday and he really hoped that he was going to get the new painting easel and brushes that he'd been yearning for. The easel was handmade from solid oak with sure-grip clips and adjustable legs. It was the Ferrari of easels and it was all he wanted for his birthday. He had a pretty good feeling about his chances from the way Mom and Dad had been so low-key at breakfast. Mom wasn't a low-key person. *She must be trying to hide something.* He reasoned that something had to be his art stuff.

He was changing his clothes in the school locker room for gym class when he was snapped out of his happy thoughts by the innate feeling that something was wrong. The locker room had suddenly gone quiet. The natural sounds of sixth-grade banter about sports, drones, homework, and girls had stopped. The same thing happened in nature when a tiger prowled through the forest. Birds stopped singing and monkeys stopped chattering until the danger passed.

This was definitely bad.

Edward finished pulling his T-shirt over his head and grabbed his shoes, ready to head for the exits when Brodie came stalking around the corner flanked by his two large, dim-witted cronies, Taylor and Wilson. Edward looked for escape routes, but they had him cornered in the dead-end bank of lockers. Brodie sneered while chuckling softly and cracking his knuckles.

Edward gulped but found that all the moisture had disappeared from his mouth. Brodie was the biggest and baddest bully in sixth grade. He picked on everyone but had a special place in his heart reserved for Edward. Unfortunately, Brodie's heart was rotten as far as Edward could tell. They had unfinished business. The last time Brodie and his cronies had used him as a punching bag, Anastasia had shown up and rescued him. She had gone all ninja on Brodie's butt.

His current predicament wasn't helped by the fact that Brodie was enormous for a thirteen-year-old. As far as Edward was concerned, no one should be six feet tall with muscles and facial hair in sixth grade. Apparently, Brodie's parents hadn't thought he was ready for school and had held him back a year before he started first grade. After failing to demonstrate any basic grasp of reading, writing, or arithmetic, the school had decided to hold Brodie back yet another year. Brodie wasn't very bright, but he could hold a grudge like nobody's business.

"I told you this wasn't over," he said. "Now that your crazy sister's not here to protect you, you're going to get it! Get him, boys."

Taylor and Wilson seemed to grunt as they advanced and started to close in on Edward. He tried to fake high and duck through Wilson's legs. It actually worked until he got back to his feet and ran right into Brodie, who crushed him in a bear hug. Soon Taylor and Wilson assumed their normal position of immobilizing his arms while they dragged him across the floor of the locker room.

"Which one did you use?" Brodie said to Taylor.

"The second one."

Brodie cackled in response. Edward continued his futile efforts to break free as he wondered what they could possibly be talking about. It started to dawn on him how bad this could be as they pulled him around the corner toward the four toilet stalls. *God, please not the toilets!*

"Time for your swirly, you geek!" Brodie said as he ran to the second stall and pushed the door open before ducking inside.

Edward panicked at the thought of his head being inserted into the toilet bowl while it was being flushed. Nothing could be more gross or humiliating. This was not what was supposed to happen on your birthday. However, telling Brodie it was his birthday would probably make things even worse.

"Where the heck is it, Taylor?" Brodie shouted with anger in his voice as he emerged from the stall. "I thought you said you had to do number two."

"I did," said Taylor quietly.

"Well, there's nothing in this toilet bowl, Taylor. How am I going to give him a poo swirly if there's no poo?" Brodie said as if lecturing about the theory of relativity.

Taylor turned a bright shade of pink. "I'm sorry. Mom says you have to flush if you do number two. It's what separates us from the animals."

Brodie looked at him in disbelief. Edward was horrified by where the conversation had gone. This was much worse than he could have imagined. He was going to be sick.

"You're an idiot, Taylor. Wilson, go in there and do number two!" Brodie ordered.

"I can't," said Wilson, shrugging his shoulders. "I already went this morning."

"I'm surrounded by morons!" Brodie shouted. He paused as he ran his hands over his flattop haircut. "Okay, a normal swirly will have to do."

Brodie was crouched by the toilet bowl as the two goons tried to drag him into the stall. Edward managed to swing his feet up at the last moment and braced them against both sides of the doorframe. It checked their momentum as he strained with everything he had.

"Get him in here! The class is going to start any minute. We're running out of time!" Brodie shouted.

"We're trying!"

Edward could feel the ligaments in his shoulders stretching as he struggled against the goons. Something was going to give, and unfortunately it was probably going to be his shoulder joints. *I really should lift weights and drink those protein shakes they show on TV.*

Just then Coach Peterlik's loud voice echoed through the locker room. "Edward, Brodie, Taylor, and Wilson, you are all officially late to gym class. You will be serving one detention after school. If you're not out of the locker room and lined up for class in the next ten seconds, it will be two detentions!"

Edward ended up sprawled on the floor as they let go of his arms and gravity took over. All three of them managed to step on him as they sprinted out of the toilet stall to avoid the second detention.

Edward dragged himself to his feet and ran toward the exit as quickly as he could while trying to catch his breath. Coach merely shook his head at Edward's awkward gait as he shambled out of the locker room. Edward didn't mind Coach's pitying look. He joined the rest of the class and lined up on the basketball court. He had avoided the ultimate humiliation and had made it back to the safety of the herd.

Chapter 8

Edward had a long history of getting on the wrong side of Brodie. At first, Edward hadn't understood why Brodie had taken such a dislike to him. It had started as soon as Brodie had moved to Washington, DC, in fourth grade and started attending the Blake Academy. He had pushed Edward off the top of the monkey bars that first day on the playground. It had been a long fall and the rubberized play surface had only absorbed so much of the force. Edward had been winded and dazed. He'd thought that there must have been a misunderstanding about something. Maybe if they talked about it, they could patch things up and even become friends. He had been wrong. Every day there had been some sort of new torment on the playground. Getting beaned in the head by the dodgeball. Getting fully tackled during the touch football game. Getting tripped during soccer. All of this while he wasn't even playing in the games.

Brodie was a typical bully in the sense that he would try to push around anyone he thought wouldn't push back—anyone like Edward. Brodie had tried tackling Anastasia once and only once. She had ducked under his charge and then levered upward to send him flying through the air. After flipping over and landing on his back, he hadn't moved for a minute or two. When he had gotten up, he'd acted like nothing had happened and skulked away. The next day he'd picked up where he had left off with Edward again. After all these years, Brodie thought of Edward as some sort of little mouse. Now it was time to show Brodie that this mouse had teeth.

The trap had already been laid. The truth was that Edward had made his preparations right after Anastasia had rescued him from Brodie the last time. Now it was time to set his plan into motion.

Edward spread the word about what Brodie and his henchmen had done that morning. According to the story Edward sent around school, Brodie, Taylor, and Wilson had tried to jump him before gym class but weren't smart enough or strong enough to give him a swirly. In fact, they had been lucky that Coach Peterlik had interrupted them because Edward had been about to open a serious can of whoop-ass. This may have been stretching the boundaries of believability, but he wanted to make sure that Brodie was in pure attack mode. He didn't want any protective animal instincts making him cautious.

Edward made sure he left his fifth period English class as soon as the bell rang. He had set the trap in an unused school locker about thirty yards away. It was the last locker on the row and he made sure it wasn't locked.

Edward ran down the hallway to the intersection formed by two corridors crossing. Brodie's Remedial Math class was just around the corner. Edward made sure to stand in the middle of the intersection in plain view of Brodie's classroom.

Brodie, Taylor, and Wilson exited their classroom, rubbing their foreheads from the recent strain of trying to think, when they spotted him. What came out of Brodie's mouth was more of a growl than actual words, but Edward fully understood the meaning: it was time to run.

He sprinted down the hallway to the partially open locker. He pressed play on the old voice recorder, turned on the motion sensor, and closed the door. He could hear his own voice coming from the voice recorder inside the locker as he raced down the hall.

As Edward hurtled back into his English classroom, Mr. Johnson raised his eyebrows and said, "Edward?"

Edward thought fast and said, "I think I dropped my pen." He pretended to look for it on the floor around his desk.

Out in the hallway, Brodie, Taylor, and Wilson had rounded the corner and had stopped in front of the locker.

Edward's voice shouted from the locker, "Hey, boneheads, you can't get me now, can you? Looks like your brains just aren't big enough to figure out what to do! What's that smell? Brodie, did you fart again? I thought we talked about the fact that your farts aren't the same as cologne. Wilson, no eating your boogers! That's gross, dude! Taylor, you should really stop kissing Brodie's butt. You just don't know where that thing has been!"

Brodie slowly looked around. All the other kids in the hallway were laughing. He turned a deep shade of red from a combination of acute embarrassment and anger. In the old-fashioned cartoons, steam would have been coming out of his ears.

"He's hiding in this locker! Let's rip the door off! I'm going to kill him!" Brodie had an absolutely manic look in his eyes, which were full of bad intentions. Everyone started to back away in anticipation of some sort of beatdown. The three antagonists all lunged forward to grab the handle of the locker door and pulled as hard as they could.

They hadn't expected the door to open like it did. They all fell backward and landed in a tangle of arms and legs. A soft spraying noise could be heard as they were enveloped in a wave of unbelievable stink. It was so thick they couldn't just smell it, they could taste the stink. It was as if a skunk had just sprayed Brodie, Taylor, and Wilson.

There were squeals of panic as the odor spread throughout the hallway. The three boys scrambled backward across the hallway to the far wall. They began shucking off their jackets, ties, and even their shirts in an effort to get away from the disgusting smell that covered them. It was no use; the smell had permeated everything. It was now part of them and it was worse than anything they could have ever imagined.

Taylor whimpered softly. Wilson looked catatonic.

"No, no, no!" Brodie screamed. "I'm so going to kill him!"

Edward popped his head out of the classroom door just in time to see the popular clique of girls round the corner and stop dead in their tracks.

"Oh my god! What is that hideous smell?" asked Celeste Aldridge, their official leader and the most beautiful girl in school.

The rest of the clique screwed up their faces and searched for the source of the terrible stink. Their eyes settled on Brodie, Taylor, and Wilson.

With a look of disgust on her face, Celeste said, "I have two words for you. Personal hygiene! You should look into it." She and the rest of the clique turned, flicking their hair for emphasis, and walked back the way they had come.

Edward slipped out of the classroom and joined the crowd heading away from the stink. Talk about a birthday present. This would definitely go down as one of the best days of his life.

By the time he met Anastasia by the front entrance of the school, the news of the skunk bomb was everywhere.

"Hey, sis. What a great day, don't you think?" Edward greeted Anastasia.

"Did you have anything to do with the whole skunk thing? People are saying they could hear your voice coming from the locker." Anastasia wore a look that said, "I know you did, so spill it."

"I can neither confirm nor deny my involvement in said skunk bomb incident," Edward said, grinning from ear to ear. "Plus I'm not sure you have appropriate clearance."

"I'm your twin sister. I don't think my clearance could be any better than that," Anastasia said.

"In that case, the answer is yes. I got Brodie and his cronies really good! They'll think twice before messing with me again."

"Edward Upston, you are going to get yourself thrown out of school! Then once they throw you out, Mom and Dad are going to kill you!" Anastasia said, shaking her head. "Besides, you're supposed to tell me about these things. We're supposed to be a team."

"Sorry, but I had to stand up for myself. I can't let Brodie pick on me anymore. I'm tired of always being pushed around, always being the weak one. He's been picking on me for three years. Enough's enough." Tears began to well up in his eyes. He paused for a moment, took a deep breath, and then wiped his eyes. "Plus they aren't going to be able to prove it was me who did it. There won't be any evidence. I rigged a big magnet to erase the audiotape when the spray bottle went off and I wore these babies," he said with a half smile, now pulling latex gloves out of his blazer pockets.

Anastasia understood now. She'd never been picked on, and it wouldn't be easy to have to rely on your sister to protect you. She hugged her brother and said, "Well, maybe next time I'll get you to protect me."

"Anytime, sis. It might not have been as cool as your MMA moves, but I had to work with the skills I have," Edward said, hugging her back.

"You know Brodie will try to get even with you," she said.

"I know. It makes me a little scared, but not too scared to fight back."

As they walked down the street toward the bus stop, she said, "Where in the heck did you get the skunk spray from?"

"It was easy to make. The Israelis first made it in 2004 for riot control. I just bought the main synthetic ingredients of methyl and ethyl mercaptan online from China with my debit card. Then I put them in an automatic spray bottle with a motion sensor that I learned how to make from YouTube."

Anastasia linked arms with her brother as they walked. "You truly are something else. I'm proud of you, my brother. Next time no more secrets, okay? By the way, happy birthday."

"Happy birthday to you too."

Chapter 9

Anastasia's mind wandered back through the day as she brushed her teeth. At Dr. G.'s request, Edward and Anastasia had stopped by the museum on the way home. Dr. G. had presents picked out for their twelfth birthday that he wanted to make sure they received. It had been so typically thoughtful of Dr. G. They had just gotten back to thinking of him as Dr. G., their friend and mentor, as opposed to some sort of time-traveling Homeland Security agent.

She had unwrapped the package he had given her to find a small leather box with a hinged lid. She had quirked a questioning eyebrow at Dr. G., who had merely nodded at her to open the box. Inside had been a silver case the size of a quarter. It had been covered with delicate engravings of what looked like a constellation of stars. She had gently opened the sliver case to find that it was a compass.

"Oh, thank you, Dr. G.! It's beautiful," she had remarked as she'd examined the compass closely. It had seemed to have two hands pointing in slightly different directions.

"You are welcome, my dear. As you can probably tell, this is not an ordinary compass. The two hands point to both the magnetic north pole and the geographic North Pole."

"What's the difference?" her brother had asked.

"They are actually different places. The north magnetic pole currently shifts by approximately forty miles a year. In fact, the earth's polarity regularly flips every two hundred thousand to three hundred thousand years," Dr. G Dr. G. had told them.

Anastasia hadn't learned about this yet in science class but found it fascinating. She'd slipped the compass's silver chain over her head as Dr. G. had continued.

"The second hand points to the geographic North Pole and can be adjusted according to the date to accommodate these movements."

Edward had opened his package to find that Dr. G. had given him a special pocket knife. It had had just about every tool in the book, including a special compartment in the handle that held flint, steel, and tinder to start fires.

"Thanks, Dr. G.! This knife's got everything. I'm going to call it the Batknife," Edward had declared, unfolding and then closing each of the tools.

"I hope that these gifts will serve you well in the years to come," Dr. G. had told them.

They had been blown away by the beautiful gifts, as they weren't the kind of thing you found at the shopping mall. When they left for home, they were already planning ahead for their next visit.

Back at home, the family had made homemade pizzas. It was a birthday tradition. Anastasia had made a margherita pizza, which had had mozzarella, tomatoes, and basil on it. Simple and delicious. Her brother had made his meat lover's pizza, which had been smothered in chicken, bacon, pepperoni, sausages, and ground meats. He'd claimed it was built for a modern-day carnivore like himself. Edward counted cow, pig, lamb, and chicken as four of the primary food groups. The pizza had had everything outside of snake, crocodile, and alligator, which he considered the fifth food group: exotic meats.

Pizza had been followed by cake and presents. Their parents had spoiled them. Anastasia had gotten an incredibly cool iWatch with a metallic rose gold band. Edward had gotten the art supplies he'd been hoping for. It had been a great birthday.

As Anastasia finished getting ready for bed, Edward came in her room with a wrapped gift in his hands.

"Happy birthday, sis," he said with a smile.

"I can't believe I forgot to give you your present!" she said as she turned and ran back to her desk to retrieve the present she had for Edward. She had gotten him a vintage hardback copy of Alexandre Dumas's *The Count of Monte Cristo*. He loved reading and had loved *The Three Musketeers* so she thought this was a good bet. Edward followed her and they sat down on the bed and exchanged presents.

Her gift from Edward was rectangular and flat in shape. It was wrapped in beautiful pink-and-white-striped paper with white ribbons and a bow. It was a far cry from the *Washington Post* newspapers in which her presents from Edward were usually wrapped. She carefully lifted the tape from the corners to open the present without destroying the paper. Her mouth nearly hit the floor. It was a portrait of her that Edward had painted. It was so vivid that she was almost coming off the canvas in midleap, doing a superman punch with her hair trailing behind her. She didn't look mean or angry. Just strong, confident, and full of energy.

"I love it! This is completely amazing. Thank you. It's going straight up on my wall," she said while throwing her arms around her brother and wrapping him in a giant hug.

"Urr arrr elcom," Edward muffled from underneath Anastasia's shoulder.

"Sorry. I got a bit excited," she said, letting go of him so he could breathe again.

"Thanks for the book, Anastasia. I love hardbacks and I'd been wanting to read this one."

"You're welcome, bro. I'm not sure if I've told you but I think you're really brave and incredibly talented," she said as she gave him a gentler hug.

"I'm not really sure any of that is true, but thanks for believing in me. I think you're pretty cool, too, sis." Edward left to go back to his room and begin reading his new book.

Anastasia couldn't get to sleep straightaway. Her mind was too busy. Her eleventh year on the planet had been a great year. So much had happened in the last year. She had started middle school at the Blake Academy with Edward and all her friends. She had even maintained her straight A average. She'd also discovered that her friend Dr. G. was a time-traveling member of a secret order whose mission it was to protect the world. She couldn't help but wonder what was in store for her in the next year. Eventually, she drifted off to sleep with a lingering feeling of hope and excitement.

Chapter 10

Edward and Anastasia sat on the bus as they traveled to the museum to see Dr. G. Edward was still enthralled by what he had learned in class from Mr. Elderton. He could hardly believe how interesting the Old Testament was from a historical context.

"Can you believe that there were five authors for the book of Genesis? I mean that probably explains the inconsistencies. Like why it says that God made Adam and Eve from clay in one part and says that he made Eve from Adam's rib in another." He was still chattering away when he noticed that Anastasia's eyes were glazing over.

"Right. Sorry about that. I'll stop talking about Biblical Studies now," Edward said, biting his lip.

"Thanks," Anastasia said as her eyes rolled back to the front of her head. "You were just beginning to sound a lot like Mr. Elderton and you know how that puts me to sleep."

As the bus pulled up to the stop behind the Smithsonian on Constitution Avenue, they noticed a number of ambulances and fire engines. There were lots of people coming around the corner of the museum and gathering by the side of the road. From the way they were rushing around, they seemed to be panicky, almost frightened. Edward looked at Anastasia to see if she had any idea what was going on, but she just shrugged her shoulders. Something unusual was definitely happening at the museum.

As they got off the bus, the twins were immediately approached by one of the firefighters who seemed to be directing people near the roadside.

"No one is going into the museum this afternoon," said the big, burly firefighter with a beard bigger than his helmet. "There's been a bomb threat called in. We have to get everyone out of there pronto!"

"A bomb threat?" asked Edward.

"Stay clear of the building. Everyone, move back!" he called to the crowd.

Anastasia had whipped out her phone. "I'm calling Dr. G."

"Oh my god, you're right! What if he's still in there?" Edward held his forehead in his hand, panic setting in as he watched Anastasia make the call. She shook her head in frustration.

"He's not answering. It just keeps rolling to voice mail. What are we going to do?" Anastasia was pale and looked every bit as worried as he was.

Edward gulped and steeled his courage. He knew what they had to do. "We have to go in and find him. He would do it for us."

The alarm was blaring and there were firefighters on each side of the front entrance of the Smithsonian directing people to exit and to move toward Constitution Avenue. They felt unbelievably nervous trying to sneak into the museum in broad daylight while the general public were trying their hardest to get out of the building. There was a virtual river of tourists pouring out of the front doors with big sneakers, belt bags, selfie sticks, and T-shirts emblazoned with presidential quotes like "I am not a crook" or "I did not sleep with that woman" and "I stand by all the misstatements I've made."

"We're never going to be able to get by the firefighters without being noticed," Anastasia said in exasperation.

Edward looked at Anastasia with a glint in his eye. "How did we do it last time?"

His sister pivoted to look at him as they both said, "Misdirection!"

Edward pushed through the exiting crowd until he reached one of the firefighters. "Excuse me, sir, but what does that skywriting mean? Is it about the bomb threat?" Edward asked as earnestly as possible.

The firefighter bent down to Edward's eye level and said, "What skywriting, kid?"

"The writing straight above us. You just have to walk down the stairs to be able to see it."

The firefighter stood up and shouted to his partner on the other side of the entrance. "Yo, Billy! There's skywriting about the code 255. C'mon!" Both firefighters ran toward the stairs in front of the building.

Edward and Anastasia bolted through the front doors, squeezing between selfie sticks and tourists who were rushing to the exit. By the time they reached Henry the African Bush Elephant on the far side of the rotunda, the bodies were starting to thin out. However, the noise from the fire alarm only seemed to be getting louder.

"Should we see if he's in his office?" Anastasia shouted as she ran for the stairs without actually waiting for Edward to answer.

Before he could follow her up the stairs, Edward registered a blur of movement out of the corner of his eye that made him take a second look. Two figures clad in black had pelted down the staircase on the other side of the rotunda. By the time he fully turned his head, they were halfway to the museum entrance. Even though he couldn't see their faces, something felt oddly familiar about the one in front. Edward quickly dismissed the thought from his mind and chased after Anastasia, taking the marble stairs two at a time. They crossed the *Hall of Geology, Gems, and Minerals*, heading for Dr. G.'s office with Anastasia well in the lead.

Edward shouted to Anastasia, "You're going to need my badge!"

He was out of breath as he caught up to her unsuccessfully trying to open the closed security door. He held out the security badge to her. She grabbed it and pressed it up against the card reader. It beeped and the light flashed green.

Edward lunged forward and yanked open the door as Anastasia shot through to the hallway. Edward let out a brief groan before plunging through the door and down the hallway after his sister. When he caught up to her, she was already at the door of Dr. G.'s office, gesturing impatiently for him to hurry up. He tapped into his fear for Dr. G. and used his adrenaline to put on an extra burst of speed to reach the door just as Anastasia opened it. As he stepped through the doorway, he could see there was no one there.

Anastasia raced across the office and checked the door to the crystal, but it was locked. She turned to Edward with a worried expression. "Maybe he's helping get people out of the museum or maybe he's working on an exhibit."

Edward yelled above the din of the alarm, hoping to put his sister more at ease. "Let's go look for him." He grabbed her hand and they ran out of Dr. G.'s office door.

They went in opposite directions and raced the loop around the *Hall of Geology, Gems, and Minerals*. Edward passed the 423-carat Logan Sapphire, which was roughly the size of an egg. He slowed a little bit more as he passed the meteorites.

"Clear!" shouted Anastasia as she rounded the corner to meet Edward.

Edward cocked his eyebrow as he looked at Anastasia. "Clear? Someone's been watching too many *NCIS* reruns!"

"Stay focused and pick up the pace! Come on," she said as she headed back toward the exit. "You head counterclockwise toward the *Live Butterfly Pavilion* and we'll meet in the middle." She took off, sprinting toward the *Garden Lounge* exhibition.

"Me stay focused? I'm not the one quoting TV shows," Edward muttered to himself. *Man, she's bossy. If we ever get reincarnated, I'm going to be the one who's born first.*

He took off for the *Live Butterfly Pavilion*. He sped toward the stairway so he could skirt the rotunda and climb up the stairs on the other side. He took them two at a time, gulping air and promising himself that he would start using the Stair Master his parents bought last year. All history and no sports made Edward an unfit boy. Edward crested the last step into the *Live Butterfly Pavilion*, sucking air and gasping like an asthmatic marathon runner.

It was a riot of color and wings everywhere, a veritable cloud of butterflies. For some reason, butterflies liked Edward. They converged on him as he gasped and flailed his oxygen-deprived arms to keep them from suffocating him. He could have sworn they were trying to fly down his throat to block the last vestiges of air entering his lungs. He lunged through the exit of the *Live Butterfly Pavilion* in time to hear a distant "Clear!" echoing from somewhere around the *Bone Hall* exhibition. *Man, she's fast.*

He picked up the pace as he entered the *Live Insect Zoo* and all of its different exhibits. There were thousands of insects. Giant grasshoppers, cockroaches, praying mantises, dragonflies, and beetles, all with their creepy, crawly antennas and legs and their crunchy exoskeletons. Edward tried not to look too closely, because he really didn't want to see any tarantulas. He wouldn't be able to sleep tonight if he did.

He rounded the corner to the Egyptian section and stopped dead in his tracks. The place was a disaster. The sarcophagi—coffins used to hold the remains of the pharaohs—were knocked over on their sides. The ancient mummies were scattered across the floor. It looked like a tornado had hit. Edward saw Anastasia across the room at the entrance to the *Last American Dinosaur* exhibition. She stared at the wreckage. Then he noticed a pair of legs in smart brown trousers with brown leather shoes sticking out from under the top of a stone sarcophagus. They were Dr. G.'s legs.

Chapter 11

Anastasia heard Edward's worried shout of "Dr. G.!" as he ran toward the sarcophagus lid that lay on the floor on top of Dr. G.

Oh my god, thought Anastasia as she felt a wave of fear followed by a rush of adrenaline through her body. She moved like a cheetah, vaulting an empty sarcophagus, a mummy, and then a toppled pillar.

Edward was already crouching down by the stone lid bearing the image of an ancient pharaoh with its long hair and stylized beard shouting, "Dr. G., can you hear me? Are you okay?"

There was no response, only the sound of the fire alarm still droning away.

"Dr. G., it's Edward and Anastasia," she said. "Are you hurt?" *Please don't be dead!* she thought.

A long second later, they heard Dr. G. groan. "My leg. I think it is badly injured."

Never before had she been relieved to hear someone say they were badly injured. At least he was alive. He was going to be okay.

"We'll go get help!" Edward yelled above the alarm.

"No, Edward. I am afraid that's not a good idea," said Dr. G. "This is the work of the Corsairs. They were waiting for me and I was ambushed. I am not sure that I want to have to explain this to the district's finest. I can't afford to be detained if I have any chance of stopping them."

"The district's who?" asked Edward, looking confused.

"The police, Edward. Dr. G. means the police," Anastasia explained.

"I expect they will be here soon anyway," said Dr. G. "Once they have fully evacuated the museum, they will need to search for the explosive device the Corsairs claimed was planted. I am afraid we don't have much time."

Anastasia was still trying to process what Dr. G. was saying. The Corsairs had staged a bomb threat and used the distraction to ambush Dr. G.

"What exactly happened, Dr. G.?" Edward asked as he bent down to Dr. G.'s level.

"I will tell you everything later but there is no time right now. We must get out of here."

Anastasia's heart started accelerating. *The Corsairs had attacked Dr. G. and the police were coming! This is bad. Are we going to get in trouble for still being inside the building? Will they find out about the Order of Time? What will Mom and Dad think? What will Harvard Admissions think? I have to get focused.* She took a deep breath and centered herself like she had learned in martial arts training. Three breaths later, her heartbeat had slowed and the panic receded from her mind.

"What should we do, Dr. G.? Can you get out from under the lid?" she asked him.

"It's just too heavy, Anastasia. I am afraid I cannot budge it."

She looked over at Edward and said, "Let's both try to lift the lid at the same time."

Edward responded by flexing his spindly arms and then slapping his hands together in preparation for lifting the lid. They both bent at the knees and grabbed the underside of the sarcophagus lid. Their upper bodies and heads were leaning over the hieroglyphs carved into the pharaoh's stone chest.

"Now!" said Anastasia and they both heaved as hard as they could.

It didn't budge an inch. Nothing happened except for Edward letting out a cross between a whimper and a squeak. The sarcophagus lid was made of solid stone.

The fire alarm suddenly stopped and an announcement came over the PA system. "This is the police. Please ensure that everyone has evacuated the building. This is not a request; it is a direct order. Anyone lingering in the building will be prosecuted to the full extent of the law."

Through gritted teeth, Dr. G. said, "Perhaps my meeting with the police is inevitable."

Anastasia scanned the room for solutions while Edward slumped against the toppled pillar, breathing heavily while rubbing the area where his biceps should be. They weren't strong enough to move the lid on their own. They needed something to amplify their strength.

Too bad they didn't have a pulley system to lift the lid. Anastasia had learned all about pulleys in her science class. She cast her eyes over the debris littering the floor. No rope or wheels but a number of broken display cases with both their contents and glass spread across the marble floor. A beautiful statue of Isis and Horus, which had sat atop the pillar, lay broken on the tiles. The stand and pole attached to the Egyptian flag also lay on the ground.

Suddenly, another image formed in Anastasia's mind. A pulley wasn't the only simple tool she had learned about in science. She had also learned about levers and fulcrums.

"I've got it!" Anastasia said excitedly. *The Egyptian flagpole will make a perfect lever. The pillar from the Isis and Horus statue Edward's leaning on could be the fulcrum. It's lying close enough to the sarcophagus lid that Dr. G. is trapped under. I'll just need to wedge the pole far enough under the edge of the lid before levering it up.*

"Get up, Edward. I'm gonna need to use those muscles of yours again."

Edward bounced up, puffing out his chest and flexing his arms in anticipation. "Dr. G., just hang in there. We're going get you out from under there."

The flagpole was made of solid oak and seemed to weigh a ton. It took both of them to wedge it under the lid while propping it on top of the pillar at a forty-five-degree angle. They climbed on top of one of the fallen display cases to reach the end of the pole jutting into the air.

"One. Two. Three!" Anastasia said as they both held on to the pole and stepped off the end of the cabinet.

The sarcophagus lid seemed to shift slightly before settling back in place with Anastasia and Edward suspended in the air. They hung there for a few seconds before Anastasia said, "That wasn't exactly what I'd planned. I'm going to have to try something else, Dr. G." She let go of the pole and dropped lightly to the floor. She ran over to where she had left her school backpack. She dumped out the contents on the floor.

"Now is not the time to do homework, Anastasia," Edward said with an exasperated tone. "How about helping me get down."

Anastasia was so focused she could hardly hear him as she scanned the debris on the floor and started picking up the largest pieces of stone debris she could find and then loading them into her backpack.

"Why are you packing rocks into your backpack? It's not the time to clean up either! I'm hanging on for my life and you're getting all OCD!" Edward shouted, still grasping the pole with his feet dangling in the air.

She couldn't resist saying, "What's the matter, Edward? You getting tired of hanging around?"

Even through his pain, Dr. G. chuckled from under the stone lid. "I thought he might have the hang of it by now."

"You both know I'm afraid of heights!" Edward squeaked. "Instead of helping me down, you're making absolutely terrible jokes. I demand you help get me down! I can't hold on much longer."

"I thought we could all just hang out," Anastasia said, now laughing at herself. "Hang on! I'll get you down in a second."

She strained to lift the backpack up onto the display case. She climbed onto the case and then slowly pulled the backpack on to her shoulders. She grabbed on to the pole next to Edward's hands and stepped off into the air. This time the added weight of the backpack created enough downward force to lever the lid into the air and off of Dr. G. It flipped over and crashed onto the stone tiles while they rode the pole down to the floor.

"Great problem-solving, Anastasia! That was very clever," Dr. G. shouted in relief as he propped himself up on his elbows.

Anastasia turned and smiled at Edward. He looked surprised to be on the ground and in one piece.

"Freed Dr. G. and saved you from falling three and a half feet to your death," Anastasia said. "Two birds with one backpack full of stones. Now let's help Dr. G. back to his office before the police get here."

"I concur," said Dr. G. with a grimace. "If you can just help me to my feet, we will be on our way."

They created a splint for Dr. G. out of a few broken timbers from one of the display cases and duct tape they had found in its remains. While it wasn't good for Dr. G.'s elegant woolen suit, it did help to stabilize his leg. The combination of the splint and Anastasia and Edward helped Dr. G. to hobble his way across the second floor of the museum. Anastasia's father had always said that the number of uses for duct tape was unmatched by any other substance created by man.

Once they made it back to his office, Dr. G. settled into his chair with a sigh of relief. He opened his desk drawer and removed a bottle of ibuprofen and shook out two tablets. To Anastasia, he appeared to pause for a few seconds before shaking two more tablets into his hand, which he subsequently popped into his mouth like M&M's and swallowed in one fluid motion. She looked at him gobsmacked.

"The two tablet thing is merely a recommendation. Current circumstances and levels of pain call for a more significant application," said Dr. G. with a wry smile. He closed his eyes, leaned back, and sat silently.

Anastasia tried to be patient and understanding. She knew that Dr. G. was hurt but she was dying to know what had happened. Dr. G. sat there with his eyes closed like some sort of yogi master in a trance. Edward was even more impatient than she was. She could see Edward getting agitated by having to wait to find out what had happened with Dr. G. and the Corsairs. *After all*, she thought, *he did play a prominent though somewhat passive role in Dr. G.'s rescue.* Edward was about to break the silence when Dr. G. spoke.

"I am just gathering and synthesizing my thoughts before they slip away from this old mind. Bear with me for just a moment and I will explain what happened."

This time, the twins waited somewhat patiently for Dr. G. to begin telling his story.

"I was in my office after lunch when my cell phone rang," he said after a moment's silence. "It was a 202 country and area code denoting Cairo, Egypt. Sem Sem, who curates the Museum of Egyptian Antiquities and leads the Egyptian chapter of the Order was on the line."

"Is there a Refractium Crystal in Egypt as well?" interjected Anastasia.

"Yes, Anastasia. There's a Refractium Crystal in Cairo. The Museum of Egyptian Antiquities is the single greatest repository of Egyptian artifacts in the world. Sem Sem is perhaps the greatest Egyptologist in the world and has been its caretaker for many years. He was calling about the Tutankhamun display. You see, while many of the artifacts on display are actual items, some of the displays are images from the Refractium Crystal."

"Are you saying that people who visit the museum can't tell the difference between the images and the real thing?" asked Anastasia, not fully convinced.

"They are historical images of the exact same objects, Anastasia. In this case, from more than 3,300 years ago but they are the same." Dr. G. paused and looked at them gravely. He leaned forward slightly in his chair, gripping the arms so tightly that his knuckles seemed to turn white. "Sem Sem told me that the images of Tutankhamun's possessions had disappeared early this morning in Egypt."

Both Edward and Anastasia gasped.

They realized those artifacts should have remained untouched and unchanged until they were discovered by Dr. Howard Carter in 1922. If the images disappeared from the Museum of Egyptian Antiquities, then something had been changed in the past. Sem Sem feared that the Corsairs were implementing another twisted plot. He was calling to ask if the images of any of the items we are purported to have here on loan at the Smithsonian had disappeared as well." Now Dr. G. lowered his head and said softly, "I was just leaving my office to check on the *Eternal Life in Ancient*

Egypt exhibition when the fire alarm went off. It was so loud that I didn't hear Sem Sem's cries for help through the phone at first. I was calling out for him when it went silent at the other end of the line. Then I heard a menacing laugh." Dr. G.'s voice seemed to catch in his throat and he stopped talking. His eyes welled with moisture.

"Are you okay, Dr. G.? Who was it?" Anastasia asked. Dr. G. was normally as steady as a rock. Seeing him like this was disconcerting.

"I haven't heard that voice in nearly a century. However, I am 100 percent certain it was Rafael Augustino. A former member of the Order of Time and now the traitorous leader of the Corsairs. He said that he was afraid Sem Sem was out of time and then cackled once more before the line went dead. I fear that I will never see my good friend Sem Sem again."

Anastasia felt tears in her own eyes at the thought of what had happened to a man she had never known and would never meet. Anastasia looked at Edward, who was wiping his own eyes with the back of his hand.

"What?" said Edward defensively. "I got some dust in my eyes."

"I ran for the ancient Egyptian exhibition as quickly as I could while everyone else was evacuating from the museum. I needed to figure out what had transpired in ancient Egypt. Between the phone call from Sem Sem and the fire alarm, I let myself be distracted. I didn't realize the Corsairs would be waiting for me when I got there." He shook his head ruefully. "I saw enough of the exhibition to know that something had been changed in the past that had eliminated the existence of Tutankhamun. All of the images of his burial artifacts were gone—it was as if he had never lived. Then two of the Corsairs jumped me. The one with the gruesome scar knocked me to the ground while his companion tipped the sarcophagus on top of me. I actually am lucky it wasn't worse."

Edward felt the hairs on the back of his neck stand up. "Did one of the Corsairs have a scar? What exactly did it look like?"

"He had a raised, purple scar that ran from the corner of his eye all the way into his unkempt beard. It looked like the result of being on the wrong end of a knife or sword. He was a very unsavory-looking character," Dr. G. said, shuddering slightly at the memory. "Why do you ask?"

Edward's mouth suddenly felt very dry. "I saw two people dressed in black running across the rotunda toward the exit just as we were coming up the stairs. I felt like there was something familiar about one of them. I think the Corsair with the scar is the same man who threatened us after DJ tackled him in the rotunda."

"I told you he was after us!" Anastasia said, smacking his arm in vindication.

"I am afraid you are most likely correct, Edward," Dr. G. said with his eyebrows drawn together and his forehead creased.

"But we've never done anything to them! How do they even know who we are?" Anastasia was rattled. The prospect of being targeted by the Corsairs was petrifying. *We're only kids.*

"It doesn't make any sense. Anastasia and I are nobodies!" Edward said with a hint of hysteria in his voice. "Most of the kids in my grade don't even know who I am!"

Dr. G. shook his head slowly as he seemed to ponder this new information. "I don't fully understand the connection between your encounter in the rotunda and today's events, including the disappearance of Tutankhamen's artifacts. However, for some reason, the Corsairs must perceive the two of you as a threat."

"But I'm the least threatening person in the world!" Edward's volume and pitch were both rising, his arms flailing about hopelessly.

"What are we going to do, Dr. G.?" Anastasia couldn't keep her voice from shaking.

Dr. G. could see how unnerved they were. He spoke slowly and calmly as he took turns looking both of them in the eye. "I promise I will do everything within my power to protect you both. I also promise that we will talk about the implications and the measures we will take to protect you from any danger. Right now I need to focus on the changes the Corsairs have enacted in ancient Egypt. I only have a small window of time to preserve the past."

Anastasia took a deep breath and slowly let it out. As her mind cleared, she knew that Dr. G. was right. Regardless of how frightened she and Edward were, they had to focus on what had happened in ancient Egypt. They had to preserve the past to protect their future. Her fear disappeared and her calm returned. "Okay, Dr. G., let's get back to King Tut," she said and nodded.

"But Tutankhamen wasn't even an important pharaoh. I read all about him in one of my Egyptology books. Why would the Corsairs want to rub him out?" Edward asked in a voice a bit closer to normal. His love of history provided an anchor in his storm of fear.

"Well, Edward, this is the complexity about changing the past. It may not have been Tutankhamen that the Corsairs were targeting. The changes wrought by the Corsairs might simply have preceded Tutankhamen. His erasure from history could have simply been a by-product of other changes." Dr. G.'s eyes lit up as he discussed the technical issues associated with time. "The extermination of any of Tutankhamen's direct ancestors would eliminate the possibility of his existence all together. Where was the line broken? Was it five hundred years before the birth of Tutankhamen or merely a decade? Did the break in the line of pharaohs occur with Ramses, Ramses II, Hatshepsut, or Amenhotep? Studying the images of history displayed by the Refractium Crystal provides the clues to where in the timeline changes were made. I believe that is part of the reason why the Corsairs attacked me and decimated the *Eternal Life in Ancient Egypt* exhibition." He was both smiling and wagging the index finger on his right hand as he talked. Clearly Dr. G. wasn't feeling the pain in his leg anymore. He was on a roll.

"Why would that be part of the reason that the Corsairs attacked you?" asked Anastasia.

"They didn't want me to get a clear view of the rest of the exhibition. They didn't want me to ascertain what had not changed in the display of ancient Egypt. The last point of constancy would inform me where the break had occurred and the changes in history had been wrought. They didn't want the Order undoing their nefarious scheme."

Anastasia found herself nodding along. That made an enormous amount of sense. Dr. G. was like a secret society version of Sherlock Holmes. The Corsairs didn't want him finding any clues. If Dr. G. had figured out where the break in the order of time had happened, he could travel back in time and fix it by preventing the change.

"What was the other part of the reason?" Anastasia asked.

"They wanted to kill me of course," Dr. G. said, shrugging his shoulders.

Edward's jaw almost hit the floor. "What do you mean they wanted to kill you? That's murder!" Edward sputtered, both terrified and outraged.

"I have been particularly proficient at foiling their plots to change history and seize power. I am sure they would prefer if I were no longer a thorn in their side. Luckily for me, they failed to erase me. Even luckier I managed to get a good glimpse of the exhibition before they clobbered me. I am pretty sure I know when the change in history occurred!" Dr. G. nodded smugly and tapped his temple.

Chapter 12

Edward was aghast that someone had actually tried to kill Dr. G. *Attempted murder happens on TV and in movies but not to someone you know. How could anyone try to kill Dr. G.? He's the nicest, most harmless man in the world. My parents will lose it if they ever find out. They won't let me and Anastasia hang out with Dr. G. if they know there are killers after him.* Edward shook it from his mind and asked Dr. G., "What exactly did you see? Exactly when did the Corsairs change the past?"

Dr. G. leaned forward and almost whispered as he said, "Nefertiti. She was the wife of Akhenaten. The famous statue of Nefertiti made by Thutmose in 1345 BC had disappeared. The statue belongs to the Neues Museum in Berlin, but we were showing it here as part of an exchange program."

Dr. G. retrieved a walking stick from a cabinet within his office to take weight off his injured leg as he limped heavily back and forth behind his desk. "Akhenaten was a famous and, in many ways, an infamous pharaoh. Akhenaten's name was originally Amenhotep when he was born. He rose to the throne after his father's nearly forty-year reign and ruled Egypt for almost twenty years. He was a very unusual pharaoh in that he didn't keep with the traditions of ancient Egyptian religion, which was polytheistic."

"Does that mean the ancient Egyptian religion supported wearing synthetic fibers?"

"Synthetic fibers?" his sister asked him in disbelief.

"Well, polytheistic. Polyester. There could be a connection," Edward said, arching his eyebrows for affect.

"Actually, Edward, polytheism has nothing to do with man-made fibers. It means a religion that worships multiple gods instead of a single god as with monotheistic religions such as Christianity or Islam. Amenhotep promoted the concept of a single sun-based god named Aten."

Dr. G. sank back into his desk chair and continued his story. "In 1346, about five years into Amenhotep's reign, he decided to change his name to Akhenaten and moved the capital of Egypt from

69

Luxor to a brand-new location. He started the construction of the city that would be known as Akhetaten or Aten's Horizon. In modern times, we now call that area Amarna."

"This guy must have had some serious issues!" Edward laughed to himself. "He moved the capital, changed the religion, and changed his name. Was this dude having a midlife crisis?"

Anastasia shot daggers at him with her eyes. She wanted to hear the full story.

"Edward's question is actually fair," Dr. G. said. "It would have taken an extraordinary level of commitment for a reigning pharaoh to fundamentally change a society that had been the dominant force in northern Africa for more than a thousand years. It was not an easy or popular political agenda. He was asking the people and the powerful priests to abandon their gods like Amun, Anubis, Horus, Ra, and Isis. Most people don't readily embrace change. The people of Egypt were comfortable with their gods and their traditions. These things were fundamental to their identity. Even harder would be asking the priests, whose position and power were tied to those gods, to give them up. History has shown this never happens easily."

"So he wasn't just having a midlife crisis," Edward said, now understanding the magnitude of what Akhenaten had done. "He was trying to create change. So what actually happened in the end?"

"Akhenaten did create sweeping change for more than a decade. However, when Akhenaten died, his son Tutankhamun became pharaoh at the tender age of eight. He wasn't in any position of strength to enforce the changes set down by his father. That being said, many scholars argue that the religion of ancient Egypt never fully recovered over the next thousand years before eventually giving way to the Romans."

"What does that have to do with when the Corsairs changed the past?" Anastasia asked, trying to get back to the question of when the change in history had occurred.

"Pardon me. I am getting carried away with the history of Akhenaten." Dr. G. gathered himself. "Prior to being attacked by the Corsairs, I also noticed a key artifact from the *Eternal Life in Ancient Egypt* exhibition. It was the ceremonial stone marker commemorating the official transition of the capital from Thebes to Akhetaten in 1345. This commemoration occurred just days before the bust of Nefertiti was completed. This, I believe, defines the boundaries within which the Corsairs must have affected their nefarious change to history—between the commemoration of Akhetaten and the completion of Nefertiti's bust. This is when I must go. Given the time that has already passed, I must go now."

Edward understood why Dr. G. was anxious. He knew they only had twenty-four hours to rectify the changes in the past before they became permanent. By his count, at least eight hours had passed since Dr. G.'s friend Sem Sem had first spotted the changes in Cairo. That being said, it could have happened anytime the night before. There was no way for them to tell without the closed-circuit TV feed that Dr. G. had said members of the Order would normally share with one another. They would have to assume that changes to the past could have been affected up to twelve hours before Sem Sem had spotted them, which meant that they had already lost twenty hours! They only had four hours left to open a portal to ancient Egypt with the Refractium Crystal. Dr. G. stood up to walk toward the room housing the Refractium Crystal when his leg buckled and he promptly fell over with a loud thunk.

Anastasia and Edward quickly rushed to where Dr. G. lay on the floor.

"I am alright. I think my body is just reminding me that it is less ready to go than my mind." Dr. G. rolled over and propped himself up on his elbows.

"Let me see your leg, Dr. G.," Anastasia said as she reached over and gently rolled up his right pant leg to the knee.

What they saw wasn't pretty. His leg was red and very swollen. The skin was also broken and still oozing blood from where the stone sarcophagus lid had landed on it.

"I think I'm going to be sick," Edward said, looking away.

"I don't think you're going anywhere or anywhen," Anastasia said with deep concern. "I think your leg may be broken."

Dr. G. sighed deeply. "That may be true, but I see no choice in the matter. Any change in time can fundamentally change the world we live in now. The changes wrought by the Corsairs are typically intended to do just that. It is possible that each of us, or even the city of Washington, DC, might never exist as a result." Dr. G. paused as he caught his breath for a moment. "I tried contacting the New York chapter of the Order but Dr. Anderson is unreachable. This, of course, is a serious breach of Order protocol. I also tried contacting the head office in London, but it's already past ten o'clock and they have signed off for the night. By the time I raise another chapter, it may be too late. We are definitely going to have to revisit our continuity of business procedures." Dr. G. shook his head in frustration, then regathered his thoughts before proceeding. "While I am injured, at least I know the history of the time period well and have dealt with this enemy many times. I must reverse the changes wrought by the Corsairs prior to them becoming fixed."

Edward shook his head slowly. "Dr. G., you couldn't stop them in the ancient Egyptian exhibition when you were healthy. How are you going to stop them on one leg?"

As the words left his lips, the spark of an idea began to grow within the recesses of Edward's mind. Perhaps Dr. G. didn't have to be the one to travel back to ancient Egypt. As the spark within his mind grew to flames, Edward stepped forward and shouted, "Stop the presses! Anastasia and I can go back to ancient Egypt to stop the Corsairs, reverse their changes, and ensure that Tutankhamun is not erased from the pages of history!"

Anastasia was the first to speak. She started slowly, "I agree that Dr. G. is in no shape to go, but how would we possibly know what to do? We don't know the history, we can't speak the language, and we're only kids." She turned with worried and questioning eyes back to Dr. G. "It's an impossible idea, Dr. G. Isn't it?"

Dr. G. didn't answer Anastasia's question. He was still lying on the antique Persian carpet that decorated the floor of his office, but he was deep in thought and seemed far away. Slowly, he came back to the present with hope beginning to shine in his eyes.

"Perhaps the idea is not so impossible, my young friends. It is an extraordinary idea but it would appear well matched to the circumstances we find ourselves facing." He looked penetratingly at Anastasia and then at Edward, as if looking into their hearts and souls.

Edward felt the hairs on the back of his neck stand up. It was almost as if the room was charged with static electricity. He had the feeling that something big was about to happen. He looked at Anastasia and she nodded her head back at him, letting him know that she was feeling it as well.

"I have known you both for some time now," Dr. G. said. "I must confess it has always been in the back of my mind that the two of you might someday make perfect candidates to become members of the Order when you were older. You both have a love of history and are highly intelligent. You are both courageous while also possessing a strong moral compass. You have your own unique strengths, which compliment each other and make you an even stronger team. Someday I hoped that you might join the Order of Time, but I never imagined it so soon or under such dire circumstances."

Edward was astounded. "Do you mean we can travel back in time to ancient Egypt and we can become members of the Order of Time?!" he asked incredulously. "That would be way cooler than being an Eagle Scout!"

"Can we really, Dr. G.?" Anastasia found her voice wavering with a mixture of excitement and fear.

"It is a very serious choice, Anastasia. One that should not be taken lightly or easily. I think you and Edward are capable and formidable in many ways. The Refractium Crystal also provides certain gifts that would further strengthen your partnership. While we still don't fully understand how, the energy from the past imparts the time traveler with a complete knowledge of the language and writing of the time."

"We would be able to speak ancient Egyptian and read hieroglyphics? That is amazing." Edward beamed. He'd never been able to grasp much beyond a cartouche, the unique symbol for each pharaoh.

Dr. G. raised his hand to slow Edward's enthusiasm. "The energy from the Refractium Crystal gives another longer-lasting gift. The energy infuses the traveler and extends their lifespan. I have lived for more than 150 years now. I can tell you the prospect of outliving one's parents is very different from the prospect of outliving one's children or grandchildren. This is why we do not normally allow such decisions to be made prior to prospective members reaching the age of eighteen."

Edward swallowed hard. He couldn't imagine the prospect of being eighteen years old let alone the idea of being 150 years old. It made his eleven years feel incredibly insignificant.

Then it dawned upon him. This wasn't just about him.

""I don't think I could ever understand what it would be like to live for 150 years. That seems almost like forever. But I do know that if Anastasia and I don't try this, we may not make it to tomorrow. You, Mom, Dad, none of us might make it to tomorrow. We have to try. For everyone's sake, we have to try."

Anastasia reached out to clasp Edward's hand. "He's right, Dr. G. We have to try."

Chapter 13

Their intervening visit to the museum costume and makeup studio was eye-opening. Anastasia hadn't really thought about all the different period costumes that would be required for the exhibits. She fidgeted with her long, white Egyptian gown as they stood in front of the purple Refractium Crystal. It pulsed softly in its golden stand.

The gown wasn't as simple as a dress. It wrapped around Anastasia's waist like a skirt and the remaining material draped over her shoulders and cinched at the waist. It made getting dressed in her school uniform seem unbelievably simple. Edward looked even more uncomfortable in the male version.

"At least you're a girl and used to wearing dresses. I'm a boy. Thank god none of the guys can see me. I would never be able to show my face in public again and that's not even the worst of it," he said, examining his outstretched arms and shaking his head.

Dr. G. had insisted that Edward apply a spray tan and colored hair spray to better blend in to the Egyptian environment. While Anastasia's olive skin and dark hair would fit in, Edward's blond hair and pale skin would make him stand out from normal Egyptians. It was likely to make it more difficult to gather information on the Corsairs without drawing attention to himself. There was no time to get colored prescription contacts, so there wasn't a lot to be done about his blue eyes. While Edward hadn't done a perfect job of applying the spray tan evenly, it was better than his super pasty self. Getting used to black hair was going to be hard.

Anastasia looked him over and couldn't stifle her giggle as she said, "At least your legs are okay. Maybe a bit skinny but still not too bad." His face fell even further as it took on a shade of deep crimson.

Dr. G. interrupted their discussion to let them know it was almost time to open the portal. "Did you finish reading the material that I printed on Akhenaten?" he asked Edward.

"I did."

"And you both still have the gold, silver, and copper pieces I gave you?"

"What gold and silver pieces?" Edward asked and then quickly looked at Anastasia to see if he had missed something.

Dr. G. sighed as he ran his hands through his hair. "In my haste, I must have forgotten them. Edward, can you retrieve them for me from the vault in my office? They are in a leather pouch on a shelf on your left as you enter the vault. The vault door is still open."

"Sure, Dr. G.," Edward said, thinking that he had never noticed a vault in Dr. G.'s office. He scampered for the door with the knowledge that they had a limited window of time before the changes to the past became permanent. As he entered the office, he saw the open door to the vault on the back wall. When he reached the open door, he discovered why he hadn't ever noticed the vault. The front of it was hidden behind a very large painting of George Washington. "That is so cool!"

Edward stepped through the thick, metal doorway into a room twenty feet long by ten feet wide. The shelves that lined the walls from floor to ceiling held all manner of crates and cases. He quickly looked to his left and spied a leather pouch like the one Dr. G. had described. He picked it up and was surprised by how heavy it was. He loosened the cords that cinched the pouch closed and glimpsed inside to make sure he had the right one. He was just about to tighten the pouch and run the ancient coins back to Dr. G. and Anastasia when he spied a familiar, brown crate on the shelf near where he had found the coins.

"Quetzalcoatl? I wonder what that's doing in here?" Edward asked himself out loud. He placed the coin pouch on the shelf next to the crate before lifting the wooden lid by a few inches to peer inside. Sure enough, the jade eyes of the small Quetzalcoatl statue glinted back at him. Even though he knew he shouldn't, Edward couldn't resist removing the small, golden statue to have a closer look. The dragon-like figurine was just as amazing as he remembered. He slowly rotated it on his palm so he could admire it from every angle. *This has to be a mistake*, Edward thought to himself. *Something this awesome should definitely be on display.*

Edward's silent reflections were interrupted by Dr. G.'s distant bellowing. "Have you found the coins, Edward? Remember we must hurry!"

Edward panicked with the realization that he had been completely sidetracked. He quickly placed the Quetzalcoatl figurine inside the leather pouch and cinched the cords closed. *Dr. G. will be really thankful that I found Quetzalcoatl*, Edward thought as he sped back to Dr. G., Anastasia, and the Refractium Crystal.

"Did you find the coins?" Dr. G. asked him as he skidded to a stop next to Anastasia. "Yeah. I've got them right here." Edward lifted the pouch in response.

"Great. Please tie the pouch to your belt. Remember—this is the currency of the time. I have probably given you more than enough, but please don't flash it around and attract unnecessary attention."

"We know, Dr. G. We'll be careful."

Dr. G. then placed silver rings into the palms of each of the twins' hands.

"These are the rings that I spoke of earlier. Each member of the Order possesses one just like these. Each have a fragment of the crystal embedded in them. This fragment absorbs the unique energy signature from the journey through the portal. By returning to your point of entry and adjusting the face of the fragment so," he twisted it counterclockwise, "it becomes the key to reactivating the portal and returning to the present."

Anastasia placed hers on her finger with the knowledge that it would be essential to ensuring that she was not trapped in the past. The mere thought made her heart tremble. The possibility of not seeing her parents or her friends. Not being able to live the life that she had been born to live. Anastasia vowed to take good care of this ring.

Edward had his ring held up between his thumb and his index finger. He squinted to examine the purple fragment of crystal in the light. He promptly dropped it and chased it across the symbols engraved on the floor. It stopped next to the levers that controlled the Order's Refractium Crystal. He scooped it up after a few attempts and looked very pleased with himself. *It's a good thing that we have two rings between us,* Anastasia thought.

Dr. G. leaned on his walking stick while making adjustments to the levers that controlled the vector of the portal that would be opened. The eight levers corresponded with latitude, longitude, year, month, day, hour, minute, and second. In other words, an exact time and place in history that they would travel to within ancient Egypt. Dr. G. paused and looked up from the dials as he regarded them seriously. "Please do remember that the past may be different than what you have learned or what you think. What we have in our textbooks is our current interpretation of what we think happened in the past. It is not always fact. We have explained away many of the things that we don't understand as being either fanciful legends or myths. The vault is full of strange and powerful artifacts that have taught me you must keep an open mind."

"Wait a minute. What do you mean the vault is full of strange and powerful artifacts?" Edward questioned, tilting his head slightly to the side.

"I was simply relaying that through the course of my travels through time, as well as my role at the Smithsonian, I have come across a number of artifacts that are not wholly of this world. I just want the two of you to keep an open mind and be wary," Dr. G. said as if it were no big deal.

"Um, what exactly does 'not wholly of this world' mean?" Anastasia asked, not at all following what Dr. G. was saying.

"It means objects that have powers that do not occur or exist naturally within our world. When we find them, we take them out of circulation and lock them away so they cannot find their way into the wrong hands and pervert the course of history," Dr. G. explained matter-of-factly, like everyone had similar hobbies.

"We could find stuff with superpowers? That is the coolest thing I have ever heard!" Edward said excitedly as his voice traveled more than an octave upward. "Like we could totally find Thor's hammer. I mean if he were Egyptian and not Norse and all."

Edward's excitement was unwilling to be deterred by factual accuracy.

Dr. G. looked back down at the dials before saying, "Everything is ready now. It's time."

"We're ready too. We're going to fix it," said Anastasia in a quiet but confident tone that she didn't quite feel. She couldn't believe that everything and everyone was dependent upon them to succeed. It felt like a huge weight pressing down on her.

"Yeah, we're going to be back in no time. Get it? It won't seem like any time has passed when we get back. We're just going to save the planet first," Edward said, doing his best to lighten the situation despite the worry she knew he must be feeling as well.

Anastasia couldn't help but smile as Edward flexed his muscles as if he were in the world's strongest man competition. *It was nice how he could take the tension out of any situation.* She glanced at the clock behind Dr. G. and noted the time: 5:37 p.m.

Dr. G. nodded as he turned a dial on the control panel and the familiar humming noise returned. The crystal slowly began to glow and emanate a purple light. The intensity built over the next thirty seconds as the glow from the crystal seemed to make the jewel expand from the size of a football to a radius of seven or eight feet that formed a purple sphere of light. The whole room, including Dr. G., was bathed in the intense purple light of the Refractium Crystal. The vibrations from the crystal hit Anastasia like bass notes from a giant subwoofer.

Just then a black crack appeared in the sphere. The crack slowly spread until it formed a black tunnel into the heart of the purple light. Anastasia felt Edward clasp her hand. She looked at him and he nodded at her. In that instant, their connection as twins kicked in and she knew that they shared the same thought: *We entered this world together; we can do this together as well.* They slowly took one, two, and then three steps forward to the mouth of the tunnel. She looked at Dr. G., who did his best to mask his fear for their safety with a confident nod of his head. In his eyes, she could see both hope and what looked like a sense of pride. They took the next step into the blackness and plummeted into the abyss of space and time. The cold was breathtaking as it chilled her all the way to the bone. The darkness was absolute, and she couldn't see an inch in front of her own face. It was like they were falling endlessly through a void. It was terrifying. Anastasia was pretty sure she was screaming, but she couldn't hear anything. The only thing that kept her sane was the fact that she could still feel her twin brother's hand. She knew she wasn't alone. They still had each other.

The world exploded into brilliant sunshine as they stumbled through the portal, still holding hands, and face-planted onto the hot, yellow sand. Anastasia lifted her face and wiped her eyes. Then she felt the heat hit her like a wave. It reminded her of when she opened the oven door to peek at chocolate chip cookies while they were baking.

They were surrounded by a sea of yellow sand as far as Anastasia could see. Dr. G. had set the portal to arrive two miles outside the city of Akhetaten so they would be less likely to run into anyone directly upon arrival. Just to their right was an outcropping of rocks that rose ten feet off the desert floor. Three lizards rested on a rock shelf about a meter off the ground. They were about two feet long and almost the color of the sand. They had wide bodies with short legs that left them close to the ground—squat really. Their tails stood out from the rest of their bodies as they had rings of spiny protrusions along their length. They regarded the twins carefully before scuttling off the shelf and around to the back side of the outcropping.

Anastasia got up and dusted the sand off her gown. Edward was still busily trying to wipe the sand off his tongue. *He looks ridiculous. He must have had his mouth open when he face-planted.* "Come on, Edward," she said as she motioned for him to get up. "We'd better get moving if we want to make it to the city and find a place to stay."

Edward stopped wiping his tongue and collected himself. "You're right. Good idea." Then his eyes went wide and he exclaimed, "Oh no!"

"What's wrong?"

"I accidentally brought Quetzalcoatl with us." Edward's face was white and he was biting his lip.

"You did what?" Anastasia wasn't sure if she had heard him right.

"Well, I saw Quetzalcoatl's crate in the vault and I thought it must have been there by mistake. I was going to give it to Dr. G. when I came back into the room but I forgot when he gave us the rings," Edward said in a rush as he shrugged his shoulders.

"You mean you took the Quetzalcoatl statue from Dr. G.'s vault—the vault full of strange and powerful artifacts that are 'not wholly of this world'? Do you mean that vault, Edward?" Anastasia was unsuccessfully trying to contain her frustration.

"Oh!" Edward's mouth formed a perfect circle. "I hadn't even thought of that."

"I knew there was something off about that statue. Honestly, Edward! Maybe you should give me the Quetzalcoatl for safekeeping. What do you think of that? Is that a good idea?" Anastasia was clenching her jaw as tightly as she could to try to keep from shouting.

"Yeah. That's probably a good idea," Edward said quietly as he removed the small Quetzalcoatl statue from his pouch and handed it to Anastasia. She quickly zipped it into the belt bag that was strapped around her waist under her gown.

"I suppose we'd better get going now," Edward suggested, trying to change the subject.

Anastasia took a deep breath in through her nose and then slowly blew it out through her mouth along with her frustration. "You're right. We should get going."

"Plus I can tell you a little bit more about what I was able to read about Akhenaten and Nefertiti before we left," Edward offered tentatively.

"Sounds like a plan." She pulled out the compass on the silver chain that Dr. G. had given her for her birthday. She had set the date for the true north hand with Dr. G. for 1345 BC before they'd entered the portal. She oriented the compass in the right direction for the city of Akhetaten, not to be confused with Akhenaten the ruler, and they were on their way.

As they walked south, Edward explained that Akhenaten was considered by most scholars to have been a really significant pharaoh due to the amount of change he introduced to ancient Egypt. "But change is really hard. People say that change is as good as a holiday, but what they really mean is it's good when it happens to someone else." He quirked his eyebrows up for emphasis, like he was letting her in on a big secret.

Edward was so excited to get to share his knowledge that he was practically glowing. "Now try to change an empire and a society that had already been around for more than 1,500 years. Akhenaten's new religion based upon the Solar Disk God, Aten, was a huge change. The same was true for relocating the capital from Thebes, which we now call Luxor, to Akhetaten. He even changed the way artists depicted pharaohs in both paintings and statues. Before Akhenaten, pharaohs were always shown in an ideal form instead of what they actually looked like. All the statues and paintings looked almost the same regardless of which pharaoh it was supposed to be. It would be like depicting every president and first lady as looking like Ken and Barbie even if they looked like Frankenstein's monster and his bride."

"I get it. Akhenaten was into change. He was a radical pharaoh," Anastasia said, hoping that the lecture was over. She was wrong.

"There's more to it than that," Edward said, waving his hands as he spoke. "You see, there were a lot of people who didn't like these changes. Most of all, the high priests who made their livelihood by representing the hundreds of different deities in ancient Egypt's religion. The move to a single god was bad for business. They called Akhenaten the Heretic Pharaoh."

"Did it really matter what the priests thought? Their opinion had to be biased anyway."

Edward stopped walking as he turned to face her. "Even most normal Egyptians struggled with the change in their religion. They knew who to pray to for different things. If you wanted protection from evil, you could pray to Bast, the Cat Goddess. If you were a scribe, you prayed to Seshat. If you wanted to be embalmed successfully for the afterlife, you prayed to Anubis. The move to one all-powerful god was pretty scary to most of them. Could Aten really look after all aspects of their lives? What would happen to them in the afterlife?"

"I guess that makes sense," Anastasia said as she mulled over what Edward had said. "People get comfortable doing what they're used to, even if a better way comes along."

"Yeah, just because there are cool ways to pay for things with your smartphone doesn't mean that Grandma is going to stop writing checks," Edward chuckled mainly to himself. "Maybe if the changes to religion had lasted long enough, the next generation of Egyptians would have embraced Aten as their single deity without ever knowing the alternative. As it happened, the changes didn't last long after Akhenaten's death in 1336 BC."

Anastasia wiped the sweat off her forehead with her hand. It was crazy hot out here in the desert with the sun radiating off the sand. The soles of her feet were hot and that was through her sandals. She uncapped her waterskin and drank deeply, feeling the cool water flowing down her throat. "So what happened to his wife Nefertiti when he died?" Anastasia asked as she started trudging across the sand again.

"Well, Nefertiti was just one of Akhenaten's wives," Edward replied.

"How many wives did Akhenaten have?" Anastasia asked incredulously.

"I think they said he had five wives," her brother said carefully. "But Nefertiti was the Main King's Wife. She was known as his beloved."

"Well, that's just great. He had five other wives, but she was still the Main King's Wife! Nothing to feel bad about at all!"

"What is clear," her brother said, walking forward and attempting to redirect the conversation, "is that by the time Tutankhamun started his reign, the single-god religion based on

Aten was definitely on the way out. As a matter of fact, most traces of the religion were essentially erased from history."

Anastasia was momentarily sidetracked by this revelation. "What do you mean they erased the religion from history? How is that possible? He built a whole city and there would have been temples and statues for Aten. It's not like this was just some trailer park or campsite."

"That's just the thing," Edward said significantly. "The city of Akhetaten, which once was the home of more than ten thousand people, was essentially left to ruins and swallowed up by the desert over time. The worship of the old gods was reinstated, and the statues and hieroglyphs of Akhenaten and Aten were chiseled away by the priests and subsequent pharaohs. They wanted to make sure that nobody remembered the heretic and his one-god religion. A lot of what is known about Akhenaten was only pieced together after his tomb was found in the Valley of the Kings."

"He was buried in the Valley of the Kings? That doesn't make sense. If he was such a heretic, why would they have put his tomb with all the other great pharaohs?" Anastasia asked skeptically.

Edward got his bright-eyed, useless-trivia look again. Even though his cheeks were red from the heat, despite his fake tan, he chatted excitedly as he explained, "Most of the pharaohs started the construction of their tombs while they were still alive and in charge of the funding. They wouldn't leave monuments of their greatness or how they would make the journey to the afterlife to chance. That was the forever. What if your son didn't like you and decided you didn't need a grand tomb or any possessions to see you through on your journey to the afterlife? Only suckers would take that chance." Edward was practically glowing with excitement in sharing his knowledge.

He's almost unbearable in this state. There's no escaping it though. It would be like tipping a four-year-old's ice cream over and watching the scoop fall onto the dirt. You just can't snatch the joy from an innocent child no matter how annoying they are at times. Anastasia sighed to herself and focused back in on what her brother was saying.

"Akhenaten's tomb was completed while he was still alive. It was the same with Khufu and the Great Pyramid of Giza, which was originally a tomb as well. They just realized that tombs were less likely to get looted if they weren't so visible."

"I get it," Anastasia said, nodding her head. "Was the Main King's Wife buried with him?" she asked sarcastically.

Edward shook his head but didn't answer as they slowly climbed the dune in front of them. It was hard work as they seemed to slide backward one step with the sand for every two they took forward. He paused, out of breath, and had a drink. Anastasia looked up at the crystal blue sky. *Even clouds don't want a piece of this heat.*

"Actually, it's still a bit of a mystery as to where Nefertiti is buried. They've never found her tomb. Some scholars think she fell from favor and was banished late in Akhenaten's reign. There are even some who think she is buried in a secret chamber behind her stepson Tutankhamun's tomb in the Valley of the Kings. There's a lot of debate even to this day. Well, I mean, the day we came from in the future."

Anastasia laughed. A realization dawned on her. The whole time she and Edward had been talking, they hadn't been speaking English. They had actually been speaking ancient Egyptian. Dr. G. had been right. The energy from the Refractium Crystal had somehow embedded this capability during their journey through the portal. The knowledge made Edward's lengthy lecture far more bearable.

"Okay. So I got things a bit twisted in my description, but you can't really blame me, can you? I haven't actually traveled through time before," Edward said sheepishly, shrugging his shoulders.

"It's not that, Edward. It's more that you just said all of that to me in ancient Egyptian," Anastasia said, smiling.

Edward shouted "Holy crap!" and clapped his hand over his mouth. He never swore. Their mother would have killed him if she had heard him say that. Even so, Anastasia saw that he couldn't hide his smile. They were speaking the language of the pharaohs.

Chapter 14

As Edward and Anastasia trudged south, chatting excitedly, they noticed that the desert of yellow sand was starting to give way to more solid ground. The earth was actually brown and sparse grasses and plants began to pop up.

"We must be getting close to the Nile," Edward told his sister. "The waters of the Nile are basically the source of all life in a country that is mostly a barren desert. Just about everyone lived—or lives, I guess—along its banks. That's how Egyptian civilization grew around the Nile."

"Look!" Anastasia exclaimed, pointing to their right.

Edward turned to his right and saw the Nile River for the first time. They could see trees lining part of the banks as well. Edward thought they looked like palm trees or banana trees. They stood out all the more given the lack of vegetation they had seen since their arrival.

"This is so cool! I can't believe it," said Anastasia, beaming before stopping suddenly and looking directly at him with a very serious expression. "The city is on this side of the river, right? We don't have to swim through crocodiles or anything to get there, do we? I don't do swimming reptiles."

Edward stifled his laugh. There weren't many things that Anastasia was afraid of, but crocodiles and alligators did the trick. She had always hated the thought of them lurking beneath the surface of the water just waiting to surprise their prey. It had been the cause of their family canceling a vacation to the Great Barrier Reef in Australia. Saltwater crocodiles, which grew up to twenty feet long and weighed a ton, were common in the region of the world they now stood in. The Nile crocodile wasn't quite as long at thirteen feet, but it was still more than big enough to eat a person. In the twenty-first century, the Aswan High River Dam in southern Egypt kept them sequestered above the dam in the south. However, in Akhenaten's time, this part of the Nile was full of those toothy critters. Edward didn't want to tell her that there were crocodiles in the Nile River. And luckily, they were on the right side of the river.

"The city is on this side." He could see Anastasia exhale with relief. "Almost all the people in ancient Egypt lived on the east side of the Nile. You see, Ra, the Sun God, was the giver of life and he rose in the east. The sun sets in the west, which is symbolic of death. This is why all the tombs like the pyramids and the Valley of the Kings are all on the west side of the Nile."

"Right, then," his sister said after regaining her composure. "Let's stop standing around. It's time to go foil a conspiracy and save the pharaoh. The city is just up ahead."

Edward looked up and saw the profile of Akhetaten in the distance. The city was less than a mile away and getting closer. They walked through the stifling heat of the midday sun. If he'd had a couple of eggs, Edward could have fried up lunch on the sandstones that paved the roadway beneath their feet. He took another long pull on his waterskin. Even though they had only been walking for twenty minutes, he'd already drunk most of his water. There were now fields of crops between the road and the river. It looked like there were canals running through the fields to water the crops. He thought it looked like chickpeas and cabbages, but living in Washington, DC, certainly didn't make a kid an expert in farming. Edward decided to explain more about Akhenaten to distract himself from the heat.

"Like Dr. G. said, Akhenaten was actually called Amenhotep when he was born. That was his given name. He was still called Amenhotep when he first became pharaoh. He only changed his name to Akhenaten when he decided to change the traditional religion to one focused solely on Aten, the God of the Solar Disk."

Anastasia gave him a slightly confused look. "What do you mean 'God of the Solar Disk'? Do you mean he was the Sun God like Apollo was to the Greeks?" she asked.

"Not really. Aten is represented by sunlight. Because he exists, he gives life to everything else. Akhenaten actually means Aten's shadow, which is essentially what he, as the pharaoh, was supposed to be on earth. He named his new city Akhetaten, which means Aten's horizon."

88

"It's a little odd, don't you think?" Anastasia asked him, shaking her head. "Changing your name like that to Akhenaten when you're an adult."

"I thought so, too, when Dr. G. first told us about it. But the more I read, the more it made sense. When you think about it, he was trying to convince all of the Egyptians that Aten was the real deal. What better way to do it than to change your own name as the pharaoh to be a reflection of Aten's. Talk about instant credibility," Edward said, knowing that it made sense. "I mean, rappers do it all the time. Jay-Z, Drake, Snoop Dogg, and Macklemore weren't given those names by their parents. Those are names they gave themselves to be more credible with the audience they were trying to connect with."

Anastasia stopped for a moment as she looked at him. "You can be surprisingly smart sometimes."

Edward felt his cheeks becoming hotter and he knew that he was blushing—and not because of the blazing sun. "I could be wrong. That flaky actress did name her kid Apple but I think I'm right about the rappers."

It was surreal, almost like a dream. They truly had gone back in time. The road was clogged with merchants and tradesmen traveling to and from the city. The men were bare-chested and wore linen kilts that were tied in a knot on the side. Dark hair framed their deep brown eyes and handsome features. Many had bundles of wares strapped to their backs and were using donkeys to carry their goods. Others carried tools such as wooden-handled hoes or hammers. The bronze or stone heads of the tools were tied in place with strips of leather. It was a far cry from the battery-powered leaf blower that Edward used to clear the sidewalk. There was a constant hum of conversation as the merchants chatted openly about their families, friends, or jobs.

Edward and Anastasia trudged along the road toward the city with everyone else, trying to ignore the heat. He noticed that all of the people seemed shorter than in modern times. He knew that people had gotten taller over time with better nutrition and health, but he hadn't realized that they'd been this short. For some reason, he'd also expected that everyone would have camels instead of donkeys. *Weren't camels the right animal for the desert? I'll have to be careful not to assume that everything I thought I knew is right. Maybe this was the type of thing Dr. G. meant when he talked about our interpretation of the past.*

They approached a large stone pillar on the side of the road with engraved and painted hieroglyphs. He knew from his reading that this pillar was one of the steles that marked the boundaries of Akhetaten. Statues lined both sides of the roadway after the stele. There were statues of sphinxes—animals with human heads atop a lion's body—that guarded the roadways to holy places.

He was used to seeing Egyptian etchings and hieroglyphs without color. Even though he knew that they had originally been painted, he hadn't realized they would be so vivid. The reds were like bright rubies while the blues were like brilliant sapphires. This was so much more amazing-looking than *The Rise of the Pharaoh, Part III* that he had been playing online. He had thought those graphics were awesome until now. This was like living in some sort of movie set.

He read the hieroglyphs out loud: "Welcome to Akhetaten. All who enter shall bask in the glory of Aten, the One True God, and his divine reflection on earth, the Pharaoh Akhenaten. May their light shine upon you as you travel upon the Royal Road and banish all shadows." Edward smiled and looked at Anastasia. "That's a pretty cool welcome sign."

She nodded her head and smiled back. "You definitely know who's in charge. Then again they aren't exactly running a democracy here, so that's not really a surprise."

The sphinxes were both awesome and a little weird. They projected a level of serenity with the placid face of a handsome Egyptian while the body displayed an underlying ferocity that was undeniable. The sphinxes guarded the Royal Road here as they did in the original capital of Thebes. There must have been a couple hundred of them as they were spaced every five yards or so along the road. While the proportions were very similar, they all were slightly different in terms of posture, features, or facial expression.

It slowly became apparent to Edward that they hadn't been made from a mold—they were each unique.

Anastasia shook her head in awe. She whispered under her breath, "I can't imagine how long it would take to carve one of these statues out of stone, let alone all of them."

"Why are you whispering?" Edward whispered back.

Anastasia giggled at his question. "I don't know. It just seemed appropriate. I guess it feels a little bit like we're in the museum," she replied at a normal volume.

As they continued south, they could clearly make out the sandstone walls rising from the ground like some kind of fortress. The road itself led directly toward a large double set of gates. They would need to traverse the entire city from north to south in order to reach the merchants' quarter. The map in Dr. G.'s office was based upon the archaeological excavations performed in their time. It told them that the temple district formed the northern end of the city and was followed by the Royal Palace, then the city's administration district, and finally the merchants' quarter. That was where they intended to stay while on their mission in Akhenaten. Hopefully the map wasn't wrong.

Anastasia caught his eye as they got closer to the gates. "Okay, are you ready?" Her jaw was clenched and her tone was serious.

"Ready for what?" Edward was confused. He was pretty sure they'd both been laughing only a minute ago.

"We don't have a lot of time to figure this out. We have to save the future," Anastasia said solemnly.

In that moment, Edward realized that everything and everyone was depending on them. He felt like he couldn't breathe. *What if we really can't do it? What if we fail?* Then he looked back at his twin and saw the fierce determination burning in her eyes. It steadied him. "Let's do this," he said and nodded at her.

Anastasia silently nodded back and they were resolved.

The first set of gates was about fifteen feet high, equal to the height of the sandstone walls on either side. The wall itself was also almost as thick as it was high. The second set of gates was set on the inside edge of the wall and stood higher than the surrounding walls at twenty feet. The gates were open, but they could see guards with long, metal-tipped spears at the gates and bowmen on top of the wall.

Edward felt a little stab of fear seeing men armed with these ancient weapons. They weren't machine guns or sniper rifles, but he was pretty sure they could kill you anyway. In some ways, the lack of modern technology actually made them scarier to him. Primitive but utterly brutal. He swallowed hard. Clearly if Aten's light didn't banish any shadows or enemies, Akhenaten's guards would make sure of it. Luckily, he didn't think he and Anastasia would be seen as the kind of threat that would require the guards to use their weapons. But that didn't keep his heart from thumping like a bass drum within his chest as they prepared to cross the last twenty yards to the first gate.

Thankfully, they passed right through the gates with the rest of the traveling procession. The guards didn't even given them a second look as they passed inside the walls of the city. Edward let out the deep breath he hadn't realized he'd been holding and looked around.

A giant garden full of fountains, flowers, and trees stretched into the distance on their left. It was easily the size of several football fields and laid out in geometric patterns that were full of color and movement. He couldn't believe all the trees. There seemed to be figs, willows, sycamores, and palm trees everywhere. It was completely the opposite of what you would expect in the middle of a desert.

Edward's eyes followed the source of the life-giving water to a canal that flowed underneath the Royal Road. Edward determined that it must have continued underground and connected to the Nile. The whole garden must have been engineered on a slight grade to enable the water from the Nile to flow through these gardens and create this oasis inside the city's walls. A mixture of Akhetaten's inhabitants were quietly strolling through the gardens, including families, laborers, and priests.

On the right of the Royal Road was a temple for Aten. It towered above its surroundings as it rose as high as a five-story building. Twin obelisks sat on either side of the temple's entrance. Mirrored paintings of Aten, depicted as a large circle emanating rays of sunshine upon the land, flanked the obelisks. Other images along the front of the temple showed Akhenaten with arms outstretched and bathed in Aten's rays. Scaffolding was still up on the southern end of the temple's facade where Edward could see artists with chisels and brushes still actively at work, many dressed in linen smocks with their hair tied back with leather bands. Dr. G. had told them to expect that Akhetaten might still be under construction as Akhenaten pushed to complete the city's construction.

Edward couldn't help but gawk at the surroundings. Anastasia tugged at the sleeve of his robe, which snapped Edward back into reality. She jerked her head south, motioning that it was time to stop goggling and continue walking down the road. He realized he was so overwhelmed by what he was seeing that he was standing with his mouth hanging open. He closed his mouth and then brought his hand up to his face to make sure it had worked. He smiled at his sister, who had been watching him and was now fighting not to laugh. She was having a hard time stifling it.

"What?" he asked, slightly injured.

Then she snorted. It wasn't a little, delicate, lady snort. This was a big, honking, truck driver snort. Now he was laughing at her.

"Shut up, you goof! I only snorted because you were being such a nerd and I was trying to spare your feelings," Anastasia said, smacking him on the arm.

"Yeah, but then you almost inhaled me through your nostrils!" Edward giggled. He quickly got moving down the road before Anastasia decided to put him in a triangle choke or some other debilitating jujitsu maneuver.

Anastasia followed after him, glowering, but was soon distracted by their surroundings.

They had moved past the formal temples and gardens and seemed to be passing a series of long, flat, single-story buildings.

Both workmen and what had to be priests in their pure white ceremonial robes were striding with purpose both in and out of the buildings. The workmen were powerfully built with their honey-colored skin burnished by the sun. Even though Edward had been really embarrassed applying the fake tan and black hair spray, he was really glad that Dr. G. had insisted. He would have stood out like a polar bear at the equator otherwise.

Edward was jostled repeatedly as he wove his way through the flowing sea of people. Despite the rush-hour traffic, he felt a pulse of positive energy from the crowd. Many called out or stopped to chat with others they knew as their paths crossed on the Royal Road. Edward could have spent the whole day taking in the sights of the city. "Come on," he said, trying to pry his eyes away from the amazing sights that surrounded them. "Let's follow our plan and find a place to stay in the merchants' quarter and then we can decide what's next."

"You're right. We don't have a lot of time," Anastasia agreed. They quickly made their way through the bustling crowd on the way to the merchants' quarter, intent on establishing their home base in this ancient and alien world.

Chapter 15

Anastasia had been debating with her brother on where exactly to start their investigations as she sat on the woven mat on the floor of the boarding house they'd found. Fortunately, the map of Akhetaten was accurate and the process of finding accommodations had gone smoothly thanks to the papyrus that Dr. G. had prepared before they'd left the museum. The fake letter of recommendation he had written in hieroglyphics said that his children were coming to Akhetaten in advance of his arrival to establish the family's papyrus and scribing business in the new capital. They were able to arrange for a simple, clean place to stay in a quiet corner of the merchants' quarter with Yemthi, the owner of the boarding house. He lived there with his wife and two children but still had two rooms for rent.

The truth was they didn't really know exactly where to begin. Anastasia searched vainly around their little room, which didn't have much more than a small table and a few clay jugs and bowls, for ideas.

"Let's go straight to the palace," Edward argued impatiently. "The Corsairs' plot definitely involves the pharaoh and that's where we'll find him."

Anastasia took a deep breath. She wasn't comfortable just rushing straight for the palace. They didn't know enough about what was going on. Where the danger was or where the Corsairs might be hiding. It was like in martial arts, it was usually a good idea to know something about your opponent before engaging. "I know we're on the clock and don't have a lot of time, but I don't want us to be careless. I think we should get a better understanding of the city before we rush after the royal family," Anastasia said thoughtfully. "Even if we went to the palace, there's no reason for guards to talk to us, let alone let us see the pharaoh."

This seemed to sink in for Edward. "Sorry. I'm just really worried. I think I was so excited to be in ancient Egypt that I kinda forgot that we were on a mission to save the world. What happens if we don't stop the Corsairs in time? What about Mom and Dad?

Everyone at school? What if they're not there when we get back?" His voice cracked with emotion and he was sniffling.

"We won't let that happen!" Anastasia said forcefully, taking his hand into hers. She was worried, too, but she focused on her breathing and felt herself getting calmer. She needed to keep it together for both of them. "We'll figure this out, together."

He tried to stop sniffling. "I'm not crying, you know!" Edward said with his voice catching even further. He was embarrassed, but trying to calm himself was only making it worse. Tears started to leak out of his eyes. "It's just sand in my eyes." Edward wiped them away with the back of his hand. "We are in the desert, after all."

She patted his hand and nodded agreeably. "Let's get that sand out of your eyes, then we can go check things out. We'll get a lay of the land and then we'll get to work."

Anastasia found herself wandering arm in arm with Edward through the market square, taking in the sounds and smells of daily life in ancient Egypt. Wide sandstone walkways were laid out in a grid with the merchants and their stalls set on the dirt squares in between. Most of the stalls were covered with cloth to provide shade from the powerful sun. It was like the ancient world's Food Channel. The smell of exotic spices like cinnamon, paprika, and a bunch of others that she couldn't name filled her nostrils. She loved the energy in the market as the inhabitants of the city haggled with vendors selling everything from oils and grains to fruits and live animals. She chuckled to herself, thinking that the chickens and donkeys wandering around the market gave a whole new meaning to fresh food. They bought some flatbread and were snacking while they walked and observed. Just then a brownish object whizzed past Anastasia's and Edward's heads.

Anastasia pivoted and followed the flight of the object while Edward let out a strangled squawk. "What the heck was that?" he said, looking left and right.

Anastasia determined it was some sort of ball just a split second before a pack of marauding children chased after the slightly misshapen, brown ball. A boy with curly, black hair and a woven sack over his shoulder was distancing himself from the rest of the pack as he gracefully caught up with the ball. He flicked the ball up into the air with his left foot and then booted the ball with his right foot directly over the top of one of the vendor's stalls. Anastasia followed the arc of the ball as it dropped from the sky directly into a large basket that seemed to be made of woven reeds. Roughly half of the kids cheered and danced about the square chanting, "Salah! Salah! Salah!"

The boy who had kicked the ball crowed "We are tied. The next basket wins!" as he ran around the square with his arms stretched out wide. The merchants paid the boys no notice. Clearly, this was a common pastime for the boys in the square.

Anastasia laughed. "They're playing some sort of ancient version of soccer! That's the other goal." She pointed to another large basket on the other side of the market.

Edward seemed to be nodding in agreement but pointed at the brown ball. It was the size of a volleyball but slightly oblong like someone had sat on it for too long and squashed it. She couldn't identify what it was, but the brown exterior of the ball didn't look like normal leather either.

"What kind of funny soccer ball is that?"

"One that's not made in China," she replied as the game raged on.

The ball popped out of the throng, and one of the boys on the other side of the market belted the ball with his foot. The ball was still rising when it struck Edward on the side of his head with a loud bonk. Edward pirouetted slowly from the force, collapsing in a heap as the ball careened off his head straight into the air. While she was instantly worried about Edward, she couldn't help it when her instincts took over. Instead of running to Edward to make sure he wasn't concussed again, her eyes followed the ball as she felt her feet shift and her knees bend slightly. She instinctively plotted the path of the ball and launched herself off the ground. Her left leg climbed up and above her head, providing the momentum to turn her body upside down with her head pointing toward the ground. Her eyes never left the ball. She scissored her trailing right leg forward, making perfect contact with the ball with the instep of her right foot. The ball changed directions by more than ninety degrees as it arced once more across the market and directly into the same basket the ball had landed in only minutes before.

For a moment, it was quiet and then the boys in the square erupted with a combination of cheers and protests. By the time she had climbed back to her feet, she found herself surrounded by a circle of boys jumping up and down and cheering. Anastasia couldn't help but be caught up in the moment and joined them in the celebration.

The curly-headed boy who had scored previously beamed at her as he shouted over the cheering, "That was the most amazing strike I have ever seen! You are truly touched by Aten's rays!" He was smiling and looking straight into her eyes, his mocha-colored skin setting off his white teeth. Now that he was standing in front of her, she could see that his eyes were almost black and matched the curly hair hanging down to his shoulders.

Anastasia felt herself blush. "Thanks. I'm sorry if I interrupted your game. I didn't mean to," she stammered as she looked down and tucked her hair behind her ears. "I just couldn't help myself when I saw the ball."

"I am Salah. It is an honor to meet one such as you. You have brought us victory. You may interrupt our game anytime as far as I am concerned."

Just then two of the boys in the circle were shoved to the ground as a very large boy pushed his way through the circle. "You and your team have cheated, Salah! You had an extra player. I will not pay a cheater!" This guy clearly had already hit puberty as he was tall and had a mustache.

Salah smiled sweetly at the angry boy and replied, "We have done no such thing. By Aten's rays, we have never met this young woman before in our lives. As you know, Bilji, everything in the market is in play. You will need to honor your wager unless you have no honor."

All this did was make Bilji much angrier. The celebrations seemed to stop as all the boys from both sides were watching now.

"You lie! I will not pay you a single piece of silver."

Anastasia interjected, "He's not lying. My brother and I just arrived in Akhetaten today. We haven't met him or anyone else before. I am sorry I interrupted the game. I didn't mean to—it just happened." She was truly sorry.

Bilji swiveled toward her and growled, "No one is talking to you. You are nothing but criminal trash. You are probably the daughter of a courtesan." He was so angry he was actually spitting. "You will speak only when spoken to!"

A switch flicked in Anastasia's brain. *Criminal trash. Speak only when spoken to.* Her eyes narrowed as she felt her own anger start to build. She found herself taking a step toward him. "First, stop spraying your saliva on me like some sort of disgusting ogre. Second, no one gets to speak about my mother that way," she said with a deathly calm. It was like someone had started a volcanic reaction deep inside her. She could feel the anger and heat rising through her body, ready to erupt.

That's when Bilji got stupid. "I will call you anything I like!"

He charged forward with his hands outstretched to shove her. She caught his wrists and used his momentum against him as she rolled backward while planting her foot in his sternum. He looked surprised as he flipped over forward and landed flat on his back in the dirt.

The crowd of boys collectively said, "Ohhh."

Bilji was stunned, winded, and humiliated as he scrambled back to his feet.

He dusted himself off and growled "Now I will give you exactly what your sort deserves!" as he reached to his belt and drew out a knife.

She could hear the boys around her gasp. She heard Salah say, "Be careful, he has a knife!" This may have been unnecessary as she couldn't help but see it. It wasn't a machete but at four or five inches, it was plenty big enough.

Anastasia automatically found herself in her fighting stance. Hands up with her left foot slightly in front of her right. There was no time to be scared. She had trained for situations like this with her MMA coach.

Bilji lunged forward and swung the knife as she ducked underneath its path and danced backward. He lunged again, this time far more quickly, and caught the edge of her gown with the knifepoint as she sidestepped. She heard a small ripping noise as the fabric was cut. She became even more alert, if that were possible.

Bilji leered maniacally. "You can keep dancing, you little rat, but I will get you in the end."

Time seemed to slow down for Anastasia as Bilji switched the knife to his left hand and feinted with it before throwing a hook with the bunched fist of his right hand. She ducked under the looping hook and pivoted backward on her left foot to sweep his front leg out from under him with her right heel. She returned to her fighting stance as she completed her 360-degree rotation and Bilji toppled backward with a surprised expression on his face. He landed in the dirt on his backside and dropped his knife, which skittered across the ground. As he tried to rise to his feet once more, Anastasia launched a roundhouse kick that planted her right instep flush on Bilji's left cheek. His head snapped to the right and more spit flew out of his mouth, this time involuntarily. He was out cold when he hit the ground.

The crowd of boys let out another low, "Ohhhh!"

A bald-headed boy rushed to Bilji's side. He looked at Anastasia with pure hatred in his eyes as he shouted, "You will be cursed for this."

Suddenly the boys started to scatter. Salah tugged her sleeve. "One of the merchants has alerted the guards. They are coming! We must leave now."

She turned to spot Edward, who was just sitting up in the dirt and rubbing the side of his head. He was still where he had fallen after he had been beaned in the head by the ball.

"We have to get my brother first," she said to Salah.

They rushed to Edward and helped him to his feet. He was still a little confused as he looked at Anastasia. "What happened? Why was I on the ground?"

Anastasia glanced across the market square and could see three or four guards just like the ones at the city gates entering the square.

"Come! We must go now!" Salah implored.

She put Edward's arm over her shoulder and said, "There's no time to explain right now, bro. I seem to have gotten us into a little bit of a mess. I'm really sorry."

Edward looked across the square and saw the guards. He let out a little yelp as he and Anastasia quickly followed Salah's lead in crouching down and weaving in between stalls.

They followed Salah through twists and turns as the sandstone-paved streets ended and gave way to narrower alleyways of hard dirt. They wound between mud-brick buildings, dodging people and the occasional animal who were going about their daily routines. Anastasia completely lost her bearings. They didn't see or hear any guards behind them, but they didn't stop running for the next five minutes. They were all panting when Salah led them through a doorway and into a quiet courtyard.

"We can rest now. This is my home. You are safe here," he said, still panting. Then his face broke into a giant and friendly smile. "Where did you learn to fight like that? That was just as amazing as the wonder basket that you scored!"

Anastasia felt herself smiling with him despite being slightly out of breath. It was probably to be expected after fighting a boy with a knife and then running for her life from the guards. They had only been in ancient Egypt for a few hours and she hadn't exactly kept the low profile they had agreed upon with Dr. G.

"Are you a goddess hiding here on earth? You must teach me," Salah asked earnestly.

"Wait a minute," Edward cut in, clearly confused. "Time to put this on pause. What the heck happened back there? Something hit me in the head and the next thing I know we're running from scary guys with swords. Someone has to fill me in, connect the dots, paint me a picture." Edward looked at her and Salah imploringly.

Salah laughed a deep and friendly laugh. He put his arm around Edward's shoulder and said, "My name is Salah. Your sister is amazing and we are all going to be fast friends!" He went on to explain the details of what had transpired while Edward had been unconscious.

The game the boys had been playing was called fasoo. The ball was made from the stomach of a donkey, which explained its irregular shape. Like soccer, you couldn't use your hands or arms but you could use every other part of your body. The objective was to get the ball into the opposing team's basket. The first team to ten baskets won the game. The game was bounded by the market square and there were no fouls. It really was anything goes.

Salah and his team were the sons of lesser artisans and workmen within Akhetaten. Bilji's team were the sons of priests and the wealthy merchants. This afforded Bilji and his friends countless advantages in life, including things like fine clothes, plentiful food, and education. Salah and his team took great pride in beating them in fasoo whenever they could. Bilji's father was the wealthiest merchant in Akhetaten. His bald-headed friend that had cursed Anastasia was the son of one of the high priests. It figured. Within hours of arriving in the city, somehow she had made two of the most powerful enemies she could have imagined.

"Don't worry," said Salah with an easy smile. "That lot of pompous fools don't like any of us who aren't in their rich and powerful club. The fasoo team will protect you both. We are like a family on the streets and you are my friends. Plus you delivered us one of the most famous victories we could have imagined. How did you flip upside down and score that basket?"

Salah bantered on about the events in the square. Edward turned pale when Salah recounted the knife fight.

"OMG, Anastasia! You could have been killed while I was unconscious," Edward said incredulously.

"Do you fight like your sister as well?" Salah asked Edward.

"Not exactly. I am more the creative type. Anastasia is the fighter in the family," Edward said sheepishly.

Anastasia felt bad for Edward. She didn't want him to feel embarrassed that she had protected him. "Edward knows pretty much everything about everything and he is really creative. You should see the picture that he painted of me for my birthday," she said.

Salah's eyes lit up. "You are an artist, Edward? You must stay for lunch and meet my father, Thutmose. He is an incredible sculptor. He has been working on his first commission for the royal family. He is going to be famous across all the lands one day. You will see," Salah said excitedly.

Anastasia and Edward couldn't believe it. Salah's father was Thutmose, the sculptor who created the statue of Nefertiti. Things were definitely looking up.

"Come on. You will love my parents. Plus it's time for our midday meal. You must be hungry."

Chapter 16

Edward, Anastasia, and Salah sat cross-legged on mats woven from reeds around a low table in the main room of Salah's house. It was nice and cool inside compared to the blazing heat from the midday sun. Food lay piled in the middle of the table on three different ceramic platters for all of them to share. The first platter was full of dried dates and fresh figs that had been split in two. The second platter held flatbread smeared with honey. The final platter had three fish, their heads still on and skin crisp and split from roasting.

Salah and his parents, Thutmose and Aneski, also sat on the opposite side of the table. Thutmose had curly hair like his son and a broad face and full lips that were prone to breaking into a smile. His eyes were dark and full of inquisitiveness. He wore a simple smock covered in dust and drops of paint that he clearly used while working. Aneski was a kind and pretty woman. She had delicate features and long, dark hair. They had gladly welcomed them to join their midday feast.

After all their walking this morning, both Edward and Anastasia were ravenous. Edward couldn't wait to dig in but couldn't spot any forks or knives. *How am I going to eat the fish without a fork?* He was quietly relieved when he saw Salah and his parents use their fingers to tear off portions and eat. Part of him couldn't wait for the next time his mother told him off for eating with his fingers. He'd let her know that if it was good enough for the advanced civilization that was ancient Egypt, it was good enough for him. By the end of the meal, he was stuffed. The food was so different from the ham and cheese sandwiches they normally had at home for lunch, but it was delicious.

Edward and Anastasia had shared their prepared story about arriving in advance from Thebes to help their father expand the family papyrus and scribing business. The family had seemed to accept the story and were now chatting amiably about the work they performed in the studio behind the house.

"I mainly work with stone these days," Thutmose told the twins. "A few years ago, I was working more frequently with clay to make ceramics, but it seems that my stonework has become more popular. I suppose you have to do the work that people will pay for. I am thankful for the fact that I have a constant stream of work," he said happily as he gazed across the table at Aneski and Salah. "I have to try to keep my family fed and clothed. Can't have them running around skinny and naked after all."

Edward couldn't help but laugh. Not so much at the joke but more about the fact that there were dad jokes over three thousand years ago. *Clearly, humanity has not advanced in all fields of endeavor.*

"Stop embarrassing Salah in front of his new friends, my husband," Aneski said, shaking her head. She turned to Anastasia and Edward and said, "He is a good and talented man, my husband, but deep inside, he wishes to be a performer, a comedian." She smiled lovingly at her husband and continued to say, "For all of our sake, please stick to the sculpture."

"Father, Edward is a painter as well," Salah said excitedly.

Thutmose smiled and examined Edward closely and asked, "You are an artist, Edward?"

"Well, of sorts, sir. I paint and sketch but I'm not that good."

"What do you mean you're not that good?" Anastasia was not having any of it. "You are really talented, Edward. Even your teacher says so."

"So you have had instruction, Edward?"

His sister spoke for him before he could even open his mouth. "He has been painting since he was three. When I was painting stick figures, he was painting pictures of people that actually looked like people."

"You and Anastasia must come and join me in the studio this afternoon. Salah is going to spend the afternoon mixing pigments while I work on my latest commission. Anastasia, perhaps you can help Salah while Edward does some painting."

Edward was really overwhelmed. "It would be an honor to see your studio, sir."

Anastasia was nodding emphatically as she said, "We would love to see your studio."

Thutmose laughed again and it was plain to see where Salah got his easy laugh. "Edward, there is no need for you and Anastasia to call me sir. You can both call me Thutmose."

Thutmose's studio was a wonder. It was divided into four different sections. The first section was for stonework with pedestals and work stools in the middle. They were flanked by stores of raw stone, chisels, brushes, and other tools for working the stone. The second section was for making ceramics, which also had the same pedestals and stools. These were supported with stores of fresh clay, tools for shaping the clay, and ovens for baking. The third section was for painting. This seemed to include both papyrus and finished ceramics. There were easels, pedestals, stools, sheets of papyrus, and shelves of pigments and brushes. Finally, there was also a long workbench with mortars and pestles that appeared to be used for grinding and mixing the different pigments. There were four men wearing smocks similar to the one Thutmose was wearing, busily working on different things or clearing up.

This was an ancient Egyptian heaven for real artists. Edward actually felt a little nervous. Thutmose and all the other men were real artists. Edward could paint a bit, but he couldn't sculpt a thing. All his art projects with clay always went horribly wrong. Instead of ending up with beautiful vases, Edward's pottery wheel invariably created crude and stumpy bowls. He hadn't even dreamed of ever trying to work with stone.

Anastasia and Salah sat on stools at the workbench, grinding and mixing ingredients to produce pigments for painting. At Salah's direction, they scraped and mixed bits of various brightly colored stones and minerals. Salah appeared to be slowly adding some sort of liquid and a bluish powder into a mortar while Anastasia continuously ground and mixed the contents with a pestle. It was vibrant blue but clearly far more involved than buying a tube of paint from the art store—something that Edward took for granted at home.

Thutmose worked on a bust in the far corner of the studio. The rough outlines of the head and shoulders had already been chiseled from the block of limestone. The head appeared to have

106

some sort of big hat on top, which Edward recognized as a royal headdress. Thutmose appeared to be at work on refining the features of the face in the stone. Edward was certain that this unfinished piece of stone was the famous statue of Nefertiti. He wanted to go over and sit and watch Thutmose, but he knew that everyone was expecting him to create something himself. Before starting his work, Thutmose had set up Edward with a smock, easel, brushes, and a palette. He had a variety of colors for painting at his disposal, including white, black, blue, red, and yellow. He was just mixing and sorting his colors on the ceramic palette when he heard a serious commotion in the courtyard.

Two armed guards entered the studio. Edward froze and his mouth went completely dry at the same time. *We're in big trouble. How did the guards find us?* He had assumed that was all behind them when Salah had said they were safe. He looked over at Anastasia, who looked equally alarmed as she looked back at him. He started to mouth the words "Get ready to run" when the most beautiful woman he had ever seen walked into the studio. She was tall and brown skinned with shiny, black hair and large, piercing eyes. She was dressed in a flowing gown of white with vibrant patterns of blue and yellow dyed into the fabric. She was the first person he had seen wearing jewelry since they had arrived. An elaborate gold necklace surrounded her long, elegant neck and golden bangles circled her arms. She had a magnetic presence that immediately erased any thoughts Edward had previously had of running.

This has to be Nefertiti! His suspicion was confirmed when he saw that everyone else in the room was bowing face down on the floor. The guards were staring at him—the idiot who was still standing. He immediately dropped to all fours, hoping they weren't going to feel inclined to beat any common sense into him.

Thutmose said, "Your Royal Highness, we are honored by your presence in our most humble studio."

She laughed happily. "Oh, Thutmose, please dispense with the formalities. I would like to think we are past that now. How many times have I sat for you in your private studio?" she asked with her eyebrows raised.

"Your Highness, I will always be your humble servant. I will try, but it will be very difficult for me to be informal with Your Grace."

Edward looked up to see they were smiling at one another.

"Alright then," said Nefertiti, now putting on a very stern-looking face. "You may consider it royal order punishable by death if it makes it easier for you to comply."

Thutmose burst into laughter and bowed his head to acknowledge his defeat. "As you wish, Nefertiti. Now let's get you seated and I will get to work."

It was one of the happiest afternoons Edward could remember. Nefertiti's timeless beauty and down-to-earth nature filled the studio with positive energy. Thutmose asked Nefertiti if she would put her hair up so that he would have an unobstructed view of her face. Similar to how it would appear if she were actually wearing a royal headdress.

"But of course, Thutmose," Nefertiti said as she twisted her long, black hair into a bun on top of her head and secured it with a long pin. "You would think it would be a habit by now after so many sittings," she laughed.

She continued to smile serenely and chat away with anyone and everyone in the room. Definitely not what Edward had envisaged from the Queen of Egypt. He was also inspired watching Thutmose at work carving his masterpiece. Thutmose had absolute focus on what he was doing but also managed the environment around him. He was friendly but firm in the constant direction he gave both to the apprentices in his studio as well as Nefertiti herself. Edward found himself halfway through his own painting without even realizing what he had been doing. He had been so caught up by the creative energy in the room that his painting had been instinctive.

Edward continued his work, not wanting to lose the moment. He mixed the blue lapis lazuli pigment with the gypsum to match the shade of blue on Nefertiti's gown and kept painting. Time flew as Edward's brush darted back and forth from the palette to the papyrus. The pattern was only interrupted when he had to stop to mix his colors before resuming his flow.

He was almost finished when he realized that Thutmose was actually standing over his shoulder. Edward suddenly became very self-conscious. He hadn't really expected anyone to look at his painting. It was something he had just been compelled to do.

Thutmose let out a slow and appreciative whistle. "Edward, this is quite remarkable. You have captured her essence so accurately it is almost uncanny."

Edward found himself both smiling and blushing at the same time. He wasn't used to getting complimented by world-famous artists or really anyone outside of his family and teachers.

Edward's mild embarrassment turned to abject fear when Nefertiti stood up and smiled at him and said, "What is that you have painted, my young artist? May I see?"

Edward felt his throat closing and it became hard to breathe. He managed to squeak out "Of course, Your Royal Highness" in an abnormally high-pitched tone before turning even redder.

She glided across the room with a fluid grace like water flowing down a stream. She gasped when she saw the picture Edward had painted on the papyrus. "It looks like me!" She beamed at Edward. "When the greatest painters in the land have painted my portrait, never once have they looked like me. They always paint Akhenaten and me in the image of our ancestors. It's quite ridiculous. They paint what they think we expect and not what is real." She turned and regarded Edward closely. "Why are you different from all the rest, my young man?"

"I guess I am not skilled enough to paint what might be expected. I can only paint what I see, what is true." He looked at her earnestly and said, "I am really sorry if I took any liberties or offended you."

Nefertiti laughed and erased any concerns that Edward may have had. "You have not offended me, my artist, you have brought me an unexpected joy. May I have this painting so I may give it to my husband as a gift?"

Edward felt his face split into a grin. "Of course you may have it, Your Highness. It would be an honor." Edward shot a glance over to the table where Anastasia was working with Salah. She was beaming back at him and gave him a big thumbs-up.

Nefertiti tried to offer Edward a commission for the painting, which he politely refused. The fact that she wanted it meant more than any money ever could.

After formal introductions to Edward and Anastasia, she insisted that they all be her guests the following day for the royal procession to commemorate the formal establishment of Akhetaten as the capital of all Egypt.

Edward and Anastasia could hardly sleep that night in their rented room. The excitement of the day was almost too much. They had made new friends, met the Queen of all of Egypt, and had been invited to a royal celebration. They weren't sure if they were any closer to stopping the Corsairs' evil plot, but it felt like they were making progress.

"How cool was it that Thutmose liked my painting?" Edward said to Anastasia happily as they were drifting off to sleep.

"It was amazing, Edward!" she answered with real pride in her voice.

"And how cool was it that Nefertiti liked my painting?" Edward added excitedly.

"It was really cool," Anastasia answered, yawning this time.

"And how cool was it that she wanted to give it to the pharaoh as a gift?" Edward asked, basking in his own glory.

"You are potentially my most awesome twin brother in the world. Now shut up and go to sleep!" Anastasia said as she faded into sleep.

He beamed at the compliment, then he remembered that he was Anastasia's only twin brother. It didn't dent Edward's mood. He still fell asleep smiling contentedly to himself.

Chapter 17

Anastasia and Edward slept soundly on the woven sleeping mats that they had unrolled for bedtime last night. Edward had been dubious about sleeping on the floor. However, when they woke the next morning, they felt refreshed and ready for the day.

After a simple breakfast of fruit and bread smeared with honey in their room, they visited the market to look for new clothes for the royal celebration that Nefertiti herself had invited them to. Anastasia didn't want to draw unnecessary attention because they were dressed shabbily. She found a merchant selling garments made from fine linen.

"No one threshes the flax as thoroughly as my family. It is the only way to get the fine thread. As you know, young lady, fine thread makes for a fine weave," the merchant said in a know-it-all tone.

Anastasia held the garments in her hands as she examined them closely. They were so much softer than what she and Edward were wearing now. The weave was so fine it was almost translucent when she held it up with the sun behind it. They were a big step up from the costumes they had borrowed from the museum.

"It is very fine, is it not? Of course this type of quality does not come cheaply." He examined them skeptically as he tried to assess if Anastasia and Edward could afford the clothing or if they were wasting his time.

Edward almost choked when he first named his price, but Anastasia convinced her brother that they should splurge so they wouldn't look too out of place.

They met Salah and his parents midmorning and chatted excitedly about the upcoming celebration. In spite of being utterly beautiful and the most important woman in Egypt, Nefertiti had been so down to earth and generous yesterday. Anastasia couldn't believe that they were going to see her again, let alone meet the pharaoh. Akhetaten had functionally become the capital of Egypt when Akhenaten and Nefertiti had moved there from Thebes, but this celebration would make it official.

They traveled north through the merchants' quarter and headed toward the palace. They would meet Akhenaten and Nefertiti before traveling on to the Great Temple of Aten for the formal ceremony. This was the same temple they had first seen when they'd entered the city yesterday. It would be a great day for all the citizens of Akhetaten who had actually helped to build the city from the ground up. They would truly make history today.

Anastasia stared at the palace. It was more than impressive. It must have been at least five stories high and every bit as large as the Great Temple of Aten. Anastasia realized that it looked even larger than it was because there were very few structures in the city that were more than one or two stories.

They started up the ramp that led toward the palace entrance, which was framed by giant pylon towers on either side. The pylons were covered from top to bottom in painted reliefs of Aten riding in his chariot across the sky to bring light and life to the people of Egypt. The guards parted and a royal attendant came out and greeted them each in turn. They passed through the palace entrance into a great entry hall, which was easily the size of a football field. The pillars and stone beams were all etched with hieroglyphs that all told stories of the greatness of Aten. When Anastasia looked up, she saw that even the ceilings had been painted the deep blue of a nighttime sky. *How is that even possible to build something so big and grand without modern technology?* The attendant then led them through a set of silk curtains to a private waiting area.

"Their Royal Highnesses will be with you all shortly," the attendant said before bowing and exiting the room.

Anastasia suddenly found herself short breath. *Nefertiti was so nice yesterday, but what if Akhenaten is different? What if he's stuffy and formal or just really mean?* She fidgeted and tucked her hair behind her ears, which was a nervous habit. She knew she got this way sometimes with authority figures. She had felt exactly the same way when they'd first met Dr. G. She hated idea of being in trouble.

Salah noticed Anastasia's anxiety and smiled at her. "Don't worry. He is a truly great and caring man. You will see."

They were only there for a few minutes before the curtains parted and in walked Akhenaten and Nefertiti.

Akhenaten dominated the room with his regal presence. He was in the full pharaoh outfit with his golden scepter and flowing robes of linen with golden threads embroidered around the trim. While his features weren't beautiful, with a nose that was slightly too big for his face, they were strong and commanding. He had a broad and well-muscled chest and shoulder-length, jet black hair. He might have only been five and a half feet tall, but he was still taller than everyone else in the room. Anastasia was silently thankful that she and Edward were still a couple of inches shorter than Akhenaten. *It would have been super awkward if we towered over the pharaoh.* Nefertiti swept in beside Akhenaten in her formal regalia replete with a jeweled headdress like the one in Thutmose's sculpture.

Thutmose, Aneski, Salah, and Edward quickly got down on their knees and began to press their foreheads to the ground in what was clearly a sign of respect and deference. Anastasia almost freaked out when she realized her mistake. Even Edward, who often had the social etiquette of a cave bear, had learned from yesterday and gotten it right. She bruised her knees as she quickly hit the ground. *I really need to get better at royal protocol,* she thought when Akhenaten said, "Please stand up, my guests." To Anastasia's relief, he smiled broadly as he greeted them. "It is a pleasure to meet such a talented group of Egyptian artists. Nefertiti has told me all about your bold and original works. Thank you for joining us on such an important day for our kingdom. It is also fitting as the city of Akhetaten is bold and original, much like your own creations."

"Thank you for inviting us to join the royal grandstand on such an auspicious occasion, Your Royal Highness," Thutmose said for all of them.

Nefertiti smiled and said, "We are all fortunate on this day. In many ways, it is a new beginning for an empire that is already more than 1,500 years old." She gestured to Edward and Anastasia as she said to her husband, "These are the young visitors to our city

I spoke of last night. Edward is the one who painted the papyrus portrait that I gave you, my husband."

The pharaoh's face lit up as he turned to Edward and said, "That painting is a gift I will cherish for the rest of my days and into the afterlife. It has captured my wife exactly as I see her, not as some historical ideal. It is her essence that I love and gives me strength. May thanks be upon you."

Edward felt caught between embarrassment at being complimented so publicly and euphoria at the very compliment—from a pharaoh—but he managed to say, "You are very welcome, Your Royal Highness. It was . . . um . . . my pleasure."

"You should know that today I will be making a royal decree that Nefertiti and I are only to be portrayed in our actual forms. It is time to ensure that we celebrate the truth of things as they are. Be that its beauty or its flaws," he said, knowingly pointing to his protruding nose with a smirk.

It suddenly dawned on Anastasia that Akhenaten's decree was the equivalent of removing the filters from Instagram. She and her friends spent a ridiculous amount of time trying to make the photos they were going to post look just right. Questions started racing through her head. *Will my followers still like my posts if I post them as is—without editing? Do the likes and comments actually mean anything if the images aren't actually real?* Everyone had insecurities, herself included. What Akhenaten was proposing was really bold.

Akhenaten turned toward the curtains. "Imhotep, have you prepared the decree as I requested?"

A short, thin man with a bald head parted the silk curtains and stepped inside. "Yes, my pharaoh. The decree has been p-p-prepared and only awaits your final review and a-a-approval," he stuttered timidly with his eyes averted before bowing deeply.

"We will leave you with General Meketre to accompany you to the royal grandstand while we finalize the decree and make our preparations for the ceremony," Akhenaten said to Anastasia and Edward as the curtains parted.

In strode a powerfully built man with a sword at his waist and a shield strapped to his back. He was dark skinned like all the Egyptians, but his hair was a mixture of black and gray. Anastasia had heard her mother use the expression salt-and-pepper hair for the look the general had going. It certainly gave him a distinguished air. He was flanked by another younger man who was also armed to the teeth with sharp things that could kill you. Anastasia could count two swords strapped to his back with their bronze hilts visible over each shoulder. He also had two daggers on his belt and one more strapped to his thigh. Those were just the weapons that were visible. He had a strong jaw and broad shoulders. Anastasia guessed that he must be a more junior officer under the general's command.

Akhenaten smiled broadly at his guests. "You will be in good hands with General Meketre. He is a true protector of Egypt, and he and his troops will be participating in the procession so he is actually on his way there as well." With that, the royal pair glided back through the curtains, followed by the timid scribe, and disappeared from sight.

The general guided them back through the great entry hall and out through the entrance of the palace. He strode next to Anastasia along the sandstone-paved Royal Road with his hands clasped behind his back. Thutmose, Aneski, Salah, and Edward walked ahead of them, chatting as they pushed thorough the gathering crowds.

"Young Anastasia, you wouldn't happen to know anything about an incident that occurred in the market yesterday by any chance?" General Meketre asked in a casual manner.

Anastasia's trouble radar starting pinging loudly in the back of her mind as she tried to imitate his casual tone. "What incident would that be, General?"

"The son of a very prominent merchant was brutally attacked. I am told it was unprovoked and he was lucky to escape with his life. The assailant was apparently a woman."

"No. No," Anastasia said slowly and thoughtfully. "I haven't heard anything about an attack in the market. That's really quite shocking in such a nice, safe place like Akhetaten," she said as lightly as she could.

"So you weren't there in the market at the time of the attack then?" General Meketre said, looking calmly into her eyes.

Anastasia fought to maintain her cool and eye contact. She measured her words carefully as she said, "No, I definitely wasn't in the market during the attack that you described, General."

The general smiled. "I would have been surprised if you had said you were there. I don't think anyone could have possibly seen the attack that was described to my guards. The victim reported that the female assailant was well over six feet tall and had a striking resemblance to an Amazon. While I have seen many things in my life, I have yet to see a six-foot, crazed Amazon within the borders of Egypt."

Anastasia nodded, then said innocently, "I have never seen an Amazon either, General. Sounds quite scary. Is the victim going to be okay?"

"Physically he is fine, but his ego is in tatters. Apparently, it was quite traumatic for the young man." He chuckled and looked at her knowingly. "I suppose this incident will likely become one of the few unsolved crimes in our city. Whoever the assailant was would seem to be quite formidable."

"Oh well. I suppose you can't solve them all," Anastasia said sweetly as her heart hammered nervously inside her chest and they strode into the temple grounds. The grounds were packed with at least two thousand people already gathered in the gardens.

The general laughed out loud at her response. "I suppose you can't solve them all. I am afraid I must leave you now to take up my duties, but I have greatly enjoyed our chat. Please do try to stay out of trouble today, Anastasia."

Somehow the general knew it was her, but he had chosen not to pursue it any further. She could actually feel her heart rate slowing as the tension leaked out of her. She happily joined Edward and Salah's family as they fought their way through the crowd to their spot on the royal grandstand.

The commemoration stone stood about three feet high and was placed alongside the Royal Road fifty yards inside the inner gates with the Great Temple of Aten directly behind it. The front of the stone was flat with hieroglyphs carved directly into the face. Akhenaten would make his speech next to the stone and directly in front of the temporary grandstand that had been erected on the other side of the Royal Road.

The stand, which sat at the edge of the garden, apparently contained the who's who of the ten thousand citizens of Akhetaten. Members of the royal family plus the most important priests, bureaucrats, members of the military, merchants, scholars, and artists were among 120 guests who could fit in the grandstand. They were all dressed in their finest garb with many adorned in golden jewelry. One man in particular stood out. He wore a jeweled circlet of gold on his head and several large gold bangles on each arm. She watched as he was greeted deferentially by all those around him. He seemed to bask in being the center of attention in the grandstand.

"That is Ementah, the pharaoh's younger brother and next in line to rule," Salah whispered discreetly in her ear.

Anastasia was overwhelmed by the pageantry. It reminded her of the red carpet at the Oscars where all the celebrities were stopped for their pictures and latest gossip. Anastasia couldn't believe that she and Edward had somehow made the cut. It had been a really unlikely chain of events that had led them from the market to Salah's house, Thutmose's studio, the Royal Palace, and now here. She reminded herself not to get too caught up and not to forget their mission. They had to figure out what the Corsairs were up to and keep Akhenaten safe. It was the only way for them to protect their time, their families, and their lives from the ripples of change.

Once the speech was complete, Akhenaten would step into his glittering, golden chariot with Nefertiti. Then, being led by General Meketre and his men, they would conduct a full circuit of the temple gardens. Afterward, they would continue down the Royal Road and past the remainder of the assembled crowds to the entrance of the palace. A select set of guests were invited to attend a function in the royal gardens while the general public would use the holiday to make merry in the streets or at home. There were even two extra jugs of beer for each working-age man courtesy of Their Royal Highnesses. With two liters in a jug, it was definitely enough to create a substantial amount of merriment.

Akhenaten appeared from the entrance of the Great Temple of Aten with Nefertiti by his side. The cheers from the citizens of Akhetaten were thunderous. It was clear to Anastasia that the rulers were truly loved by their people. Akhenaten and Nefertiti strode down the front steps of the temple with everyone's eyes upon them. Akhenaten's staff, topped with its giant blue sapphire, blazed brightly in the sunshine while his white robes trailed behind him in the breeze. Nefertiti actually glittered in the sunshine. She appeared to glide next to her husband and was nearly as tall as Akhenaten in the jeweled headdress.

Akhenaten ascended the temporary dais that been erected next to the commemoration stone and a hush fell over the collective crowd. He began to speak and his voice seemed to carry loudly across the temple grounds as it echoed off the stone buildings and pathways. He was easily heard and understood by all.

"How does he do that? He's not even using a microphone," Anastasia whispered.

"I dunno. Maybe it's the acoustics?" Edward shrugged.

Akhenaten praised Aten for providing the life-giving rays of the sun to all of Egypt. He also praised the citizens of Akhetaten for building this great city in Aten's honor. It was a sign of a new beginning within Egypt—one that would provide equal opportunity to all Egyptians.

"Wealth and access to the afterlife will be the providence of all people, not just those who can afford to be embalmed," he told the crowd. Akhenaten's voice resonated like thunder through the gardens as he declared, "Today is a day for all to reflect on their achievements and celebrate their future together!"

The royal grandstand applauded politely after Akhenaten finished his speech. However, the general public cheered wildly. While the rich and powerful already had access to the things promised by Akhenaten, the general public did not. Akhenaten was giving them and their children a chance for a better future and afterlife.

Akhenaten signaled to General Meketre, who nodded back and started the procession. Pulled by two white horses, Akhenaten and Nefertiti smiled and waved at the crowd from their chariot. They greeted well-wishers with enthusiasm. Anastasia could hear snatches of their conversations.

"Praise to Aten and praise to Akhenaten! You make our world a paradise here on earth, Your Highness," a working man said, grasping the pharaoh's hand.

"May Aten's rays shine upon you and your family," Akhenaten smiled benevolently.

The crowds pressed in closer, encouraged by the royal couple's openness. It looked like it was going to be a pretty slow journey for the royal couple on their way back to the palace. Thutmose let them know it would be a good time to start walking back to the palace.

"The crowds will be really thick. It will restrict our pace to that of a leisurely stroll, so it may take us some time."

Edward chatted with Thutmose and Aneski on their way back. He was clearly enjoying himself. He was getting to hang out with one of the greatest artists of the time and he was getting to witness history as it happened. He was essentially a pig in mud.

Anastasia didn't mind, either, as she got to chat with Salah. He was funny and kind, plus she could tell that he thought she was pretty cool. Most boys were usually intimidated by her knowing martial arts or being a good athlete. But Anastasia's conversation with Salah was easy, and she soon forgot the crowds around them.

"We are all different, but we truly play as one team. You should come play with us. You would fit right in. Plus they already love you after what happened last time!"

"I'm not sure it's a good idea, especially after what happened the last time. What if the general's men are in the market and realize that it wasn't a six-foot Amazon who flattened Bilji," she laughed.

"Okay. Okay. You are probably right, but both you and Edward should meet them anyway. You could use a few new friends. What if you tire of me?" Salah said with laughter in his eyes. "It's most unlikely but it could happen."

They slowly made their way down the sandstone-paved Royal Road past the temple warehouses when the crowds began to swell behind them. It was as if a rolling wave of people had suddenly caught up with them. Anastasia thought that Akhenaten and Nefertiti must be getting close. She looked back over her shoulder and, sure enough, she saw the General leading two dozen of his finest men and parting the crowd in advance of the chariot carrying the royal couple. She turned back to tell Salah that they were approaching when she realized that something was very wrong.

They were just passing a small alleyway behind one of the temple's warehouses when she noticed a purple light emanating from the dark recesses of the alley. It glowed from behind the back corner of the warehouse. It instantly struck fear into the pit of her stomach. She knew exactly what that light was—a portal from a Refractium Crystal. A portal was being opened around the corner of the warehouse, just like the one that had carried her and Edward back to ancient Egypt.

The adrenaline now coursing through her veins gave her the feeling that her body had been struck by a bolt of lightning. Her senses were heightened as time slowed and she could sense every one of her nerve endings. She frantically looked at Edward, who was walking right in front of her and chatting to Thutmose and Aneski, unaware of what was happening in the alley just to his left. She screamed his name at the same time she grabbed his shoulder and quickly spun him around. He looked at her, confused.

"Look!" Anastasia shouted as she pointed down the alley.

Edward's face moved from confusion to fear as a large group of men dressed in dark clothing came running around the corner toward them. They each had long, curved swords in both hands and wore masks that looked like some sort of snarling, black dogs with razor-sharp teeth.

Assassins coming to kill Akhenaten and Nefertiti!

Anastasia nudged Thutmose and Aneski forward and clear of the alleyway before turning to shove Salah and Edward clear in the opposite direction. The masked men were no more than twenty-five yards away when Anastasia plunged into the street, running as fast as she could in General Meketre's direction.

This is it! This must be what Edward and I came back through time to stop! She was vaguely aware she was screaming as she was running and that people were looking at her. She spotted General Meketre less than fifty yards down the road. He watched her with concern as his eyes narrowed and his hand went to the hilt of his sword. She was now less than forty yards away from him and closing fast.

"They're coming!" she shouted at the top of her lungs. "You have to save Akhenaten and Nefertiti!"

Finally, a look of alarm crossed General Meketre's face. Anastasia glanced over her shoulder to see a dozen of the dog-masked men flooding into the street behind her and moving fast. She saw General Meketre and his men drawing their weapons as her eyes once again swung forward. She realized that some of the general's men must have bows the instant arrows started whizzing past her head. She could hear a few groans and curses behind her and the sound of swords clattering on the road, but she didn't dare stop to look back. She just crouched lower and ran as if her life depended upon it, which it did.

General Meketre and his men surged past her toward the attackers. Two of the guards stayed with the royal chariot, swords drawn in a defensive posture, while the rest of the guards engaged the enemy. Akhenaten remained in the chariot, shielding Nefertiti behind him. Anastasia ran until she was right in front of them before pivoting back toward the battle in her fighting stance. It felt like the right thing to do. The truth was that she had no idea what she would actually do if the assassins made it past the general and his men.

By the time she had surveyed the battle scene, several of the guards were down on the ground but only four of the dog-masked attackers remained standing. Three of the fallen assassins had arrows protruding from their bodies while the others simply lay in a heap on the ground with crimson pools of blood forming around them. The same was true for the bodies of the guards. Anastasia couldn't believe how quickly it had happened.

The general and his men had the masked attackers surrounded, thanks to their superior numbers. Their swords were drawn and their shields were up as they attempted to close ranks and finish them off. Two of the men charged the general in an attempt to break through with their four blades flashing in the sunshine. The general was incredibly fast, parrying one blade on his sword while catching another on his shield and then leaping over a third blade. As he landed, he kicked the first attacker in the knee, which buckled as the man toppled to the ground. He ducked under the second attacker's blade and spun backward with his sword extended. Suddenly, the dog-masked man's head separated from the rest of his body. Without losing a beat, the general turned and brought the pommel of his sword down on top of the first attacker's head as he tried to scramble back to his feet. The dog-masked attacker went limp and collapsed to the ground.

By the time the general looked up, the remaining attackers had already been dealt with by the rest of the guards. An eerie silence hung over the scene of the battle with six guards and eleven dog-masked assassins lying on the ground dead and one assassin unconscious. The silence was interrupted by a squawk and then the sound of bodies crashing to the ground.

****

Edward had fallen hard after Anastasia had shoved him out of the way. He had accidentally rolled into the group of people that had been walking behind them. They had gone down like bowling pins with several of them falling on top of him. He tried to get back to his feet, but his legs were pinned under the tangle of other bodies. He looked up and saw the dog-masked men running past with their swords drawn. His mouth went dry as terror gripped him. His adrenaline kicked into high gear as he tried to wrestle his way out.

He imagined that this is what it was like when the Incredible Hulk guy got angry and turned all green and muscly. He felt himself roaring as he twisted and turned and eventually fought his way to his feet. His fight-or-flight instinct kicked in, which in Edward's case was definitely the flight instinct. He shot back down the street the way they had come, determined to get as far away from the assassins as he possibly could.

He ran and shoved his way through the crowd shouting "Run for your life!" when his toe caught a raised stone in the street. Edward let out a squawk as his momentum launched him through the air like a bullet fired from a gun. He would have kept flying if not for the black-clad figure with a mask that emerged from a doorway directly in front of him. Edward slammed directly into the man's stomach, and he could hear the air whoosh out of him and his two swords clatter to the ground. Edward tried to get up so he could run away but tripped and fell directly on top of the man's head, inadvertently slamming it to the ground. Edward sprang to his feet, but the man didn't budge. He had been knocked out. It occurred to Edward that he was usually the one lying on the ground unconscious. This was a nice change.

He looked to his left and saw that the royal chariot was only yards away. Edward realized that none of the guards would have seen this man coming from behind them. It suddenly dawned on him that the dog-masked assassins from the alleyway must have been a diversion to attract attention of the soldiers and the crowd. The assassin he had run into by accident was the one who was actually meant to kill the pharaoh. He looked up and saw Akhenaten and Nefertiti staring down at him in wonder and admiration. Someone from the crowd next to him shouted, "Did you see that unarmed boy take out that assassin? He saved the pharaoh! He is a hero!"

Chapter 18

Edward stood stunned with the masked man—the would-be assassin—conked out at his feet. The crowd closed around him, cheering and slapping him on his back. It was a collective nervous release for the crowd, who only moments before had been both surprised and terrified. Edward felt like he had to tell them that they were wrong. He hadn't meant to save Akhenaten; it had been an accident. Thankfully, General Meketre's strong hand landed on Edward's shoulder and helped to guide him out of the crush. He was pulled into an inner circle of guards that had formed ranks around the royal couple and Anastasia. It was like the ancient Egyptian version of the Secret Service. A few of the guards were securing the two attackers who were unconscious but alive. The general was in a hurry to get the pharaoh back to the palace and out of danger. However, Akhenaten was not ready to retreat.

The pharaoh held up his hands to silence the buzzing crowd. Edward saw the hush spread up and down the Royal Road in a matter of seconds.

"Fear not, citizens of Akhetaten, citizens of Egypt. We are too strong for our enemies, for those corrupt forces who would like to drag us backward. We will not be cowed. Aten is too strong, our soldiers are too strong, and our future is too bright! They will be shattered against the granite that is our resolve!" His eyes were filled with steely determination as his voice rang strongly across the crowd. He seemed to grow taller as he prowled defiantly in front of the crowd. "We now have two reasons to celebrate today! Not only have we officially launched Aten's city as the capital of the land, we have also sent a resounding message to anyone who stands against our future and our destiny as a nation! We are Egypt and we will not be stopped! Praise to Aten!" Akhenaten's fists were clenched as he tilted his head back and thrust his arms upward toward the sky.

The crowd answered back with a roar so loud that Edward could actually feel their wall of sound. The pharaoh snatched a clay jug of beer held out in offer by one of the people in the crowd. He raised it in triumph of the foiled attack, then drained its contents before smashing it emphatically on the ground. The crowd roared its approval and the pharaoh climbed back in the golden chariot and signaled General Meketre to proceed.

The crowd continued to celebrate as the procession got underway again to complete its journey to the palace. As Edward jogged along, trying to keep pace with the guards and the chariot, the gravity of what just happened began to sink in. *People died. We're lucky it wasn't Akhenaten or Nefertiti, let alone myself or Anastasia. This wasn't a movie. This was real. Who were those men? How are they related to the Corsairs? Does this mean everything is safe now and Anastasia and I can go home?* Part of him wanted nothing more than to run back to the rock outcropping in the desert and summon the portal to get back home. The rest of him knew that they couldn't go until they were sure they had actually fixed the problem. Otherwise, there might not be anything or anyone to return to.

As he watched the chariot, Edward saw a flash of concern pass between Akhenaten and Nefertiti. Edward had the strong feeling that the pharaoh was a lot more worried than he had just let on to the crowd. Edward wondered if that impromptu speech was a show that was intended to salvage the celebration of the new capital. Certainly, the general's face was like a mask of stone.

Edward's head was still spinning and his heart was racing as they reached the palace and proceeded up the ramp to the entrance. The pharaoh and Nefertiti climbed out of the chariot and hurried into the palace.

The general collected Edward and Anastasia and said in a hushed voice, "Please come with me and refrain from speaking until we reach the private chamber."

The General shuttled them through a side door off the great entry hall. They followed a series of twists and turns before they arrived at another door with a pair of guards standing at attention. The guards stepped aside allowing the general, Anastasia, and Edward to pass through.

"Please stay here," said the general. "I will be back momentarily."

Edward let out a deep breath. Deep inside the palace within this private chamber, he felt safe for the first time since the attack. He looked around the room and saw a table set in the center that was laden with fruits, breads, and meats, as well as pitchers of wine and beer. The table was surrounded with comfortable chairs and cushions. It was quite a spread, and looking at it reminded him that it had been a long time since breakfast. *Would it be bad manners to make a sandwich while we wait?* he wondered. Just as he started to relax, he was squashed in Anastasia's embrace.

"What exactly were you trying to prove, tackling that assassin? You are a total idiot!" she said, releasing him and stepping back to look at his face.

"It was all an accident," Edward said to her sheepishly. "I was actually trying to run away. I didn't mean to knock him out. Now all these people think I'm some sort of hero, but I'm not."

Anastasia shook her head and smiled at him as she said, "Oh, Edward. You are the only person in the world capable of stopping a transmillennial conspiracy to assassinate a pharaoh through pure lack of physical coordination. You are one of a kind."

Edward shrugged sardonically as he said, "Yeah. They must have broken the mold after they made me."

"Technically, I think the mold maker tripped over his own feet and the mold broke when he fell over, but that's probably just splitting hairs," Anastasia giggled.

Edward felt slightly wounded but couldn't help but laugh himself. *Goodness, what a day it's been.*

Their conversation was interrupted when the general reentered the room followed by Akhenaten and Nefertiti. Akhenaten stepped forward and took them each by one hand. Looking into each of their eyes in turn, he said, "Thank you for your protection today, my young friends. I might not be alive without you."

Nefertiti nodded in agreement as she said, "You two are a miracle. You truly have been sent to us by Aten."

Edward said, "Anastasia is the true hero here. She figured out what was happening and saved all of us. Thutmose, Aneski, Salah, yourselves, and me. I just happened to run into one of those dog guys."

"I just did what anyone would have done," his sister replied, shrugging her shoulders.

General Meketre chuckled deeply. "You are both heroes and you, Edward, are far too modest. You subdued an assassin with two poison blades while unarmed."

Edward felt his stomach drop straight to the floor. "Poison?"

"Yes. The edges were coated in poison from an asp, the deadliest snake in Egypt."

"I think I'm going to throw up," Edward said weakly, sitting down on a bench.

Nefertiti placed a comforting hand on Edward's shoulder. "It's always the hardest after the adrenaline has left your system. It's natural to feel this way. I am certain your valor will return shortly," she said with a confident smile.

Edward tried to smile back at Nefertiti, knowing that this was his natural state.

Nefertiti turned back to Akhenaten and General Meketre. "At least Anubis has shown his hand. We suspected he was behind this all along."

Akhenaten nodded. "The jackal cannot abide the fact that his time has passed. He clings to this world like a leech."

"What do you mean 'Anubis'? Isn't he supposed to be the God of Embalming and the Dead? How could a god be behind this?" Edward asked, confused.

"Do you mean that the men who attacked us are Anubis worshippers?" Anastasia cut in.

Now that made sense to Edward. Some people did violent and terrible things in the name of religion. Maybe the Corsairs had found a group of crazy Anubis worshippers to do their dirty work by rubbing out Akhenaten and Nefertiti.

"It is all a little bit more complicated than that, my young friends. The men who attacked us today are priests of Anubis. That is why they wore the jackal masks. They are not merely loyal worshippers acting on their own. They are Anubis's foot soldiers and they are following his directions."

"But why would a god want to kill you?" Edward asked, not really following either why or how Anubis could do this. *Aren't the gods just myths anyway?*

"It is because of my decision to have Egypt worship only one god—Aten," Akhenaten said in a somber tone. "Perhaps you should both be seated before I explain. This may take a while."

Chapter 19

Akhenaten guided Anastasia into a chair next to Edward and began pacing. She didn't really understand everything Akhenaten had been saying or how all of these things were linked together. She sat forward in the chair, listening intently and waiting for the pharaoh to explain.

"When I became pharaoh, I realized that there was a dark force weighing down my kingdom. While many of our gods were still looking out for the best interests of Egyptians, some of our gods were abusing the powers they had gained from more than a thousand years of worship."

Anastasia was only getting more confused the more Akhenaten explained. "The gods have gained power? Are they more powerful now than they were a thousand years ago?"

"Our gods are more powerful than they used to be," Akhenaten said. "The prayers and rituals performed for the gods provide them with a form of energy. The more prayers they receive and rituals performed in their honor, the more powerful they become. This is something that is understood by the priests, but it isn't generally understood by our people. While this increased power is most evident within their specific temples, it is also evident in the way gods are able to influence people and events here in our world."

"But how were they abusing their power? What exactly were they doing?"

Nefertiti stepped in to answer Anastasia's question. "We all like to believe that our gods are all-powerful and all-knowing beings; however, the reality is that they suffer from many of the same shortcomings as any ordinary person. Some can be spiteful, some can be lazy, some can be arrogant." She sat down on her own chair next to Anastasia. "As they have grown more powerful over the last millennium, some of these traits have become more pronounced."

"Take Toth, the God of Knowledge and Wisdom," Akhenaten said, adjusting his robes, which were still slightly disheveled from the commotion on the Royal Road. "He was clearly a bit of a know-it-all to begin with, but he has become truly unbearable over the centuries. If you ever ask him a question now, he just lectures you and goes on and on."

Edward gulped in a moment of reflection as he saw Anastasia sniggering out of the corner of her eye. "That doesn't sound all that bad," he said largely to himself.

Akhenaten didn't seem to notice their exchange as he continued the story. "Take Bast, the Cat Goddess for example. She has always been somewhat fickle but as she has become more powerful, she has developed quite an attitude. It's not unusual for anyone who had upset Bast to find cat feces in their sandals or, even worse, on their pillow."

"She has the cats poo on her command? That's disgusting!" Anastasia said.

"Yes," agreed Nefertiti. "But largely harmless."

"That is not the case with all of the gods," General Meketre said grimly as he joined them at the table. "In Anubis's case, he became both jealous and power-hungry. As we know, eventually all men and women meet their end. Some sooner and some later than others. Despite gaining enormous power from the prayers made by the dying, their loved ones, and the priests, it wasn't enough for Anubis. He was jealous of Aten, whose rays of sunshine give life, and he was jealous of all men who got to live and walk the earth. It ate at him that he was bound to graveyards and tombs. Anubis wanted enough power to become master to the living world as well."

Anastasia scratched her head. It was a lot take in. *Gods are real. They aren't just stories that ancient people use to explain situations or occurrences they can't understand.*

"What did Anubis do? What actually happened?" Edward asked.

"Over the last century, Anubis started exacting a greater and greater toll on the dead who wished to complete the journey into the afterlife. It was no longer only about embalming and weighing of the heart to balance the scales and pass judgment. Anubis's role became that of a blackmailer or extortionist. He demanded more prayer, more elaborate rituals, and greater tithes for anyone to pass judgment and enter the afterlife. All to build his power in the hope that he might take form wherever he wanted on earth," Akhenaten explained.

"But that's not right! The judgment and passage to the afterlife is sacred. Plus Osiris oversees the entry to the afterlife. Anubis plays a lesser role in the whole process," Edward shouted indignantly.

"You are correct, Edward. What Anubis did to all Egyptians is unthinkable and motivated by the worst of selfish intentions. Withholding access to the afterlife in order to demand more power-building worship is nothing short of extortion. He was incredibly jealous of Osiris's role as the Lord of the Afterlife. Through his actions, he became more powerful than Osiris and eventually usurped him to rule the afterlife. He had to be stopped," Akhenaten said firmly.

Nefertiti stood from where she sat next to Anastasia and glided effortlessly across the room to stand with her husband. "Given how powerful Anubis and his army of priests had become, it was far easier said than done."

"Anubis was not to be reasoned with. I went to his temple in Thebes and summoned him for an audience. I asked him to give up his jealous pursuits and return to his traditional role. Anubis flew into a rage. He and his priests set upon me. It was only thanks to Aten's grace and power that I was able to escape his temple with my life. That was almost six years ago," Akhenaten said.

Nefertiti clasped her husband's hand, clearly remembering the events that Akhenaten had described.

"We had to stop Anubis before he plunged all of Egypt into darkness. This is why we decreed that there would only be one god to be worshiped in Egypt—Aten. If we could stop the prayers and rituals, we could eliminate the fount of his power and weaken him over time," Akhenaten explained to them.

It finally dawned on Edward. "The change in religion wasn't about you believing only in Aten and not in the other gods. It was just the only way to check Anubis's power."

Nefertiti spoke now. "It was a desperate measure to fundamentally change a religion as old as ours. But we did what we had to do. Thebes was no longer safe for us given that it was the stronghold of Anubis's priests," she said with her voice cracking. "We had no choice but to create a new capital in Akhetaten."

Edward watched as the pharaoh gently took Nefertiti into his arms and tenderly embraced his wife.

"While it was initially very difficult, the plan was working well," General Meketre said. "Anubis's influence was diminishing. He was losing priests from his temples and the rituals were becoming less elaborate. We thought things were better until about three months ago."

"It was small things at first," Akhenaten said. "Animals being poisoned, irrigation canals collapsing, accidents occurring as the temple for Aten was being constructed. They all seemed like random occurrences at first. We told ourselves it was nothing, but events kept escalating. We feared Anubis might be making one last attempt to snatch the power he so desired. It is why we have been in such a hurry to complete the capital over the last thirty days." Akhenaten thumped his fist down on the table, causing the food on the platters to actually leap into the air.

"We have been on high alert, suspecting something might go amiss. I have had my spy network working overtime and my troops quietly patrolling every corner of the city," General Meketre explained. "While I am not surprised that Anubis attacked, I just can't understand how his minions managed to slip into the city unseen. I am sorry that I let you down, my pharaoh," the general said, looking to Akhenaten and shaking his head apologetically.

Akhenaten looked the general in his eyes as he said, "The jackal moves in the shadows and is a very tricky adversary. Our faith in you does not waver, my old friend. We will defeat this foe together."

The general clasped Akhenaten's forearm near his elbow, and Akhenaten returned the same gesture. It was like some sort of Egyptian fist bump as far as Edward could tell.

The twins left the palace after lunch. They gave the royal couple and the general their assurances that they would be careful and would keep their eyes open for anything suspicious. After the day's events, the general had asked them to check in with him every day so he could be sure that they were okay. He was worried that Anubis and his followers might not take kindly to Anastasia's and Edward's roles in foiling their plot.

On the way back to their rooms, Anastasia took hold of Edward's hand. "There are still a couple of things that are bothering me, Edward."

"Are you including the whole gods-are-actually-real thing on your list or is this a completely separate list?" Edward asked, still a little freaked out by the whole concept.

"I'm not even touching that one right now. I was putting that onto a separate list of things that I can't even process," Anastasia said seriously. "I was thinking more about why are the Corsairs and Anubis working together? Is it just because they both want Akhenaten dead? Also, how did they know exactly where and when to open the portal? Did the Corsairs have someone watching the procession from the crowd who provided them the intelligence?"

"Or," Edward cut in to finish the thought, "do they have someone working on the inside of the palace? Someone who's within Akhenaten and Nefertiti's inner circle? Someone who would have known today's plans at a very detailed level?"

Anastasia stopped and turned to Edward, nodding with a worried look on her face. "I don't think we can rule that out. I think we have to consider the worst-case possibility that there's a traitor in the palace."

Chapter 20

Edward and Anastasia sat in a circle inside the single room of the partially completed mud-brick building that served as the secret clubhouse for Salah's fasoo team, the Desert Foxes. It was on the outskirts of the southeastern edge of Akhetaten, which was the city's version of the wrong side of the tracks. Smashed bits of pottery and crumpled papyrus were strewn about the room, and the furniture was a hodgepodge of battered and broken items that had clearly been thrown out from one of the reputable establishments in the city. It was a dump and it was exactly how Salah and his friends liked it.

Edward and Anastasia had found Salah waiting for them outside their accommodations when they had returned home from the palace. After swearing him to secrecy, they filled Salah in on the highlights of their conversation with Akhenaten, Nefertiti, and General Meketre. Without giving away the secrets of the Order or the Refractium Crystal, Edward and Anastasia had shared with Salah their concerns regarding a potential traitor within the palace.

It amazed Edward that Salah seemed to take the news that Anubis was trying to kill Akhenaten so in stride. Personally, Edward was still struggling with the idea that there was an angry god who wanted a piece of the pharaoh.

Instead of questioning their sanity, Salah said, "That's terrible! Akhenaten and Nefertiti are the heart of Egypt. There has to be a way to stop Anubis!"

Then it occurred to Edward that Egyptians really did believe their gods were present in their everyday lives. They weren't an inaccessible concept to them.

At the end of their story, Salah let out a low whistle. "I had a feeling it was going to be a big day when I woke up this morning, but this is ginormous!"

While the general had his network of spies working on stopping Anubis and his followers, the three friends thought it wasn't enough. They all agreed that they needed to help find the traitor, but Edward and Anastasia weren't sure how.

"Akhetaten is too big," Salah said. "We need more eyes and ears on our team. That I can deliver. I'll be right back," he said excitedly before running off at full speed.

Thirty minutes later, Salah returned with company and made the introductions to the promised "eyes and ears." "Edward and Anastasia, these are my friends—no, my brothers Smuz, Israh, and Bethrek."

As Edward's vision cleared, he saw the motliest of crews smiling and staring back at him. The first of Salah's friends, Smuz, had long and greasy hair that framed his dirt-smudged face. He was short and a bit chubby around the middle. The only thing dirtier than his face was his crumpled and stained clothing. He smiled self-consciously at Edward with yellow teeth and proceeded to pick his nose. He was quite possibly the most disgusting boy Edward had ever seen. Edward looked sideways at Anastasia and could see that she was physically recoiling.

Israh was the complete opposite of Smuz. He was tall, handsome, and immaculately dressed. He swept forward in a flourish and bowed deeply as he introduced himself to Edward and Anastasia. "I am Israh. I am honored to meet you both. The hero who thwarted the attack on the pharaoh and the heroine of our fasoo match." He seemed to linger too long in front of Anastasia until Salah pointedly cleared his throat.

Salah's third friend, Bethrek, was plain in every way. His straight, black hair framed an open face. He was neither tall nor short and neither fat nor thin. His clothes were clean but unremarkable. He stepped forward and politely said hello to Edward and Anastasia before turning to his left to say, "Israh, you must give Edward his money pouch back. It isn't right to steal, especially not here. Inside our clubhouse, everyone is a friend."

Edward felt for the pouch under his belt and realized that it was gone.

"You must be kidding me!" Salah said. "You just can't help yourself, can you?"

"Forgive me." Israh shrugged nonchalantly as he handed Edward's coin pouch back to him. "It's instinct. No hard feelings I hope," he said to Edward as if it were perfectly normal to steal someone else's money.

Edward hadn't felt a thing and would have had no idea. *What is Salah getting us into? This is going to be a total disaster.*

"Salah is the kind one, Smuz is the gross one, Israh is the con man, and I am honest to a fault. That is who we are," Bethrek said with a shrug.

This is going from bad to worse. Edward looked at Anastasia. She shrugged at him and said, "Not exactly the Justice League of superheroes, but it'll have to do."

They spent the next hour brainstorming how they were going to succeed in catching the traitor where General Meketre had failed. The general had highly trained men, the best weapons, and almost unlimited resources. They had none of these things. It dawned on Edward that they were going to have to rely upon their own brand of superpowers if they were going stop the Corsairs.

"Nobody knows more about what goes on in Akhetaten than Smuz. He's the extra eyes I was talking about," Salah said with passion. "You must trust me on this."

Although Edward wanted to believe Salah, he couldn't help but look at Smuz skeptically.

"My disgustingness is a cloak of invisibility. Everyone looks away. Nobody sees me, so I get to see everything," Smuz said matter-of-factly.

This actually made a weird kind of sense to Edward. Anastasia couldn't even look in Smuz's direction. Nobody else would be able to look at him either.

"Smuz will be able to find things nobody else can. Once he does, Israh will get us through the doors that would otherwise be shut to us," Salah said with conviction.

"How exactly is he going to do that?" Anastasia asked sarcastically. "Is he going to steal the key?"

Israh chuckled softly as he plucked a speck of dust off his flowing robes and smiled a golden smile. "I would prefer to talk my way through the door. Of course if I can't, I have no reservations about stealing the key. I am a facilitator. I simply get things done."

The tumblers were starting to align in Edward's mind. *This could work.* "So what role does Bethrek play in all of this?" Edward asked Salah.

"He tells us the truth. Sometimes that is very important."

Edward nodded thoughtfully. "Do you think this is enough for us to find the traitor?"

"No, my friend," Salah smiled and laughed. "You and Anastasia are both the brains and the muscle of our little gang."

Edward had never been included in the same sentence as the word "muscle." "And what exactly is your role in all of this, Salah?" he asked, raising his eyebrows in a question.

"If things go badly, my role is to outrun everyone as I go to get help," Salah said quietly with a very serious look on his face.

Edward paced around the dirty floor of the clubhouse with a laser focus while the others sat in their chairs, still deliberating. They had been debating back and forth for the last twenty minutes. Anastasia was convinced that the traitor had to be someone within Akhenaten and Nefertiti's circle of trust to know the details and timing of the procession. All they had to do was follow the potential suspects until they found them doing something suspicious, and then they could alert the general. The general and his men could deal with the Corsairs and worshippers of Anubis. After that, the plot to alter history would be foiled, the ripples in time would be smoothed over, and Anastasia and Edward could go home. The problem was that they didn't know who was in that circle of trust outside of General Meketre. They needed a place to start in terms of identifying suspects. They were getting frustrated. Edward's pacing was disrupted when he heard someone clear their throat. He looked up and was startled to see Israh standing in front of him.

"I apologize for interrupting your pacing," Israh said, deferentially placing a hand on Edward's shoulder. "However, with your assistance, I believe I can have the list of potential suspects from the royal inner circle within thirty minutes."

"You can do that?" Edward said, his frustration turning to excitement. "How?"

137

Israh paused as he used his index fingers to smooth a few dark hairs on his upper lip that couldn't quite be called whiskers. "I know someone who knows someone who knows someone inside the palace," he said.

"If you know someone, why do you need Edward's assistance?" Anastasia cut in with a warning edge in her voice.

"I will need a few silver pieces to grease the wheels of commerce," Israh replied, looking away while pretending to shoo away an invisible insect.

"Of course he needs your money," Anastasia said in an exasperated tone. "Have you already stolen everyone else's money in Akhetaten?" she asked as she rounded on Israh.

To his own surprise, Edward found himself jumping to Israh's defense. "Anastasia, we don't have a lot to go on here. I think we're going to have to trust each other if we're going to solve this. We are all on the same team after all." He walked over and sat down next to Anastasia. He took her hands into his own. "What else are we going to do anyway?"

She looked him straight in the eye, but he could see her resolve wavering. "Okay," his sister said as she threw her head back in exasperation. "Give him the silver pieces."

Edward reached for his coin bag when Israh cleared his throat again. Edward turned and found Israh smiling sheepishly at him. "I may have already taken the liberty of lightening your coin bag in anticipation of our reaching this agreement."

Edward quickly reached for his bag, which was now appreciably lighter and smaller than it was previously. "I can't believe you did that. You stole my money again! I was sticking up for you," Edward squawked, only to hear all the others laughing.

They started softly, but it was building. He turned to Anastasia questioningly.

"We'd already worked out our plan, bro, when you were doing all that pacing. So we all decided we would have a little bit of fun," she said, trying to speak between laughing.

He looked over at Salah to see tears of laugher streaming down his face as he said, "Israh said it would be too hard as you would already be on alert, but Anastasia said you were in Edward's world and that you wouldn't notice."

Smuz was doubled up, rolling around on the floor, and even Bethrek was giggling.

"This is great. We've been together for an hour and everyone's already decided that I get to be the guy on the team who gets pranked. Unbelievable!" He could feel his cheeks turning red with a combination of embarrassment and general grumpiness. *This never happens to James Bond.* Edward pointed at Israh and said "You just go get that list" and stalked off.

This, of course, only made them laugh harder.

Chapter 21

True to his word, Israh was back within a half an hour with a list of people who were part of the royal couple's inner circle. He was clearly pleased with himself and was preening like a peacock. Anastasia had to admit that it was very impressive and a little bit scary at the same time. She was glad that he was using his power for good.

However, when Anastasia read the list of names within Akhenaten and Nefertiti's inner circle, her heart dropped in disappointment. *It's just too long!* There were twenty-five names on the list. *How are we ever going to identify the traitor in time?*

"This will not do; it is simply too many. It will take forever to work our way through a list as long this one," Smuz grimaced, echoing her own thoughts while Bethrek threw his hands in the air.

"Oh no! We are back to where we started. This list hasn't helped us at all," Salah said as his shoulders slumped.

"It's not my fault," Israh said, ceasing to preen as he raised his hands defensively. "I did exactly as you asked."

"It's okay," Edward told them. His face was untroubled and his eyes full of confidence. "We're just going to have to prioritize. You know, pick the ones who we think are the most likely to be a traitor."

They all seemed to pause as one before collectively turning to Edward with a look of hope in their eyes.

"You are right, Edward!" Salah said with a momentary burst of excitement before he paused to ask, "How exactly do we do that?"

"Well, I'm still working on that part," Edward admitted, but his confidence didn't waver. He quickly turned to Israh. "Did your source say anything else that might be helpful?"

"Well, he asked if I wanted the pharaoh's inner circle from the palace or if I wanted to include the Royal Residence as well," Israh said and shrugged, not sure if it was helpful.

"Why would your source ask that? What's the difference?" Edward asked, transitioning into Sherlock Holmes mode.

"Well, Akhenaten's other wives and children all live in the Royal Residence. They don't have much to do with the goings-on at the palace. That's where all the work happens," Israh explained.

"That's it!" Edward exclaimed.

"It is?" Israh asked hopefully.

"If they don't spend time in the palace, we can deduce they probably wouldn't know all the details of the celebration. Therefore, we can remove them from our immediate list of suspects," Edward said, beaming.

"What does deduce mean?" Smuz asked, his forehead creased in confusion.

Edward was on a roll and didn't even hear him. "How many of the names is that, Watson?" Edward said gleefully, looking in Anastasia's direction.

Anastasia tried to roll her eyes at Edward, but couldn't hide her own excitement as she reviewed the list of names and titles. "That must be twenty names between his wives and children!"

"Yes!" both Salah and Bethrek shouted.

"It is as I always expected—I am the greatest!" Israh said, puffing up again.

"You're smarter than you look," Anastasia told her brother as they high-fived.

Things were looking up. After eliminating Akhenaten's other wives and children from consideration, they were left with a shorter list of only five names. They quickly ruled out the general, as they knew he had put his life on the line in defending the royal couple during the attack. That left Akhenaten's younger brother, the royal scribe Imhotep, the general's aide, and Nefertiti's personal attendant. Now this was much more manageable.

They decided to divide into two groups of three with each group following a suspect for a day. This meant they could cover all four potential suspects over the course of two days. They planned to start with what they thought were the most likely suspects first, including the general's aide, Djedi, and Akhenaten's brother, Ementah. Djedi would have access to all the plans and was also likely to know how General Meketre's spy network was deployed.

He was an ideal target for the Corsairs and the priests to turn. Ementah was also an obvious suspect. So many times in history a younger brother had cut a deal to get rid of their older brother to get their hands on the throne. Edward teamed up with Smuz and Israh to follow Djedi while Anastasia teamed up with Salah and Bethrek to follow Ementah. With their strategy set and plans to meet up later in the day, they left the clubhouse excited and focused.

They all met in the market square later that afternoon. They wanted to make sure that they were in position to follow their targets when the day ended. Anastasia noticed that Smuz was carrying some sort of large cloth sack over his shoulder. It made her curious because she hadn't brought anything.

"What do you have in there?" Anastasia asked.

"Essential items for this type of investigative work," Smuz answered, nodding sagely.

"What exactly are these essential items?" Anastasia asked, thinking about ancient Egyptian stakeout items like ropes and grappling hooks.

"It's food," Smuz replied, looking at her like she was a complete idiot.

"Leave it to our rotund one to think only about his stomach when we are getting ready for a stakeout," Israh said with a mild look of contempt on his face.

Smuz's cheeks turned red as he tried to suck in his belly. His eyes hardened slightly as he looked at Israh and shot back with, "Most of our time will be spent sitting around and waiting. Nothing is worse than being hungry. I brought it to share with everyone, but I can see now that you are not interested. Don't look to me when you are done oiling your hair and plucking your eyebrows and your stomach rumbles with hunger."

Now it was Israh's turn for his cheeks to turn red.

Anastasia didn't want this to escalate further, so he quickly stepped in and said, "That was incredibly thoughtful of you, Smuz."

Smuz, who was not used to receiving compliments, absolutely glowed in response.

Anastasia turned to Israh and said, "I was so focused on the idea of following people and solving this mystery that I hadn't really thought it through either." This seemed to appease Israh slightly and set everyone back on course.

The streets had grown quiet in the aftermath of the foiled attack and subsequent celebrations. Anastasia's team left to stakeout the Royal Residence. Edward, Smuz and Israh set themselves up outside the side entrance to the Palace, and directly across the street from the guard's barracks, to wait for Djedi. They began pretending to play a game with dice that had symbols instead of numbers as they sat huddled against the wall, facing the gate. They couldn't exactly wait inside the palace for Djedi, so this seemed like the most logical place to find and then tail him.

"Are you sure you know what he looks like? It would really suck if we followed the wrong guy," Edward said anxiously. He felt like the clock was ticking on their mission and that this might be their only chance to make a difference.

"He is the general's aide. He is the second-best well-known soldier in the city. He is wherever the general is. Djedi is General Meketre's second shadow," Israh explained to Edward.

Smuz nodded in agreement while trying to use his little finger to vigorously extract some sort of lump of wax from his ear. So they settled in to the role of watching, waiting, and playing dice.

After waiting for a few minutes, Edward's heart raced with anticipation the first time someone came out of the side gate. *Could this be him? Is it time to spring into action? Is it go time?* He could feel his heart rate accelerating inside his chest as a man stepped through the gate. It wasn't Djedi. It wasn't even a soldier. *Talk about disappointment.* This repeated itself more than a dozen times over the next thirty minutes, and he realized that it was a lot harder to play it cool than he'd expected. Smuz and Israh, on the other hand, barely even raised their eyes from the dice game to examine whoever walked out the gate. *Okay. I can play it cool as well. Think Bond, James Bond,* he told himself.

It was boring. It was really boring.

Edward sighed and decided to go against his better judgment as it related to the cleanliness and edibility of food. He said to Smuz, "Pass the sack. I need something to take my mind off the waiting."

Smuz shook his head disapprovingly and placed the neck of the sack in Edward's outstretched hand.

"You are never going to make it as a spy if you are bored and restless after less than an hour, Edward. Stakeouts are mainly about patience."

As much as it stung, Edward knew Smuz was right. He needed to chill out. "Thanks, Smuz. I needed that," Edward said in response to both the advice and the sack.

The actual sack was a bit grubbier than he would have liked. He took a deep breath and reached inside to grab some sort of smallish apple from the sack. Edward gave it a good but subtle wiping on his robes to try and remove any traces of dirt and Smuz. He took a bite and found that it was crisp and delicious. It was time to take back any negative thoughts he might have had about Smuz's grubby food sack. The thing was a godsend. He proceeded to munch noisily away with small sounds of appreciation escaping from his mouth. Israh had clearly noticed his rapture and was eyeing up the sack as well.

Smuz, who had not forgotten Israh's comments from earlier, took a long look at Israh and said, "Don't even think about it."

Israh smiled back a Cheshire cat grin in response. "I am definitely thinking about it, my little round friend."

"I said don't think about it!" Smuz snarled.

It was like watching two three-year-olds, and Edward couldn't help but laugh until he saw Smuz.

Smuz was clenching his fists and his face was turning a very deep shade of red. He looked like a boiling kettle about to whistle when he suddenly went slack. "It's him. It's Djedi," he said quietly under his breath.

Chapter 22

Edward was so surprised that he accidentally dropped his delicious apple in the dirt. *Rat farts!*

He looked up and immediately recognized the man exiting the gates. It was the same dark-haired, broad-shouldered man who had been with the general the day they had first met Akhenaten before the commemoration ceremony.

Duh! Edward thought to himself. *Of course that's the general's aide.*

Djedi moved with purpose as he crossed the street and walked straight into the unguarded entry to the barracks. Israh and Smuz had already gotten to their feet and were heading the same way.

Edward scrambled to his feet, thinking *There's no way I'm getting left in the dust by these two clowns* when the God of Uncoordination returned and struck him down. As he attempted to plant his right foot to push off and chase after Israh and Smuz, he stepped on the apple he had dropped. Given its roundish shape, the apple rolled backward when he pushed. For a split second, he found himself suspended in the air. In that moment, he realized two things with great clarity. The first was that he was not going to run through the entryway with Israh and Smuz in the next two or three seconds. The second was that this was likely to hurt. He landed flat on his stomach with a thud in the dirt. The air was expelled from his lungs and a cloud of dust was sent billowing into the air around him.

His thoughts were confirmed as the dust settled. First, Israh and Smuz were nowhere to be seen. Second, the reintroduction of air into his lungs was a painful and wheezing affair. He was thankful for the adrenaline in his system that allowed him to stagger back to his feet and lurch toward the door while he was still bent over like a smaller version of Quasimodo. This was not nearly how he had imagined his career as a spy would begin.

As he rounded the corner with his back pressed up against the wall, he saw that the barracks were actually more of a compound. There were about two dozen long, single-story, mud-brick buildings to his left. Each of the buildings was labeled with a hieroglyph. The closest one of them had the cartouche for the royal family next to the symbol for guard. Another had a symbol for a crocodile next to the symbol for guard. These buildings had to be the actual sleeping quarters for the soldiers.

Another long building sat perpendicular to the barracks. There was a hum of chatter coming from the building. When the smell of bread and beer reached him on the breeze, he guessed it had to be the mess hall. To the right and in the center of the compound there was a series of rings outlined with a single row of mud bricks in the dirt. The rings were flanked by a large building. Edward wasn't sure what those were yet.

Farther to the right was another series of long buildings. *They must be another set of barracks,* he thought until he saw a man leading a horse from one of the buildings. *Correction. Looks like the stables.* Just then he saw someone emerge from the shadows by the large building near the dirt rings. It was Israh, who signaled to quickly join him. Edward mustered as much dignity and oxygen as he could to scuttle across the open space between himself and the building.

Israh and Smuz were tucked in the shadows behind several large clay containers.

"Thanks for watching our rear, Edward. Good thinking," Israh said earnestly.

They must not have seen what happened outside the entrance. Edward had just gotten enough breath back that he could squeak out an almost normal-sounding, "No problem."

"Djedi is inside the armory. As far as we can tell, there is only one way in and one way out," Smuz let him know.

So that's what this is. Now I only need to figure out what the rings are.

He was getting excited again now that his breathing was returning to normal. His mind raced with what might come next. He didn't have to wait long before Djedi exited the armory. The soldier had his shield strapped to his left arm and his sword in his right hand. He was a big unit. He strode into the middle of the ring and began to practice different sequences of fighting moves. Then it hit him. *They're training rings. I'm getting good at this.*

Edward looked around and saw that there didn't seem to be anyone else around the armory or the training rings. He didn't know if this was odd, so he asked, "Why isn't there anyone else training?"

"Most of the soldiers only train during the day before their evening meal. He must be putting in extra work," Israh replied.

Edward watched Djedi do his thing again. Then he heard both Israh and Smuz let out a sigh as they both sat down on the ground. "What's wrong?" Edward whispered.

"He is doing the ninety-nine forms of the sword master. We are going to be here for a while," Israh said dejectedly.

Smuz opened his sack again and started to feed his face.

Israh wasn't wrong. The practice session just kept going and going. Edward found it interesting at first because he never really got to see anyone swing a real sword around and Djedi was clearly good. He moved like a big cat on the Discovery Channel. Big, powerful, and incredibly graceful. Definitely best not to mess with this man unless you really had to.

An hour and a half later and Edward was over it. He wasn't even sure which of the ninety-nine forms Djedi was up to, having lost count a long time ago. *When is this guy going to finish? How much better can he actually get? Isn't he already a master?*

Then, covered in sweat and breathing hard, Djedi completed his final form and stopped. It was approaching dusk now and the light began to fade. *Maybe whatever is going to happen is going to happen now. Maybe it had to be dark before Djedi could enact any of his devious plans.* Israh and Smuz started to rise in anticipation of Djedi leaving the armory. Edward made sure not to step on anything round as he stood up this time. They remained tucked silently in the shadows, waiting while Djedi stowed his training gear back in the armory.

Djedi exited the armory at a light jog and turned toward the stables. *Maybe he's late for his meeting with the Corsairs or the Anubites,* as Edward had started calling them in his own mind.

Smuz was the first to scurry after Djedi, keeping to the shadows around the edges of the armory and crossing the open space as quickly and quietly as possible. Edward and Israh were right on his heels. They saw Djedi enter the stable and waited for him to come out. After five minutes, he still hadn't emerged. Smuz pointed to himself and made a walking motion with his fingers and then pointed to the stable. Edward and Israh both nodded back in understanding. They had to figure out if he was still in there or if he was on to them and had given them the slip. Smuz dropped to all fours and shimmied along the dirt next to the wall until he reached the entrance of the stable. He looked back at them once before he disappeared inside. *This is definitely more like it. The game is afoot, as Sherlock Holmes would say.* They waited for another minute before they saw Smuz's head emerge from around the corner and he motioned them in. They both imitated Smuz's shimmy as they dropped to the ground and made their way into the stable.

Even if they hadn't seen the horses, Edward would have still known it was a stable by the smell alone. He wasn't an expert in horses, but he knew the smell of horse manure. Smuz guided them into a dark corner next to a row of stalls. The building was enormous, like an airplane hangar for horses. There were two rows of stalls going as far as he could see. There could have easily been a couple hundred horses in here.

Smuz whispered under his breath, "He is grooming his horse. I don't think he is going anywhere. Not unless this is all an act to make us let our guard down."

"You have to be kidding me. Sword practice and now horse grooming," Edward said in frustration. "We have chosen to follow the most boring man in all of Egypt. This is killing me."

"He is right. We should have been the ones watching the pharaoh's brother. We have been dealt a bad hand tonight," Israh agreed.

No one was happy picturing the others on a serious spy chase with Ementah, the pharaoh's brother. They all silently worked their way over to a crack in the fence at the back of the stall and settled in to watch. Edward thought that Djedi took excessively good care of his horse as he fed, watered, and groomed it for the next forty minutes. When he finally stopped, their relief was momentary. As soon as he put away his brushes and picks, Djedi started mucking the stable. He was scooping horse manure into a large earthenware pot. It had actually gotten worse.

Edward's sulking was interrupted when Smuz whispered sharply, "Did you see that? I think he put something into the pot."

"Of course he put something into the pot, you idiot. It's horse poo. So thank you for that very insightful update," Israh whispered in a tone dripping with sarcasm.

"If you spent less time fixing your nails and more time watching, you would know I wasn't talking about the horse poo!" Smuz whispered indignantly. "It was something shiny. Something made of metal. Maybe it's some kind of message."

"A message in the poo? For real?" Edward asked doubtfully.

"Well, it could be. We don't have any other leads," Smuz said earnestly.

"I am not going to be the one to check," Israh said flatly before nodding at Smuz and adding, "You can be the poo boy."

It wasn't the nicest way to say it, but Edward didn't want to be the poo boy either.

"Don't worry, Israh. I wasn't going to ask you to. I know you don't do any real work yourself," Smuz retorted, shaking his head.

Djedi hung his shovel on a hook on the wall, then hefted the big pot onto his shoulder like it didn't weigh anything. He walked out the gate to the horse's stall, turned right, and went about twenty yards farther to an open window, out of which he dumped the contents of the pot. He held the pot upside down and banged it on the window frame to make sure it was empty before putting it down. He wiped his brow and stretched before coming back to the stable to shut the gate. After which, he shouted good night to someone at the far end of the building, who they hadn't seen, before walking back out the way he had first come in.

They silently followed him back to the main entrance to the stalls and then proceeded to trail Djedi past the armory and training

149

rings and back to the barracks. He went in and didn't come back out. The truth was that there was barely any noise coming from the barracks. It seemed like just about everyone was or had already settled in for the night.

"Okay. Looks like he is going to sleep, so our boring work is done for the night," Israh said.

"What about the shiny item I saw him put in the horse poo?" Smuz asked. He turned toward Edward and said, "I think we have to see what it was."

Edward had a bad feeling about this. He wanted to say no, but he knew now that spy work wasn't always glamorous. It required patience and thoroughness. "Okay," Edward said after a pause. "Let's go."

They left Israh, who waited outside the gate for their return, and stole back to the horse stalls. They circled around the back to the window they'd seen Djedi at as quietly as possible so as not to disturb any of the horses in the stalls. They came upon what Edward could only describe as a very large pit full of horse manure.

There was a narrow ledge of land that ran between the building and the edge of the pit. Edward watched Smuz carefully scoot himself onto the ledge to the window. He put one hand on the window frame and leaned over to peer into the pit. After a moment, he bobbed his head up and looked at Edward as he pointed excitedly to the pit. *He actually found it!* Smuz took a small, pointy knife out of his belt and leaned over the pit as he reached out with the dagger. The narrow ledge he stood upon suddenly gave way, and Smuz became one with the poo.

Edward was still trying to process the horror of what had happened when Smuz's head emerged from the pit, sputtering and gagging. Smuz waded slowly to the edge of the pit but he was too short to pull himself out. He tried three or four times, and Edward could see that he was just getting more and more tired. He waved at Edward for help. Edward looked behind himself just in case there was someone else standing there. Nothing. *Rats! He is waiving at me.*

"Come on. Get me out of here," Smuz whispered loudly and desperately. One of the horses in the stalls began to make noise. The combination of his friend in need and the fear of getting caught set Edward in motion, and he hurried over to the edge of the pit to help Smuz.

He crouched down, bracing his feet, and extended his hand toward Smuz's when his feet slipped. Next thing he knew, he was falling into a sea of poo. Luckily, shock seemed to kick in from there. It was like an out-of-body experience. In his mind's eye, he watched a calamity of errors as he and Smuz thrashed around in the pit. Eventually, he climbed onto Smuz's shoulders without really asking and used him as a human stepladder to escape. Fortunately, his nervous system seemed to have shut down, because he couldn't really feel anything or smell anything. In his condition, he would have just walked away if Smuz hadn't nailed him with a blob of manure in the back. He turned around and realized that he had to have another go at getting Smuz out of the pit. He braced himself again and told himself the worst had already happened, so just stay focused. He managed to pull Smuz out of the pit with some considerable effort.

"Um, sorry about that, Edward," Smuz said as they lay on the ground at the edge of the pit, trying to recapture their breath.

"Tell me you at least found the metal thing," Edward said.

"Yeah. I found it. I don't think it was a secret message though. It was just a broken broach from his uniform," Smuz laughed uncomfortably. "Good to rule it out, though, don't you think?"

"It's just freaking fantastic! Glad we ruled that out. Totally worth it!" Edward said with a hint of hysteria in his voice as the shock started to wear off and reality set in. He was coated in horse poo from head to toe. He knew what he was about to say was pretty crazy but couldn't stop himself. "I will be swearing both you and Israh to secrecy about this. If anyone ever finds out, I will have to kill you."

The poo-covered Smuz tilted his head to look Edward in the eye as he glumly said, "Why would I ever tell anyone what happened tonight? I have no incentive. It is the honey-tongued asp Israh that we need to worry about. He will lord this over us forever when he sees us."

Chapter 23

Anastasia couldn't believe just how strange their night had been. She, Salah, and Bethrek were snacking on some bread and olives and chatting about the night's events when Edward, Israh, and Smuz walked into the clubhouse.

They all seemed to be slightly grumpy, as if they had just stopped bickering before they'd entered the room. Edward and Smuz both looked like their hair was wet, which didn't make any sense. As she examined them all more closely, she noticed that Smuz looked unusually clean, although his historical benchmark for cleanliness was pretty low in her book.

"How did things go for you guys tonight? Did you find Djedi?" she asked.

"Oh, we found him alright. We followed him all night, but we got nothing," Edward said bitterly. "He was a complete Boy Scout. All he did was train for sword fighting and groom his horse."

"Don't forget that he mucked the stables as well," Israh said sweetly to Edward.

Edward shot Israh a dangerous look.

"What's wrong with mucking stables?" Anastasia asked, wondering exactly what was going on with the three of them.

"Nothing!" Edward and Smuz said in unison.

"Let's just say this wasted evening has left a very unpleasant smell in our nostrils," Israh said in a very compassionate voice.

Anastasia unconsciously inhaled deeply and thought she detected the faintest hint of horse manure, which made sense if they'd spent time watching Djedi in the stables. "Do you think we should cross Djedi off the suspect list?" Anastasia asked them.

"I don't think we can be 100 percent certain. We only followed him for one night, but I think we should investigate the other two suspects before we spend any more time on him," Edward said thoughtfully.

"Well, it sounds like your night was less weird than ours," Salah said. "Wait until we tell you what happened to us! You won't believe it."

Anastasia, Salah, and Bethrek all pitched in as they excitedly told the story of their night following Ementah. They had found the pharaoh's younger brother sneaking out of the Royal Residence, which was an entirely different building than the formal palace. He had been dressed as a servant, and they wouldn't have recognized him if not for his very prominent hook-shaped nose.

"You can spot that thing anywhere in the kingdom. You would think he was the one who had actually modeled for the Sphinx at Giza," Bethrek added earnestly.

It occurred to Anastasia that she had never seen a picture of the Sphinx with a nose. She had always pictured a cute, little nose. She'd never thought that it would be large and hooked. She looked at Edward and saw that his eyes were wide and his mouth was slightly open as he processed this new piece of information.

Anastasia relayed how they'd managed to follow Ementah all the way through the city to the far edge of town.

"We were certain he was up to something between the disguise and the fact that he kept checking over his shoulder every few minutes. It was a miracle that he didn't spot us," she said.

"Or just really incredible detective work!" Salah added with a big smile.

"We were good, weren't we?" Anastasia smiled back at Salah and Bethrek.

"Ahem," Edward cleared his throat. "Maybe we could get back to the story."

Anastasia looked at her brother questioningly. *Something has definitely gone wrong tonight.*

"I think Edward is worried that you might be implying we stink in comparison," Israh said in a conciliatory tone. He then turned to Edward and Smuz and said, "Don't worry, my friends. I am sure no one can match your achievements this evening."

Israh's kind words didn't seem to make Edward or Smuz any happier; however, they did cause Anastasia to start reassessing her opinion of Israh. *Maybe he's not completely self-centered*, she thought to herself before she continued with her story.

"We followed him all the way to an amphitheater on the far edge of the city. When we arrived, Ementah seemed to be talking to four or five other people on the stage. It was pretty dark, so we really couldn't get a good look at them at first," Anastasia told them.

"So the pharaoh's brother is up to something devious?" Israh asked her excitedly.

"Well, we certainly thought he was part of a conspiracy that was meeting to plot their next move against Akhenaten," Anastasia said. "Out of nowhere, music starts playing and we became a little less certain. Then the torches were lit and we saw that everyone on stage was wearing these colorful pink costumes and we became even less certain. Then they all started dancing and we were downright confused." Anastasia, Salah, and Bethrek laughed together at the memory.

"Was it some sort of ritual for Anubis?" Edward asked, reaching for an explanation that might fit.

Anastasia smiled widely at Edward as she told him, "It wasn't an Anubis ritual. It was a rehearsal for a performance for the harvest festival. Ementah is the lead dancer in the *Dance of the Pink Flamingos*!" Anastasia told them, letting her own astonishment show.

"Ementah is a dancer? Do royals do that kind of thing?" Edward asked skeptically.

"He's not just any dancer. He's an expressive dancer and a very good one at that. It's like a mix of modern and interpretive dance," Anastasia said, as if that made it clearer.

Bethrek looked slightly confused by Anastasia's explanation as he cut in, "I don't really know anything about dance, so Anastasia probably has a better idea than I do about him being a good dancer. What I can tell you is that it didn't seem very dignified or royal."

"Yeah, he seemed to be hopping around a lot on one leg," Salah said, imitating the motion while simultaneously extending his head forward and then back.

Israh agreed with an uncomfortable grimace. "No one looks royal doing that."

155

"He saw us when I clapped at the end of the performance," Anastasia told Edward. "He recognized me from the commemoration ceremony and came to talk to us because he was terrified that we were going to tell Akhenaten. Apparently, it's very unlike a royal to be an expressive dancer. The men are all supposed to be warrior scholars. I told him we weren't there to judge, and Ementah said it's just in his blood. He's hoping his brother can see him perform in the festival and see how good he is and how much he loves it. Maybe then he'll let him dance, and Ementah won't have to hide it anymore." She could see that the boys were having a hard time taking the whole expressive dancer thing in.

"This cannot be right. I have seen him compete in the sword contests. He is a trained fighter," said Smuz, shaking his head and apparently completely unconvinced.

"Being good with a sword doesn't mean you can't be good at dancing as well. Don't be such a caveman. Real men are allowed to dance if they want to," Anastasia said with more force than she had intended. *Why were boys always such boys?*

"So Ementah is not involved in any conspiracy then?" Smuz asked as if just to make sure.

"The only conspiracy going on with Ementah is the one to be himself."

"Where exactly does that leave us then? Was this all just a wasted night?" Edward asked despairingly as he threw his hands in the air.

Clearly, it had been a bad night for Edward. Anastasia elected to use the Band-Aid method. *No point in beating around the bush. Tell him plainly and quickly. It always hurts less that way.*

"Sorry, bro. It's stakeout duty again tomorrow night as well. I think it's time for all of us to grab a broom and clean this place up and then call it a night. Tomorrow night could be a really big one."

Chapter 24

The boys had all told their parents that they were sleeping over at each other's houses, but in reality, they were all sleeping at the clubhouse tonight. It had been the only way for them to conduct the reconnaissance they'd performed tonight without someone having to answer to their parents. They spread the sleeping mats on the floor, including the extra ones brought for Edward and Anastasia. Edward realized that his mat was next to Israh's. His first reaction was that he was going to move. The veiled references and jibes he had been receiving from Israh since they'd returned to the clubhouse had gotten on his nerves at first. He knew now that his best course of action was to just not worry about it. He needed to sing like Elsa and let it go. He decided not to blame Israh anymore for his bad night and left his sleeping mat where it was.

Edward's mind ran at high speed. They really hadn't gotten any closer to stopping the Corsairs and the Anubites today. The only real progress had been ruling out suspects. He whispered to Anastasia quietly as everyone else was drifting off to sleep, "Do you think we'll have better luck tomorrow?"

"I'm sure of it. You can't try to assassinate a pharaoh without leaving some footprints, no matter how shallow," she said with an underlying note of steel and determination. She rarely ever seemed to waver. She was so confident and determined. It was something he both admired in her and was jealous about.

He stared at the stars through a small hole in the clubhouse roof as he started to think things through out loud. "Given that the assassins wearing the Anubis masks came out of a portal made by a Refractium Crystal, I think it's likely that the Corsairs and the priests of Anubis are working together. But I still can't understand why the Corsairs would want to work with them. It just makes things more complicated. It means more people who might reveal secret plans. More people who need to be persuaded and coordinated with. The more moving parts there are, the easier it is for something to go wrong. There must be something more to it."

157

He turned his head to look at Anastasia, who was stretching sleepily now.

"I think you're onto something, Edward. What can the priests possibly offer the Corsairs? I'm not sure that they actually need someone else to help them kill Akhenaten if that's their objective. There's something else here that we need to figure out." Anastasia yawned as she gestured to their friends who were sound asleep. "Maybe we should figure that out tomorrow. You know, after we get some sleep too."

"I'm not sure if you knew this, but there was a time when I was pretty obsessed with ancient Egypt and its mythology," Edward said, not letting her drift off.

"Yeah, I seem to remember the piles of books on Egypt, the models of the pyramids, and you trying to learn to read hieroglyphics. It was kind of obvious."

"You know in the myths, Anubis normally sat in judgment of the dead to see if they were worthy of the afterlife. Through the embalming process, the dead person's organs were separated from the body and preserved in canopic jars. Anubis's judgment was tied to weighing the heart of the dead person to see if it was virtuous. If it was lighter than a feather, they were judged to be good and they got to enter the afterlife and everything was great. If the heart was heavier than a feather, the person was unworthy and Anubis gave them to Ammit." Edward paused to see if she was still listening.

"Got it. So what did this Ammit person do with them?" she asked him sleepily, prompting him to continue.

"Well, Ammit is a demon not a person. A really scary one with a crocodile head, a goat's arms, and a hippo's butt. Once Ammit got them, he ate them. So they got to die again and this time forever. Game over, you know."

This got Anastasia's attention. She propped herself up on her elbow and looked Edward directly in the eye. "That's pretty scary, Edward. Anubis got to determine who got to bask in the afterlife and who got eaten. He's the last person you'd want to be corrupt."

"It actually gets worse. I read this one story about Isis, who was the Goddess of Magic and Motherhood. She's beautiful and powerful and pretty much loved by everyone."

"Edward, I know who Isis is. Just get on with the story, please."

"Well, one day she saw this woman and her husband in Egypt, who loved and cared for children. Not just their own children but all children. They fed them if they were hungry. Cured them if they were sick. Gave them a home if they had no place to live. They were amazing. Well, Isis decided to cast a special magical spell upon them. If their lives were to end before they had lived a full life, they wouldn't die. They would be brought back to life."

Anastasia cut him off as she asked, "What do you mean 'a full life'?"

"If they died before old age from being sick, having an accident, or really for any reason. If that happened, they would be brought back to life so they could keep doing good deeds on earth."

"Okay. I got it now," she told him and gestured for him to continue.

"Well, it happens in the story that the wife and her husband die from a plague that strikes the land, and sure enough, the spell brings them back to life. The problem was that Anubis was so enraged that he didn't get to sit in judgment of the dead as was his right that he decided to take matters into his own hands."

"Define taking matters into his own hands." Anastasia was fully sitting up now.

"Well, Anubis didn't wait for them to die again of old age. He made two identical magical sarcophagi out of gold that could transport the living to the land of the dead."

"Remind me again what exactly sarcophagi are," Anastasia asked.

"They're like our coffins, except for fancy. Like pictures you always see of King Tut."

"Okay, I remember now."

"When one of their relatives passed away, he ambushed the wife and husband when they entered the graveyard to mourn. He caught them and put each of them into one of the golden sarcophagi. Once there were living souls within the golden sarcophagi, the magical spell instantly pulled the couple with Anubis back to the land of the dead."

"They weren't dead. Couldn't they just climb out?" Anastasia asked, shaking her head.

"Even though their loved ones tried to rescue them, the sarcophagi couldn't be reopened in the land of the living. When Anubis got back to the land of the dead, he fed them to Ammit without even weighing their hearts. He wanted to prove a point to Isis and everyone else that this was his territory. If anyone crossed him, there would be serious consequences," Edward finished.

"What exactly is the point of this story?" Anastasia asked, both frightened and confused.

"Just that if Anubis does exist, this is not a god we want to ever have angry with us," Edward said, shrugging his shoulders defensively.

Anastasia gulped and stared at him with wide eyes as she said, "I can't say that was my favorite bedtime story ever. I hope I don't get nightmares."

Edward, on the other hand, suddenly felt better for having gotten things off his chest. "Sorry, sis. Great chat though. I feel much better now," he said with a big yawn as he rolled over and fell asleep.

Chapter 25

Anastasia woke up slowly, stretching and reaching for consciousness after a restless night. She had foggy recollections of bad dreams filled with jackals, golden coffins, and other dark images that left her feeling a little on edge and slightly grumpy. She really wanted to be at her best today, but as her kindergarten teacher always told her, "You get what you get and you don't get upset." It usually applied to what snack was packed in her lunch bag, but it seemed to apply just as well to the situation this morning.

Her stomach growled loudly. Even if she was tired, her stomach was not going to skip a meal. When she rolled over and looked at Edward, he was already sitting up, watching her and grinning happily. He clearly must have slept like a baby after unloading that terrible story about Anubis on her last night.

"Salah and the others have already gone home this morning to do their chores. They said to say goodbye and that they'd be back after lunch. Speaking of food, it sounds like someone is as hungry as Ammit this morning," Edward quipped, flashing a cheeky grin.

"Are you calling me a hippo-butted demon, Edward Upston?" she asked, arching one eyebrow dangerously at her brother.

"Um . . . no, I don't remember saying anything like that. I did say that I thought you might be hungry for breakfast. Maybe we should go to the market. What do you think?" Edward said as he hopped up and quickly scooted out of striking distance.

They made their way through the winding streets of Akhetaten as the sun was still beginning its morning journey into the sky. The streets were still relatively empty of people. Only those who had to be up at this hour in order to avoid the midday heat were up. The weather was cool and beautiful, belying the fact that the temperature would soar into triple digits. Farmers and laborers walked the streets on their way to tend crops and animals or to the various construction sites that remained around the city.

They made their way to the market to find breakfast and organize their thoughts. They once again purchased flatbread but this time added an assortment of fruits, including dates and grapes. They sat on a low sandstone wall, munching on their food. Edward grumbled openly about the lack of meat in his Egyptian diet.

"Look on the bright side. I'm sure it's improving your cholesterol," Anastasia mused.

"Anastasia, I'm a twelve-year-old boy with the physique of a beanpole. I need every bit of protein I can get. Cholesterol is not my issue," Edward laughed ruefully.

Their relaxing morning was interrupted when Djedi suddenly appeared in front of them. Anastasia froze the moment she saw him. *Oh my god. Does he know that Edward, Israh, and Smuz followed him last night? Are we in really big trouble?* She could feel the color draining from her face as she nervously tucked her hair behind her ears. She glanced sideways at Edward, who appeared to have stopped breathing altogether.

"Apologies for the interruption, but General Meketre, Akhenaten, and Nefertiti have requested your presence at the palace," Djedi said cheerfully, not at all like a potential jailer.

"Do they need us now?" Anastasia asked while cheerfully thumping Edward on the back so he could start breathing again.

"If it doesn't inconvenience you," Djedi said.

Djedi led them across the city toward the palace under the increasingly stifling heat that now blanketed the land. Anastasia wiped her brow with a feeling of certainty that this was going to be the hottest day yet during their time in Egypt. She was still a little worried about why they were being summoned. She hoped that nothing was wrong.

Djedi completely put them at ease as he chatted to them about the people of the city, his role in the guard, and his open admiration for General Meketre.

"He's a great man, General Meketre. I owe him my life," Djedi told them.

"Do you mean in battle?" Edward asked, making slashing and cutting motions with his hand to illustrate his question.

"The general has certainly saved my life more than once in combat. However, I was referring to the fact that he accepted me into the Royal Guard. You see, I was a troubled young man and the general took a chance on me. He gave me a new life and taught me everything I know. In many ways, he is the father I never had," Djedi explained.

The story brought a tear to her eye. She felt guilty for ever considering him a potential traitor and for deciding to have him followed last night. Even Edward had gotten over his initial panic and was chatting happily with Djedi about the city's layout and architecture.

Anastasia smiled to herself as she ascended the ramp toward the front entrance of the palace. While part of her was still anxious about their mission and how quickly time was passing, it wasn't every day that your presence was requested at the palace. Certainly not in her life anyway.

She noticed that there seemed to be a lot more guards at the entrance today than there had been the last time they'd been here. They were actually frisked by the guards before entering. Djedi apologized for the inconvenience but didn't elaborate any further or make a big deal out of it. She wondered if that was a bad sign.

They found Akhenaten, Nefertiti, and the general seated around the table in the same chamber where they had talked after the attack by the masked assassins. They all rose from the table to greet Edward and Anastasia.

"How are you, my young friends?" Akhenaten's powerful voice boomed as he strode across the room with his scepter in hand. "I hope Aten's rays find you well today and that we have not disturbed your morning too greatly."

"We are both well, Your Highness. You haven't disturbed us at all," Anastasia replied happily.

"Yes, we are blessed by both Aten's rays and your presence, Your Highness," Edward added, bowing with a flourish.

Anastasia looked sideways at Edward. He smiled back, raising his eyebrows as if to say, "Look at my royal etiquette!"

Akhenaten didn't even seem to notice Edward's newly acquired flair as he slid his scepter into a sheath on his back and put his arms around each of them. "We must thank you again for your service yesterday. You likely saved our lives. It was incredibly brave to put yourselves in the path of danger for our sake. It is not something we take lightly."

"We have a small gift for both of you as a token of our and Aten's appreciation," Nefertiti added as she embraced both of them in turn.

Anastasia couldn't believe their luck. She certainly hadn't been expecting anything in return for their actions.

Nefertiti placed a golden necklace with an intricate sun medallion around each of their necks. Anastasia realized it was the same as the hieroglyph they'd seen on the temple, the one of the sun disk with the long rays of light. They were exquisite.

"Thank you, Your Highnesses," Anastasia beamed delightedly as she tilted the medallion's face upward so she could study it more closely. She could see that the sun's rays were actually fashioned like long arms with delicate hands at their tips as though Aten was reaching out and offering a hand. "It's the most beautiful thing I have ever seen."

"Yeah, thanks. These are really cool," Edward added, holding his up for inspection as well.

"These necklaces are more than just beautiful. They have been blessed by Aten and will keep you safe from the forces of darkness in a time of need," Akhenaten added.

Anastasia could have sworn the jewel in his scepter turned a golden yellow for the briefest of moments before returning to its normal blue. She wanted to ask exactly what had happened with the scepter and what he'd meant about the necklaces protecting them, but it didn't seem right to ask questions after receiving such a special gift from the pharaoh.

"Now that we have that out of the way, we also wanted to keep you updated on our progress and hopefully put your minds at ease," Nefertiti smiled at them. She gestured to the general, who had been hanging back slightly, to come forward.

"The good news is that as of this morning, we believe we have defanged the asp," the general smiled with his chest puffed out and hands on his hips.

Anastasia knew this metaphor was supposed to be a good thing based on the general's expression, but she still wasn't exactly sure what he'd meant. She looked at Edward, who shrugged back.

"That sounds great, General," Anastasia said as enthusiastically as she could before adding, "But . . . what does that mean exactly?"

Nefertiti laughed, shaking her head. "You men are all the same. Always making things sound complex and dangerous when simple speech would do. No more riddles. Just tell the girl what happened."

The general cleared his throat and said, "We located and confiscated a secret cache of weapons that we believe the priests were planning to use in another attempt on the pharaoh. There were enough weapons for more than a hundred men. It would have been impossible to sneak that many armed men into the city without being noticed. Instead, they snuck the weapons in first bit by bit over time with the hope of surprising us and taking us unaware. By capturing their weapons, we have taken away their ability to stage any significant military operations in the immediate future."

"Oh, I've got it now. The asp's fangs are like the priest's weapons. No fangs, no poison. No weapons, no attack. Good one, General," Edward said, smiling and nodding at the general.

The general smiled and nodded discretely back to Edward. Nefertiti looked at Anastasia and rolled her eyes affectionately.

"Pardon me, General. The priests may not be able to launch a military attack without their weapons, but what if they try something more subtle? Couldn't they still send one or two assassins?" Anastasia asked, not convinced that the asp no longer had any fangs.

"That is a good question, Anastasia. Now that we have eliminated their military options, they may be forced to utilize whatever evil means they have left. We must all remain alert and on guard," the general conceded.

"The general is right, and we have prepared for this accordingly," Akhenaten interjected with confidence.

The general expanded on Akhenaten's statement by explaining, "As you probably noticed when you entered the palace, we have tripled the number of guards at each entrance to the palace and the Royal Residence. Akhenaten will also refrain from making public appearances for the time being until we have time to locate the asp's nest and cut off his head." The general looked at Nefertiti and quickly added, "I mean until we find the priests' lair and we destroy their ability to threaten Akhenaten and Nefertiti."

Anastasia still wasn't convinced. She wanted to say "What if the threat is already inside the palace?" but she didn't feel comfortable making that type of statement without proof. After all, they had thought that Djedi could have been a traitor less than twenty-four hours ago.

"We know the jackal will be desperate," Akhenaten added stonily. "We have also prepared for the fact that he may choose to attack us directly instead of through his agents. We have not been idle, my friends. Aten's wards will make it impossible for him to breach the palace."

"Pardon me, Your Highness, but what do you mean by 'Aten's wards'?" Anastasia asked, completely confused.

Akhenaten smiled confidently as he explained, "Aten's wards are his symbol, the solar disk, which have been infused with his rays. We have warded all entrances and exits to the palace. Anubis's dark essence cannot abide Aten's light, so he will not be able to pass. Nefertiti and I will be safe here until we exterminate his evil agents and put Anubis in his proper place. Only then will the people of Egypt receive fair judgment and access to the afterlife. Only then will we be free from his pernicious ways."

Chapter 26

Edward and Anastasia hadn't been able to shake their sense of unease since they'd left the palace. Akhenaten, Nefertiti, and General Meketre were very confident that they had thwarted Anubis and the efforts of his priests. But Edward and Anastasia knew they weren't just dealing with Anubis and the priests—they were also dealing with the Corsairs and their ability to travel through time.

Edward felt so conflicted. He wanted to shout it out and tell them what he knew. That the threat wasn't really over. The Corsairs were out there and they still had a Refractium Crystal. He wanted to be loyal to the Order of Time, even if he wasn't an official member, but he also felt like he was being disloyal to his new friends in Egypt by not saying anything. *What if something happens that could have been stopped if they'd known?*

"I know the general and Akhenaten think they've eliminated the threat, but I think we have to keep looking for the potential traitor," Edward said to Anastasia as they walked toward the marketplace to meet the guys. "If there's a traitor on the inside, they might be feeding the Corsairs and the priests information about their defensive plans. What if they're able to use the Refractium Crystal to get inside the palace without them being aware? This could be a disaster."

"You're right. We have to keep our guard up. We can't tell the guys that the threat is over, because it's not. We need to keep following our plan," Anastasia answered quietly but with the same urgency.

They entered the marketplace, walking quickly. They were keen to meet up with the rest of the guys and get started. It looked like a normal day in the market with the usual buzz and banter of commerce filling the square. If trade and barter were an Olympic sport, Egypt would undoubtedly be a gold medal contender.

Edward craned his neck left and right, but he couldn't spot the other kids.

"It's not like Salah to be late," Anastasia said with a hint of concern in her voice.

Edward and Anastasia kept walking until they reached the middle of the market, looking for their friends. That's when Edward noticed a group of a dozen or more boys crowded into a narrow alleyway off to the right. They were agitated and jostling around like a pack of wild dogs. As Edward looked more closely, he spotted a familiar figure in the middle of the pack towering above the others. It was Bilji. He also spotted the heads of his four friends appearing intermittently through the ring of boys that had them surrounded.

This is bad. This is very bad.

Edward reached for Anastasia's hand to get her attention. He pointed to the alleyway and said one word, "Bilji!"

The edge of the outer ring parted briefly and they could see Salah, Israh, Smuz, and Bethrek standing in a tight circle with their fists up, ready to defend themselves. Bilji was standing directly in front of Salah, who had blood dripping from his nose.

Edward watched as his sister transformed from a normal girl to Super Anastasia in a split second. She didn't need a cape and tights. Her body tensed, bristling with energy, and her eyes glowed with an intensity that was frightening. She bolted like a streak of lightning for the alleyway. Edward threw himself into action and sprinted after her, yelling for her to wait for him.

"We're trying to save the world. I don't have time for this nonsense!"

Edward heard Anastasia's angry words as he searched in vain for another gear to help close the gap.

She approached the entrance to the alleyway, running at full speed toward the ring of boys with her legs pumping like pistons. At the last moment, she stepped on an overturned crate with her right foot and vaulted herself into the air toward the alley wall. As her left foot planted against the wall, she drove herself higher, like she'd decided to run on the wall instead of the ground. She was over five feet above the ground when she pushed off violently toward the center of the alley. Edward watched in slow motion as she cleared the heads of the boys circling their friends. He could see Bilji's head turn just in time to see Anastasia's left foot heading straight for his temple. The thump was unmistakable as Bilji toppled sideways and

Anastasia somehow managed to land gracefully on her feet with her fists up. She was the most awesome thing Edward had ever seen.

Bilji's gang was stunned. A moment before, they had clearly been in charge of the situation and had been enjoying tormenting their captives. Suddenly, their leader was down, felled again by the same girl who had knocked him out when he'd attacked her with a knife. The same girl who was now ready to kick each one of their butts.

A number of them also spotted Edward, who had taken out Akhenaten's assassin, still running and screaming as he approached the alleyway. Sensing that the tide had changed, Bilji's gang broke and ran, even though they outnumbered Edward, Anastasia, and their friends. As the gang ran, their four friends started hooting and laughing.

"You had better run, you sons of dogs!" Smuz shouted while Israh and Bethrek both did some sort of celebratory jig.

Salah wiped the blood from his nose as he faced Anastasia. "I have no words to describe how I feel. You are more than just a friend, Anastasia. I will never forget this."

For a moment, he and Anastasia seemed frozen, looking into one another's eyes. The moment was lost when Israh clapped Anastasia on the back and said, "Even though we had the situation under control, you were truly amazing! You sent those dogs running for the hills!"

Bethrek and Smuz enthusiastically concurred.

Salah turned to Edward and said, "You played your part as well, my friend. I think they knew better than to wait for you to arrive."

Edward was caught off guard. No one was ever afraid of him. "Yeah. Well, I guess word spreads, you know," Edward tried to say nonchalantly as he looked over at Anastasia and saw her wink at him. He winked back at his sister and smiled sheepishly.

They left the market to avoid any unwanted attention from the guards and regrouped in a small, public park outside of the market.

"Have you found out anything new?" Salah asked them.

"They haven't caught the traitor yet. They did find a stockpile of weapons, but things are still dangerous. We are going to need to follow our last two suspects and see where it leads," Edward told the group.

"They've increased security at the palace, but it may not be enough," his sister added.

"Okay," said Salah as he nodded in agreement and dabbed his nose. "Let's get started."

Bethrek stepped forward and put his hand on Salah's shoulder. "I hope you do not take this the wrong way, Salah, but I think we should change the groups. Bilji and his gang may come looking for you when they recover. I think Anastasia and Edward will be able to protect you better than we can."

"That is completely unnecessary. Everything will be fine," Salah said confidently.

"I think Bethrek is right," Smuz added quietly. "We cannot afford to be sidetracked again by Bilji and his rabble. Anastasia and Edward will provide a serious deterrent."

Salah looked at Israh, who nodded in agreement.

"That's settled then. Edward, Salah, and I will follow Imhotep, the scribe, and you three can follow Nefertiti's attendant, Lysandra," Anastasia said as she nodded at Smuz, Israh, and Bethrek.

"If we get started now, we might be able to pick them up if they leave the palace for their midday meal. We should meet again at the clubhouse in the middle of the afternoon. Probably best for us to stay away from the square for a while," Edward added to finish the conversation.

They set up camp across the street from the main entrance of the palace to wait for Imhotep, the scribe. They were debating how, with all the heightened security, they could possibly sit outside the palace and Royal Residence for hours without attracting attention. Then Salah snapped his fingers.

"I've got it," he said. "You two wait here and I will be back in ten minutes." He took off down the street at full tilt.

Edward looked at Anastasia and asked, "Where is he going?"

"I have no idea, but I bet he'll be back quickly," she responded, smiling and watching Salah disappear into the distance.

Sure enough, they spotted Salah coming back up the road at the same pace a few minutes later, holding some sort of bundle under his arm. As he came closer, Edward could see that Salah was smiling from ear to ear and that he was carrying a small satchel and several rolled up sheets of papyrus. Salah slowed his pace over the last fifteen yards but didn't stop smiling.

"What's all this stuff for?" Anastasia asked.

"Tools for the great artist of course. How can he sketch the palace and the Royal Residence without charcoal and papyrus? After all, that is why we are here," Salah said, winking at Edward and Anastasia.

While sketching the palace Edward decided that this was his favorite kind of stakeout. Unlike the night before, he was having a great time. Even the intense heat of the midday Egyptian sun didn't bother him. All the drawings or paintings he had ever done of ancient Egypt had always been based on pictures. Getting to use the actual palace as the model was surreal. He was so absorbed with trying to capture the lines and perspective accurately that he was surprised when Anastasia shook his shoulder gently and said, "Earth to Edward. Come in, Edward."

"I'm sorry. What's up, sis?" Edward said, surfacing from his own little world.

"It's time to meet the others at the clubhouse. Come on," Anastasia told him.

Edward sighed. It had been nice being distracted by something that wasn't life-threatening for a little while. "But I'm not finished yet," Edward started to complain before he was stopped by her raised eyebrows and the look on her face. "Right. Drawing is just our cover and not the reason we're actually here."

"I couldn't have said it better myself," Anastasia said as she and Salah helped him pack the satchel and roll up the drawings.

"Um, so did we see the scribe, by the way?" Edward asked Anastasia and Salah as they started down the Royal Road.

"Unfortunately, we have seen nothing, including Imhotep. Perhaps the others will have had more luck," Salah said, smiling as usual.

They beat the others to the clubhouse, where they put their feet up and enjoyed relaxing in the shade and its relative cleanliness. Edward was about to unroll his papyrus to continue working on his sketches when Israh, Smuz, and Bethrek arrived. Something was wrong. They were quiet and Israh and Smuz weren't arguing with one another.

"How did it go?" Salah asked, springing to his feet.

"Yeah. Did you see Nefertiti's attendant, Lysandra?" Edward asked hopefully.

Bethrek shook his head as he said, "I think we may have seen too much."

Neither Smuz nor Israh seemed to want to make eye contact or to add anything.

"What does that mean?" Anastasia asked, examining them each closely. "What happened?"

"We saw Lysandra when she left the side entrance of the palace around midday. She seemed to be nervous and was looking around a lot," Israh said in a subdued tone.

"Okay. That's a good start. And . . .?" Anastasia asked expectantly as if waiting for one of them to continue.

"She wound her way through town, looking back over her shoulder every five minutes like she was afraid of being followed," Smuz added to the story.

"Technically she was being followed. So that bit makes sense," Edward said.

"She stopped by a grain store that is under construction and looked around before ducking inside. It was empty because all the workers were having their midday meal. At least we thought it was empty," Bethrek said but then didn't continue. He just looked down at the floor.

"What are you guys hiding?" Anastasia asked, seemingly short on patience. "Out with it!" She marched directly up to Israh and poked him in the chest with her index finger.

Israh spoke slowly while grimacing and rubbing his chest. "Well, it was a delicate situation."

"What does that mean? You boys are so annoying!" Anastasia shouted.

"I don't want to talk about it," Israh said flatly.

"Me either," said Bethrek, folding his arms across his chest.

"Fine!" Smuz said. "If you wilting flowers will not tell them, I will. We snuck inside the grain store to see if she was meeting with the priests. She wasn't. She met a workman there. She has a secret boyfriend."

Edward looked at Smuz, searching for more. He looked at Anastasia, who seemed to be waiting for the same thing. "What's so bad about that?" Edward asked, not fully understanding.

Smuz looked up, red-faced. "There was a lot of kissing happening. A *lot* of kissing. They had their tongues out. I thought they were going to swallow each other's faces. It was disgusting! As you know, it takes a lot for me to say that," Smuz said emphatically.

"It was terrifying. I didn't know that's what happens with girls. No one tells you these things. I am never going to have a girlfriend!" Israh added, sniffling quietly.

"That's it? That's your horrible story?" Anastasia asked them with an incredulous look on her face.

"You were not there. It was not pretty. I will not talk about this again. I need some fresh air," Israh said.

Bethrek could only nod in agreement as they left the clubhouse together. Edward guessed that this is what happened when you didn't have cable television or the internet. You ended up very sheltered.

"So Lysandra is not the traitor?" Edward asked.

"She is not the traitor unless there is some sort of secret code only spoken with tongues," Smuz said after the other two had left.

"I guess that leaves us with Imhotep. We struck out on the first three suspects. What if it's not him?" Edward said to Anastasia.

"It might mean that there is no traitor. If there's no traitor, we may have a different problem on our hands," Anastasia said with a scowl.

"Maybe we should get back out there," Edward said, resolved that they needed to find out one way or another.

Chapter 27

Anastasia watched the palace entrance as both Edward and Salah continued to work on their sketches. Salah had gotten bored and decided to join Edward in drawing.

Anastasia took her eyes off the entrance and glanced at Salah's drawing. The people didn't look like normal people. Their features were bizarre with different-sized eyes, crooked mouths, and misplaced noses. They actually looked a bit scary. Maybe charcoal pencils weren't really Salah's medium.

Salah seemed to reach the same conclusion when he grimaced at his drawing and said, "It's not exactly what I pictured in my mind when I started."

She thought Edward was trying to be encouraging when he said, "I think you may just be ahead of your time. It looks like a Picasso to me."

"What's a Picasso?" Salah asked with a confused look on his face.

Edward seemed to realize that he probably hadn't used the right reference, given that Picasso wouldn't be born for another 3,500 years. "Don't worry about Picasso. The important part is that I like it," Edward smiled at Salah, who was still unconvinced.

They had to wait until the early evening before they spotted the small and slightly hunched figure of Imhotep exiting the palace. He was wearing the typical linen kilt worn by most upper-class Egyptian men. He shuffled his sandal-clad feet timidly down the ramp away from the palace entrance. He was carrying a small, cloth bag slung over his shoulder as he turned north on the Royal Road toward the Great Temple of Aten. Anastasia motioned to Edward and Salah to be quiet and follow her.

It was still early enough in the evening that the Royal Road was crowded with people, donkeys, carts, and an occasional horse. Imhotep made his way through the traffic and seemed to shrink away from everyone, sticking to the edge of the road. Anastasia was pretty sure that he would have happily given way to a horsefly if it had cut across his path. *Not exactly the profile of a daring traitor or secret agent.*

Anastasia, Edward, and Salah were following about fifty yards behind Imhotep so they wouldn't be spotted. As they neared the Great Temple and the gardens, he quickly turned right and exited off the Royal Road. Imhotep had gone down an alleyway between two long, flat warehouses. Anastasia quickened her pace with Edward and Salah right behind her. They couldn't afford to lose track of their last suspect, even if he was an unlikely one. As she turned the corner, she caught a brief glimpse of someone she thought was Imhotep ducking through a doorway into one of the warehouses. Something didn't seem quite right. Whoever had ducked through the door had moved quickly and decisively.

"Where did he go?" Edward asked as he and Salah turned the corner and caught up with her.

Anastasia pushed the uncertainty out of her mind. "He went through that door," she said, pointing to the entrance forty yards ahead on the left.

It was a heavy door made of wooden planks that were bound together with copper. Anastasia tried the door.

"Oh no! It's locked!" she exclaimed. "What do we do?"

Salah took his satchel off his shoulder and stepped forward. "Allow me, but please do not hold this against me. I have been friends with Israh for many years, and as a result, one learns things. I can assure you that I would never use these tools for self-interest." He reached into his satchel and removed a thin wooden lever that was shaped like a spatula and a small bag of angled wooden pegs.

"What is that thing?" Anastasia asked.

"This door is locked with a tumbler lock. Inside the door there are three or four wooden pins that are keeping this wooden beam locked into place within the doorframe. Normally, you must have a key to open the lock," he said, pointing to a hole in the wooden beam in the middle of the door. Holding up the items he had taken out of his satchel, he said, "The lever and pegs will serve as a key when adjusted correctly. This will allow me to lift the pins and slide the wooden beam to the left, which will disengage the beam from the doorframe and allow us to open the door." He smiled while inserting the key.

"Are you telling me you can open the door with that thing?" Anastasia asked, still not quite understanding.

"Yep." He extracted the lever and removed one of the pegs. "I designed this as a master key for all locks. I have just determined that this lock has three pins and therefore requires only three pegs."

"That is so cool. You designed this on your own?" Edward said with open admiration.

Salah smiled mischievously at Edward. "Israh's style is to pickpocket the keys. I thought it would be simpler to make a single, adjustable key once." Salah lifted the lever, slid the beam, and then pushed the door open.

Anastasia's mouth dropped open in amazement. "Salah, you're a genius!"

She paused and listened for a moment at the open door. Hearing nothing, she silently entered the dark warehouse with Salah and Edward trailing behind her. Her eyes slowly adjusted to the darkness as the musty smell of the warehouse entered her nostrils. She could just make out the floor-to-ceiling shelves that lined both sides of the corridor as she slowly inched forward. After thirty seconds of walking, she became aware that her heart was beating loud and fast. She had to pause for a moment and center herself. She slowed her breathing and forced her mind to focus. Then she heard the voices. They were faint, but she could definitely hear them. She felt someone softly touch her shoulder. It was Edward checking to see if everything was okay. She held up her hand, motioning for him to wait while she locked her senses in on the direction of the voices. They were coming from the left. She started forward again, searching for the passageway that would lead her to Imhotep and whoever he was talking with. She placed one foot in front of another while listening intently to the conversation that was slowly growing louder. The outline of a doorway came into focus.

She passed through the doorway and found herself in another corridor that was also lined with shelves on both sides. The corridor turned to the right and she descended a flight of stone stairs.

The air was cooler and slightly damp below ground level. Edward and Salah were right behind her as the flickering light from a torch reached them. She could see the outline of another doorway at the end of the corridor. Whoever was talking was right through that door. She held her right hand up to signal for Edward and Salah to stop. She could hear two men speaking clearly now.

"Have you left the passageway open as commanded?" the first man said.

"Yes, of course. It is exactly as asked," the second man answered.

"Very well then. Take this papyrus and return to your post, but read this before the moon has risen. You will need to make preparations," the first man said.

"What kind of preparations?"

Before the first man could reply, Edward sneezed. Actually, it was more than a sneeze. It was one of the loudest sneezes Anastasia had ever heard. She and Salah both froze as the sound echoed like a clap of thunder through the stone corridor. As the ensuing moment of silence hung in the air, she turned to face Edward as he mouthed the word "Sorry" and then everything went crazy.

It turned out that the sound of a sword coming out of its sheath sounds a lot like the sound of a chef drawing their knife across a blade sharpener: metal against metal. While Anastasia wasn't sure what the noise was at first, it became perfectly clear when a man with long, black hair bounded through the doorway. He held a torch in one hand and the aforementioned sword in the other. A cutlass. One of those short swords with a curved blade and a wraparound handguard just below the hilt.

In the light being cast from the torch, Anastasia could see that he was dressed from top to bottom in black, including his cloak, tunic, pants, and soft leather boots. He looked like some sort of swashbuckler. He was both out of place and out of time. He was definitely a Corsair.

Another man stood just behind him. It took a split second for Anastasia to realize that this was Imhotep, the scribe. Although he was the same height as the Imhotep she knew, that was where the similarities ended. Where he had once looked thin and timid, he now looked wiry and aggressive. His clean-shaven head reflected the torchlight as he crouched in a fighting stance with a dagger held in each hand. Anastasia felt the hairs on her neck stand up as her whole body went into high alert. She heard a squeak and a gasp behind her that she took to be Edward and Salah respectively. The man in black smiled a malevolent smile.

"I was expecting General Meketre and his men. To my great disappointment, I find three children instead. I was hoping this would at least be sporting. I am afraid this won't even be a contest," he said as he assumed a fighting stance with the tip of his cutlass slightly raised.

"Don't be fooled. Two of them helped to foil the last attack. They are more than meets the eye," Imhotep explained to the black-haired man.

"Well then, killing them should make my trip here through the portal all the more worthwhile."

Out of the corner of her eye, Anastasia noticed a pile of long wooden poles on the shelf to her left. She felt her hand close around the hard, smooth timber before she even processed what she was doing. She sensed the balance and weight of the pole as she held it with both hands and crouched in a defensive stance. Her eyes tracked the man in black as he sprang forward like a panther. She barely had time to bring her left hand down while driving her right hand up and across to parry the tip of the cutlass plunging toward her chest.

She drove her left hand low and forward in an attempt to strike the shin of his lead left leg, but he danced back out of range. The man in black smiled as he darted forward again, his sword thrusting, slashing, and lunging in a blur of movement with his long cloak swirling behind him. She managed to defend the first two moves, but felt the wind from the cutlass pass her cheek as the man in black's lunge barely missed its mark.

She countered forward with her own lunge. The staff met nothing but air, but it did buy her space. *He's too fast.* She knew that she was going to have to use the staff's extra length to keep him at bay. *Letting him get too close is likely to be fatal.* He sallied forward again, feinting left and then right, hoping to get Anastasia to overcommit. She stayed focused and managed to defend his next three attacks.

She felt the sweat dripping down her forehead while she waited for the next wave. She could see Imhotep jockeying around behind the man in black, trying to figure out how to join the fight. Anastasia knew that she was lucky that he was constrained by the width of the narrow corridor. She was barely keeping out of reach from the one assailant.

"Very impressive," the man said. "You have the ferocity of a young lion cub. It will actually be a shame to put you down."

"What should we do, Anastasia?" Salah yelled from behind her.

"You and Edward should run for help. I'll keep them here until you get back." Although she answered calmly, Anastasia was desperately worried that she wouldn't be able to hold off the man in black for much longer. She thought that if Edward and Salah could get to safety, she could pick a time to try to make a run for it.

"No way, Anastasia! We're not leaving you!" Edward shouted.

The man in black laughed an evil laugh. "You fools. She is trying to save your skins. I suppose your staying will only make my job simpler." He darted forward again to deliver a flurry of powerful blows, which drove her backward as she parried with the staff.

Her back foot slid on a patch of sand as she went down to one knee. The man in black's eyes widened with anticipation as he swung his sword overhead in a downward arc toward Anastasia. She managed to raise the staff with both hands spread wide above her head in time to catch the blow. However, the force of it knocked her onto her back and split her staff into two pieces. She lay on the floor of the corridor, slightly stunned from hitting her head and with a piece of the broken staff in each hand. The man in black raised his sword to deliver the final blow when he was distracted by a loud noise coming from behind her.

Anastasia swiveled her head in the direction of the sound to see a miracle unfold. General Meketre came clattering down the stairs, crouched on top of his shield and riding it like a surfboard. His left arm was extended with a bow in hand and his right hand was drawn back next to his ear with an arrow knocked on the bowstring. Edward and Salah dove to either side to avoid being run over. The general's right hand released the arrow with a twang just as he reached the bottom of the stairs and vaulted off the shield to land lightly on the floor.

Anastasia looked back toward her assailant to see the man in black with an arrow lodged deep in his chest and his sword still raised above his head. His hand slowly lost hold of the sword, which clanked harmlessly to the ground. His eyes locked on Anastasia's as he smiled and quietly said "You are too late" before slumping to the ground dead.

Standing behind where the man in black had been, Anastasia saw that Imhotep had frozen as he'd eyed his fallen conspirator. Anastasia looked behind her as she heard the sound of many feet coming down the stairs. Half a dozen of General Meketre's soldiers arrived, including Djedi. Imhotep had clearly seen the same thing as he dropped his daggers and reverted to the role of the timid scribe, exclaiming, "Oh, thank you for rescuing us from this terrible man! I feared for both my and the children's lives."

Anastasia's jaw dropped. "He's lying! He's a traitor! He was working with that other man."

The expression on the general's face hardened. "The penalty for treason is death. Take the scribe into custody," he ordered.

Before they could take him, Imhotep fled in the opposite direction for the doorway. A wave of anger swept through Anastasia at the thought of him getting away. She remembered that she still had both pieces of the staff in her hands. She sat up in one fluid motion and threw the half of the staff in her right hand at the legs of the retreating Imhotep. It spun end over end through the air and struck him on his right heel, causing his feet to cross and knocking him down in a heap. The soldiers rushed by and pinned him to the ground before he had recovered from the fall. Imhotep laughed maniacally as the soldiers bound his arms.

Anastasia exhaled. *It's over.* The gravity of the situation began to hit her, and she could feel tears coming to her eyes. If the general hadn't arrived, she would have been . . . She couldn't even let herself think about death or dying. Still, her body started to shake. Before she knew it, both Edward and Salah had their arms wrapped tight around her.

"I love you, sis. Thank you for saving us," Edward choked with tears in his eyes.

"Twice in one day you have saved me, Anastasia. I owe you my life," Salah said solemnly.

She looked up and saw the general standing in front of her with a very serious and concerned look on his face. "Are you hurt, Anastasia?"

"No, sir. I'm not hurt but I guess I am a bit shaken. I didn't know what I was going to do. Thank you for saving me," Anastasia said, still a little bit teary.

"You are welcome, Anastasia. Do not think a thing of it. We can talk about why you kids were following this spy on your own later. I am glad that I assigned someone to watch you today as an added security measure. I cannot tell you how thankful I am that I was able to arrive before it was too late," the general said, using giant arms to pull her delicately into a protective embrace.

"Me too," Anastasia said, not wanting to imagine what might have happened.

Anastasia heard Edward clear his throat with an "Ahem." The general released her from his embrace and gave her a rub on the head before they both turned to Edward.

"Before all the fighting started, we heard Imhotep talking with the other man about a message on a papyrus. We need to check his bag," Edward said to the general.

The general regarded Edward for a moment before nodding and projecting his strong voice across the room. "Djedi, can you please search Imhotep, or whoever he may actually be, for a papyrus?"

Anastasia watched as the general then turned to examine the man in black. He had a puzzled expression on his face as he said to himself, "Who exactly are you and what are you doing here?" He picked up the cutlass and examined the steel. He then looked at the man's clothing and his boots. "A sword made of a metal I have never seen and strange garments that I cannot identify. You definitely are not from Egypt. Are you a foreign spy? If so, from where?"

As the general continued to closely examine the man in black, Edward whispered under his breath to Anastasia, "I think we need to tell them he's a Corsair. They need to know what's going on—that we're dealing with more than just Anubis and his disciples."

"We can't! We swore to Dr. G. not to tell anyone. It could change the future. Plus we may have already stopped them by breaking this meeting up. We may not need to do anything," Anastasia whispered fiercely.

"But what if this didn't stop the Corsairs? What if this isn't over?" Edward whispered back, not giving up.

"They would never believe us anyway. If we tell them we're from the future, they're gonna think we're crazy."

"We can trust them," Edward implored.

"They'll probably lock us up," Anastasia answered, locking eyes with her brother.

Edward didn't look happy. He was about to respond but stopped whispering as the general turned toward them and asked, "What can you tell me about this strange fellow?"

"We hadn't ever seen him before, General, but Imhotep didn't meet him here by accident. He seemed to be giving Imhotep orders," Edward said.

"He asked if Imhotep had left the passage open and he told him to read the papyrus so he could prepare for tonight. We don't know who this man was, but they were definitely planning for something to happen tonight."

"We need to find that papyrus," Salah added.

Djedi dashed across the room with a small and tightly rolled papyrus in hand. "It was hidden in a secret pocket within the shoulder strap of his bag. We wouldn't have found it if we didn't know to look for it."

The color seemed to drain from the general's face as his brow furrowed in concern. "Have the men secure this body. Let's get the papyrus and Imhotep back to the palace. With this type of treason afoot, I am not comfortable being away from the pharaoh any longer than necessary. Let's move out."

Chapter 28

They returned to the palace in the fading light as the sun prepared to set across the west bank of the Nile. Upon their arrival at the palace, Djedi and the soldiers took Imhotep to the dungeons for questioning. Anastasia, Edward, and Salah joined the general in Akhenaten's secret council chamber to update the pharaoh on Imhotep's treachery and plan their next steps.

The chamber was underneath the main palace with a single heavy wooden door and no windows. The walls were thick and made of sandstone. There was a large, round wooden table in the center of the room that was surrounded by two chairs and a dozen low stools. Given how rare large trees were in this desert city, this table must have cost a fortune. Overall the room looked a bit like a dungeon or a military bunker. It would be very difficult for unwanted ears to gain access to the conversation inside.

Akhenaten stormed into the council chamber. His face was impassive but his eyes burnt with intensity like smoldering coals. General Meketre summarized the events of the evening for Akhenaten, who listened intently.

"Blast the man!" Akhenaten exclaimed. "He lived under our noses and as part of our family for years. All this time he has been undermining us and what we have been trying to achieve for all Egyptians. Even worse, he was willing to kill children to achieve his evil ends." Akhenaten shook his head.

"It is the worst kind of treachery, my pharaoh," said General Meketre with his head bowed. "Something I should have undoubtedly discovered before now. By failing to do so, I have put you and all of Egypt at risk. If you have lost faith in me, I will understand and tender my resignation immediately."

"Nonsense, General. He fooled all of us, including myself. While the price of this lesson is not yet clear, I cannot see how it would be prudent to squander these hard-earned learnings and remove you from your post. Outside of Nefertiti, there is no one I trust or rely upon more than you, my friend." Akhenaten placed his hand on the general's shoulder. "We face this together. Put any self-doubt aside and let's see what this secret papyrus has to say."

Akhenaten and the general clasped arms in what Edward once again took to be a 3,500-year-old version of the fist bump.

"Now let us take a look at this papyrus. Let us see what treachery they have planned," Akhenaten said, raising his eyebrows as he extended his hand toward the general.

The general extracted the papyrus from a small pocket in his linen kilt and handed it to Akhenaten. Edward was riveted as Akhenaten unrolled the papyrus and held it up to the light. It was blank.

"It just can't be blank!" Edward exclaimed.

"Edward's right. The man who tried to kill us told Imhotep that he needed to read it in order to make preparations for tonight," Salah said, nodding his head in agreement.

Akhenaten held the papyrus up to the torchlight, but there was nothing to be seen. To make matters worse, Djedi returned to the council chamber to let them know that the scribe was not talking. The only sound to come from Imhotep's mouth was the same cackling laughter that had started right after his capture. The general let out a growl of frustration.

"Has Anubis taught his disciples how to read invisible messages, or can this all be a ruse to simply distract us?" the general added, thumping the clenched fist of his right hand into the palm of his left hand.

Edward looked over at Anastasia, who was quiet and seemed deep in thought. "You were there, too, Anastasia. What do you think?" Edward asked.

The conversation paused as the others also waited to see what Anastasia might have to add.

"Well, I don't think this is a distraction. Why would Imhotep go to the trouble of sneaking across the city to meet in secret? Why would he hide the papyrus in a secret pocket that would be so hard to find? Why try to kill all of us if it were simply a distraction? I think there's definitely something bad happening," she said in a level voice.

186

"While your logic makes sense, the papyrus remains blank," Akhenaten said with frustration creeping into his voice.

Then two thoughts connected for Edward as if completing a circuit, and a light bulb went on.

"What if both Anastasia and the general are right?" Edward said with a sense of excitement building inside him.

"What do you mean? Aren't Anastasia and the general saying two different things?" Salah said as he spoke for the group.

"I mean, what if Anastasia is right that Imhotep didn't go to all that trouble for a blank papyrus? What if the general is also right that Anubis has taught his disciples to read invisible messages?" Edward looked around the room at each of the others.

"I am sorry, Edward. I wasn't being completely serious when I posed that question. I was frustrated," the general said apologetically.

"I know you weren't being serious, but it struck me that it was the only thing that made sense. What if there really is a message written on the papyrus and we just can't see it? What if we aren't looking at it in the right way? What if we need to try a different perspective?" Edward was excited but sensed that the others thought he was a bit loopy. "Can I inspect the papyrus, Your Highness?" Edward asked.

Akhenaten extended his hand with the papyrus, even though he still wore the same skeptical expression that everyone else in the room was wearing.

Edward felt the fibers of the papyrus under his fingertips as he held it lightly and carefully. He inspected it closely but saw nothing in particular that stood out. He then brought the papyrus to his face and inhaled deeply. *There it is.* The faintest trace of the smell he was hoping for reached his nostrils. He couldn't stop it as a smile spread across his face.

"Djedi, could you bring the torch over here?" Seeing the questioning expression on Djedi's face, Edward quickly added, "I promise I'm not crazy."

Djedi looked at the general, who nodded his consent. Djedi removed the torch as requested and brought it to Edward.

"If you could just lower the torch to about here," Edward said, holding his hand at the level of his chest. "I am not going to burn the papyrus, but I am going to heat it," Edward explained to make sure that no one was alarmed by what he was going to do next.

After Djedi lowered the torch, Edward extended his arms and placed the parchment about three inches over the flame. He slowly moved his hands in a circular motion to ensure that the whole sheet of papyrus was heated evenly. Almost magically, brown lines and shapes started to appear. Within a few seconds, they became a full hieroglyph. One became two, then three, then four hieroglyphs. Edward heard everyone gasp as the papyrus was soon filled with lines of brown hieroglyphs. Edward removed the papyrus from the heat of the flame and held it for everyone to see.

"Is this magic?" Djedi asked Edward with his mouth gaping open in disbelief.

"No. Just a different way of looking at the same papyrus."

"That's brilliant, Edward!" Anastasia shouted, reaching forward to give him a big high five.

"How can this be?" Akhenaten asked Edward, apparently still trying to understand what had happened.

"It's lemon juice, Your Highness. The message was written in lemon juice. When it dries, it is completely invisible. That's why I smelled the papyrus. To see if I could make out the scent," Edward explained.

"Lemon juice," Akhenaten said, smiling and shaking his head.

"So why did the flame make the invisible message reappear?" General Meketre asked.

"When the juice dries, it is invisible but the acid in the juice weakens the papyrus. The heat from the flame turns the weakened areas brown first. You were right, General. Anubis has taught his disciples to read invisible messages. Or at least messages that were once invisible." Edward smiled at the general.

"You are a marvel, young Edward," Akhenaten said.

"Not really, Your Highness. I just had a good science teacher," Edward said as he felt the heat rising in his cheeks from the pharaoh's compliment. "I guess we should see what it says," he said, realizing that he had been so caught up in figuring out how to find the message that he hadn't even read it. He looked down at the papyrus to focus on the brown writing and began to read out loud: "The pirates will open their gate under the temple at midnight. That is when our brotherhood must do their part. Anubis, Lord of the Afterlife and the True King of the Gods, will come to the city of the infidel. He will deliver his reckoning and create a new order for the Kingdom of Egypt."

The general and Djedi didn't share the same worried looks, but they clearly were not happy to hear the message that he had just read aloud.

"So the jackal comes for me tonight," Akhenaten said, breaking the silence, his face the picture of resolve. He dispatched a runner to summon Nefertiti to the council chamber before turning back to the others. "He will find it much more difficult to breach the palace than he thought. The tether between the underworld and graveyards is very short, but the tether to the temple is much longer. The jackal is weakened and he will have very little power left by the time he arrives, if he makes it at all. Aten will preserve us." Turning to the general, he asked, "Who are these pirates he speaks of and what is this gate?"

"I don't know, my pharaoh. There are no pirates operating on the Nile nor have there been for centuries," the general answered.

"It is no matter. Let the jackal obliterate himself against Aten's wards. We can end this once and for all tonight," Akhenaten said, dismissing any potential risks associated with pirates.

Edward was starting to panic inside. *Akhenaten doesn't understand what we're dealing with. He can't. We have to warn him.* Edward looked at Anastasia. In that moment, they didn't actually need to speak. He fully understood exactly what she was thinking. It was a twin thing. They opened their mouths at the same time and both said, "There's something we need to tell you."

Everyone stopped. There was a moment of silence before Akhenaten said, "I believe you have our attention, Anastasia and Edward."

Anastasia looked at Edward and said, "Should I start?"

Edward nodded at his sister.

"The pirates in the message aren't pirates operating on the Nile. They're called the Corsairs. They are evil. The man in black that the general killed tonight was one of them. They may have the ability to help Anubis travel to Egypt without expending his power. He may not be weakened when he arrives."

"How do you know this?" Akhenaten asked with a slightly suspicious expression on his face.

"We aren't from here. We're from another time. So are the Corsairs," Edward answered.

Akhenaten stared at Edward for several seconds before saying, "Are you saying you are not from Thebes? Do you mean you and these Corsairs are from another country?"

"Yes and no, Your Highness. We're from another country but we're also from another time. We're from more than three thousand years in the future," Edward said, knowing how hard this would be to believe. It had been hard for him to process even though he had actually seen Dr. G. walking out of a glowing, purple portal.

Salah let out a long whistle. "I definitely didn't see this coming."

Akhenaten and the general were silent, as though they had been frozen by what Edward had said.

"That's not possible," the general finally said, shaking his head like it hurt. "No one can be from the future. No one can travel through time."

"I know it seems crazy. I wouldn't have believed us either a few months ago," Anastasia said calmly, establishing eye contact with the general and trying to make sure he knew she wasn't crazy. "It's true, though, we are from the future."

Akhenaten slowly turned to Anastasia like he was starting to thaw. "I want to believe you but—time travel? Even Aten has never told me of such a thing. Plus three thousand years is a very long time. Why is it that you have traveled here and now?"

Anastasia stepped toward him and answered him slowly and clearly, "To understand that, I think you have to understand the

Corsairs. They are a band of outlaws who have the ability to travel through time. They travel back in time to effect changes in history that will benefit them in the future. These changes create ripples in time just like how a stone thrown into a pool creates ripples. The ripples in time have the ability to reshape the future just like ripples in a pool have the ability to reshape the shoreline. They aren't pirates on the Nile. They are pirates of time."

Edward could see that Akhenaten was still struggling and that the general and Djedi looked completely unconvinced.

Anastasia didn't seem to be deterred and kept going. "The Corsairs are our enemies. We have traveled back to stop them. To try to preserve the natural order of time and hopefully the future that we come from. To be honest, we don't fully understand why they are trying to help Anubis. We're not sure how they will benefit from it," Anastasia said as she looked at each of their new friends.

The general spoke with skepticism, "You have shown more than once since your arrival in Akhetaten that you are supporters of Akhenaten and Nefertiti. However, this tale is too much to believe. Suddenly in one of the direst times in the history of our kingdom, you have traveled three thousand years through time to protect us from these time pirates, these Corsairs? I think this is a child's tale of make believe or something even more sinister."

Edward felt a spark of anger ignite within him. *I can understand them having a hard time believing us. Who wouldn't have a hard time believing us? But suggesting we're up to something sinister? After everything we've been through to get here? We had to rescue Dr. G., travel back through time, get attacked by Bilji's gang, tangle with assassins, almost get killed by Imhotep and the man in black, wear fake tan and colored hair spray, and fall into a giant pit of horse poo. How dare he doubt our intentions!*

"We've actually been sworn to secrecy so we really shouldn't be telling you anything, but you're our friends. You can't face Anubis without understanding what you're walking into!" Edward was aware that he was speaking very loudly, but he couldn't stop himself. "The Corsairs can open a portal, or gate, to any place and any point in time. How do you think Anubis's assassins managed to sneak into the city without you noticing them? The Corsairs opened a portal for them from Thebes and then one to Akhetaten. We don't know why they're working together, but they are. If they can open a portal for Anubis to come through tonight, it could change everything!" He seethed with indignation as he marched right up to the general. "He might not be weakened. He could appear directly in the palace behind all the precious wards you laid to keep him out. You aren't as safe as you think you are and you need to know all of this if we're going to beat them!" Edward realized that he was now standing way too close. He took two very self-conscious steps backward and looked down while he quietly said, "Sorry."

Edward felt two hands rest gently on his shoulders and looked up to see Akhenaten smiling down at him. "I can't say I fully understand everything you are saying, Edward, but I hear the truth in your voice. Well said to both you and Anastasia. Please accept both my and the general's apologies for doubting you."

The general nodded at Edward and then Anastasia in concurrence before adding, "What would you two suggest we do?"

"I'm not sure," Edward said. "I wish we had had a chance to question the Corsair, the man in black, before he died. I wish we knew what the Corsairs are planning and why they're working with Anubis."

Akhenaten had a mysterious glint in his eyes when he said, "I may be able to assist with that."

Chapter 29

Anastasia was a little creeped out. The dead body of the Corsair, the man in black, was laid out on the table of the council chamber.

Akhenaten stood next to the table near the dead man's head, mixing liquids from two small ceramic containers into one large one. Despite the arrow protruding from the dead man's chest, he still looked remarkably normal except for the fact that he was definitely a little pale. She was pretty sure that happened when you bled a lot from a wound, like an arrow to the heart for example. *It's hard to keep your color without any blood inside you.* Aside from that, he looked very much like he did when he was alive, including his glossy, black hair and the nasty sneer on his face. Prior to traveling through the portal, the frog she'd dissected in science class was as close as she had ever gotten to something dead. Between the dead Corsair and the casualties from the attack on Akhenaten, it was getting a bit too commonplace for her comfort.

I'm a little creeped out—okay, maybe a lot creeped out— right now, Anastasia admitted to herself. Nevertheless, she still stood next to Akhenaten. He had tried to explain how he was going to animate the body of the dead Corsair for questioning, but she still didn't really understand it. She actually needed to see it. Just saying that he would pour a mixture of asp poison, consecrated oil, and Aten's rays down the man's throat wasn't quite enough of an explanation. *Logically, ingesting a mixture containing asp poison is likely to make the man more dead, if that were technically possible.*

Edward, on the other hand, was completely creeped out. He sat in a corner of the room as far away from the dead Corsair as possible. He was quite happy for her to watch for the both of them.

Salah stood next to Anastasia, peering over her shoulder. He had said that he wouldn't miss a chance to see Aten's power in action. The general and Djedi had the air of people who had seen this type of thing before as they sat relaxing on stools on the other side of the table.

"I am mixing the poison of the asp and the consecrated oil. It is important that they are mixed constantly throughout the process, or else they will naturally separate," Akhenaten said while agitating the mixture with an implement that looked like a whisk made from dried reeds. "In a moment, I will use the power of Aten's rays to infuse and bind the mixture together. The power of the rays will temporarily reverse the power of the venom. Instead of causing death, the potion will summon the jb, or the part of the soul represented by the heart, back to our world. This will compel the body to think and communicate with us for a short period of time," Akhenaten explained.

"That's amazing. Does this work on any dead body?" Anastasia asked, curious if there were any limitations on the power of the potion.

Akhenaten smiled and paused momentarily to look at her. "That is a very good question. This potion only works on the recently deceased. If the body has already received judgment from Anubis and moved to the afterlife, it is too late to recall the jb." Akhenaten resumed stirring with his left hand while picking up his scepter with his right hand from where it lay resting on the wooden table. He started to chant softly.

Anastasia couldn't understand what he was saying. It seemed that he was speaking some older, more fundamental version of ancient Egyptian.

The large, blue gem on the top of the scepter started to glow. It transformed from a light blue like the sky to a golden yellow. A beam of the golden yellow light leaped off the surface of the gem and shot straight into the clay pot. The previously dull mixture took on the color of the sun as its light shone from the ceramic container.

"Aten's rays," Anastasia said to herself in a mixture of both understanding and wonder. *It's like something from Harry Potter. It's magic.*

"Yes, child. Aten's rays," Akhenaten said with a smile.

Akhenaten parted the dead man's lips and slowly poured the glowing liquid into his mouth. "By Aten's will, I command you to return to the land of the living to answer my questions."

Nothing happened at first. Then the dead man's skin started to change, turning brighter and brighter until it glowed. It was as if

194

sunshine were leaking out through his pores. The man's eyelids opened to reveal two luminous, white eyes without pupils or irises. Salah grabbed Anastasia's arm in fright, and she couldn't help but gasp.

Then the dead man opened his mouth and spoke. "I am here as commanded, Pharaoh." It was the same voice as when he was alive but empty and devoid of emotion. It was chilling.

"Who are you and who do you work for?" Akhenaten inquired.

"I am Philipe Angel. I am a Corsair and second-in-command under Dr. Rafael Augustino," the dead man replied with a glow of light leaking from his open mouth.

OMG! The dead man worked directly for the leader of the Corsairs.

"Why are the Corsairs working with Anubis and his disciples to kill my wife Nefertiti and I?" Akhenaten questioned the dead man.

"The Corsairs are not here to kill you. You are not our fight. We merely have a business arrangement with Anubis and his followers. They will kill you on their own. Anubis is not happy about you changing the religion. Your people do not worship him in the same manner they used to. You have checked his power and weakened him substantially, but he will not fade quietly into the night. He will reestablish his dominance among the gods and will rule over Egypt," the dead man smiled eerily.

Akhenaten went slightly off script as he seemed to adjust to the Corsair's last answer. "What is the nature of your business relationship with Anubis?"

"It is simple. We will use the Refractium Crystal to open a portal that will enable Anubis and his disciples to carry their fight to you here in Akhetaten. In exchange, once you and Nefertiti are dead, Anubis will ensure that Dr. Augustino never dies. He will never face the ultimate judgment. He will always be returned to the land of the living. He will become immortal and the Corsairs will be unstoppable."

The implications hit Anastasia hard. If Dr. Augustino could travel through time and couldn't be killed, the Order of Time wouldn't stand a chance.

Akhenaten's face registered his worry at the Corsair's response, but he pressed on. "How will Anubis travel to Akhetaten tonight?"

"Anubis will travel to a graveyard outside of Thebes where the tether to the afterlife is its shortest." The glow emitting from his skin and mouth began to wane. The dead man's speech was stilted as he continued, "Dr. Augustino will then enable Anubis to circumvent his normal boundaries by opening a portal between the graveyard and the chamber underneath the Great Temple of Aten."

"How does Anubis intend to kill Nefertiti and I?" Akhenaten attempted in a rush.

However, the light in the dead man's eyes went out completely and he spoke no more.

Akhenaten cursed their misfortune. "I thought we would have more time to question him before he was pulled back to the other side," he said, pounding his right fist on the wooden table and causing the dead man's head to jump inadvertently.

"We have significantly more insight into the jackal's plans than we did before, my pharaoh," the general reminded Akhenaten.

"The jackal will be at full strength when he arrives in Akhetaten, which is not something we ever envisaged," Akhenaten said, clearly still frustrated.

"At least we know that the Corsairs won't be joining Anubis and his disciples in trying to kill you," Anastasia tried to add as cheerfully as possible. As she saw Akhenaten's expression, she realized that not everything works with the glass-half-full approach.

The general spoke practically, "We have approximately ninety minutes until midnight by my reckoning. We must decide if we will seal the palace or if we take the fight to Anubis. Either way, we should have our men recheck our fortifications."

"My instincts tell me that we should let the jackal spend his might against our wards. Aten's rays will banish him back to the afterlife when the sun rises in the morning. That being said, rechecking the wards would be prudent," Akhenaten said, recognizing the value of the general's words. Akhenaten paused as he looked at Anastasia and Edward. Then he said, "Thank you for confiding in us with your secret. We would have severely misjudged the situation without this information. I am not sure how I will ever repay your loyalty. Suffice it to say that I am forever in your debt."

"You are welcome, Your Highness. The truth is it's just what felt right for both of us," Anastasia replied.

Akhenaten smiled before turning to Djedi and saying, "Please check on what is keeping Nefertiti. I would also seek her counsel on these matters."

Djedi nodded in acknowledgment before heading for the door and exiting the chamber.

A commotion ensued with the sound of sandals shuffling to and fro outside the door and the confusion of several voices speaking at once. Edward couldn't make out exactly what was being said, but it seemed very intense.

Djedi returned to the room ashen-faced. He was followed by another young soldier whom Edward did not know. Djedi's voice seemed to shake slightly as he spoke, "Nefertiti is missing, my pharaoh."

Chapter 30

There was a collective gasp from the room. *Nefertiti missing!* The news struck Akhenaten like a mighty blow as he appeared to stagger before the general braced and steadied him with his arms. Akhenaten recovered quickly and shrugged the general off.

"What happened to my wife? What did you find?" he asked the young soldier next to Djedi. It was the first time Edward had ever heard fear in the pharaoh's voice.

The young man appeared to hesitate.

"You may speak, Kheti," General Meketre prompted him firmly with an urgency in his voice. "Include all the details you can remember."

"When we arrived at Nefertiti's quarters to summon her to your council chamber, she was not there," Kheti stammered. "There appears to have been a struggle, my pharaoh. Some of the furniture was knocked over and several clay pots were smashed on the floor. We found Lysandra, her attendant, unconscious. Her left eye is swollen shut and she has a large lump on her head from where it struck the floor. There was no trace of Nefertiti," the young soldier said as both his voice and hands shook.

A strangled noise halfway between anguish and a roar emanated from deep within Akhenaten. His muscles were tensed, his body rigid.

Edward was reeling. He was still off balance from the news of Anubis's impending arrival and the whole dead-man-talking episode and was not prepared for Nefertiti to have been abducted. A terrifying thought struck him. *We have only ninety minutes to find Nefertiti before a very angry god arrives to smite us from the face of the earth.*

The general set Djedi in motion, his voice booming, "It is very hard to make a queen disappear without a trace in her own palace. Have it searched from top to bottom. Nefertiti may still be in the palace or we may at least find clues as to where she has been taken. Now, man!"

Djedi left the room at a run and could be heard barking out orders for the palace to be searched from top to bottom. Edward heard the sound of feet running down the stone hallway.

Akhenaten's face twisted in agony as he sat down heavily on his chair. He was silent as he appeared to struggle to control the rage and fear coursing through his body.

Edward watched Akhenaten for what seemed like an eternity. He felt terrible. While no one had said it out loud, he was sure they were all thinking that Anubis was definitely behind Nefertiti's disappearance. *After the failed assassination attempt, this must have become his plan B for getting to Akhenaten. Anubis is not going to give up on destroying Akhenaten's new religion and regaining his power. Maybe we should have told Akhenaten and the general about the Corsairs sooner.* He couldn't help but wonder if they could have prevented Nefertiti's abduction if they had been more honest.

Edward approached Akhenaten and knelt on one knee in front of him. "I am so sorry she's missing. I promise we will do everything to help find Nefertiti and stop Anubis. You can count on me," Edward told him.

"You can count on me too," Edward heard his sister say as she knelt beside him.

"You can count on all of us, Pharaoh. We will not rest and nothing will stop us from rescuing Nefertiti," Salah said emphatically.

The pharaoh looked up at each of them and his face brightened slightly. "You give me strength in my moment of need, my young friends. Your courage is a beacon that has shown me the path." Akhenaten got back on his feet. "General, we will not wait here. Let us prepare to take the fight to the jackal!"

The palace had been searched top to bottom, but Nefertiti was not to be found. Although Nefertiti was gone, the general ordered that Kheti and his team continue to search the palace for clues about her abduction. Akhenaten and the general had decided that they didn't have time to organize a full company given how little time they had left. The general had chosen a dozen of their finest soldiers to accompany them on their mission to recover Nefertiti. Initially, the general had tried to forbid Edward, Anastasia, and Salah from joining the party, but they flatly refused to be left behind. Anastasia had stared the general down with her arms folded across her chest.

However, it was Salah who had won the argument. "You can't afford to go anywhere without us. Who spotted and helped stop the assassination attempt? Who figured out Imhotep was a spy? Who discovered that the message was written in invisible ink? You need us."

When Akhenaten nodded his assent, the general reluctantly agreed. The general had quickly led the party to the armory, where they all prepared for battle. They were armed with all variety of weapons, including swords, clubs, bows, daggers, and shields. Edward recognized a number of the men as the same soldiers who had fought off the jackal-masked assassins. They were a seasoned group with large muscles, battle scars, and grim faces. There wasn't much talking as the group seemed to prepare themselves for what they might face tonight.

Edward was struggling to get comfortable with the short sword and shield he'd been given. They didn't feel natural in his hands. He didn't want to drop them or, even worse, stab himself. Anastasia, on the other hand, was pumped about their trip to the armory. She had selected a sword-proof staff that was encased in bronze in the middle and at both ends. Edward watched her test the staff by twirling it around and jabbing the ends forward. The staff was spinning so fast in her hands that it practically looked like a propeller from a helicopter. He just didn't want her to put herself in danger after her fight with the man in black. He couldn't bear the thought of anything happening to his twin.

With Anastasia and Salah by his side, Edward watched Akhenaten and the general debate their plan of attack. They only had sixty minutes remaining before midnight when Anubis would arrive here in Akhetaten to kill the pharaoh.

"If Anubis is to arrive in a chamber under the Great Temple of Aten, then that is where his disciples will have taken her. We will have to enter the temple, locate, and extract Nefertiti before Anubis arrives. With the limited time we have, I see no other options," Akhenaten said calmly to the general.

The general seemed unconvinced. "Even without Anubis there, they will be prepared for us. If we come through the front door, we will need a much larger party to fight our way through to Nefertiti."

"I would prefer to fight his disciples rather than Anubis himself. The jackal is no fool. He will use Nefertiti as bait once he arrives. He knows it is the only way to force me outside of the palace and Aten's wards of protection," Akhenaten said ruefully.

"I don't like it, but you are probably right, my pharaoh," the general grudgingly agreed.

The soldiers filed out of the armory with the general in the lead. Edward followed toward the back with Akhenaten, Anastasia, and Salah. The general had determined that if Anastasia, Edward, and Salah were coming, he was going to keep them as safe as possible. Djedi and one other soldier were at the rear of the procession to guard against any attacks from behind. Edward could hear the sound of footsteps running in their direction down the stone corridor.

A soldier came tearing around the corner and had to stop himself abruptly to keep from running headlong into the general. It was Kheti, the young soldier who had reported that Nefertiti was missing. He righted himself and stood at attention. "Sir, we found one of Nefertiti's gold bangles on the floor in the cellar where the grain and wine are stored. There was no other sign of her, but we thought you should know."

The general clapped Kheti on the shoulder excitedly.

We have a lead! Edward looked at Anastasia and Salah hopefully.

"Good work, Kheti. You have done the right thing to let me know." The general turned to Akhenaten, who had made his way through to the front of the column, and said, "What would you like to do, my pharaoh? Should we investigate the cellar or proceed directly to the Great Temple?"

201

Akhenaten appeared to consider the implications of what Kheti had reported. "It is our first clue as to how she was taken. While time is against us, I believe we must investigate for ourselves. If we find nothing, we will make haste to the Great Temple."

The general led them through the torchlit maze of passageways underneath the palace at a run. The sound of the company clanking and pounding on the stone floors echoed loudly down the corridors. Edward found himself struggling a little to keep up. He was still trying to figure out how to run properly with the small, round shield that Djedi had strapped to his left arm and the short sword sheathed on his belt. Despite their small size, they were still really heavy. Part of him had been excited at first to have the armaments. That was until he actually thought about what it would mean to have to use them. He was very content with his place near the back of the column.

Salah was struggling as well. The small shield probably weighed almost as much as he did. His normally smooth and easy stride was laboring under the additional bulk and weight.

Edward found himself slowing down as the corridor opened into a large room illuminated by torches at regular intervals around the walls. It was filled with rows of ceramic containers as tall as Edward. Like everywhere else in the palace, the walls were made of sandstone.

He was sweating profusely and had been getting a stitch in his side, so he was very happy for the opportunity to stop and catch his breath. Anastasia wasn't sweating or breathing hard at all, which he thought was ridiculous. The only by-product of her run across the palace was a healthy glow in her cheeks. He promised himself that if they made it home, he was going to spend more time playing sports.

The round ceramic containers and their heavy lids were both brown in color. He guessed that these were the ones for grain and that the lids were designed to keep out the rats. The wall on the left was covered in shelving and held much smaller ceramic jugs that appeared to be sealed. He figured that these must be for the wine that Kheti had referred to. He could see the royal seal—a picture of

Akhenaten and Nefertiti in profile—embedded in iridescent blue wax on the top of each jug. Edward also noticed three cats lying on the shelves near one of the wall brackets that held a torch. They looked lazily at him without getting up before closing their eyes and going back to sleep. This confirmed Edward's suspicion about the rats.

The general was already crossing the room and approaching a single soldier at the end of one of the rows of grain containers.

Edward was too far away to hear, but he could see that the soldier was speaking to the general and pointing to something on the ground. Edward guessed that it must be Nefertiti's bangle. *We should get over there so we can hear what's going on.* He caught Anastasia's eye and discretely pointed toward the general. Anastasia nodded in agreement and they started across the room.

The general was crouched low with a torch in his hand in the middle of the walkway between the containers, examining the floor when Akhenaten arrived by his side.

"What have you found, General?" Akhenaten asked in an anxious tone.

"I am sorry, my pharaoh, but there seems to be nothing else out of the ordinary at the moment. We will need to expand the search radius in the room, and we need to do it quickly," the general growled in a slightly frustrated tone.

Edward turned to Djedi and asked, "Djedi, can you please get us one of the torches from the wall? We're going to help the general with the serch."

"After what happened with the invisible ink earlier, I will happily get you a torch anytime you ask for one, young Edward," Djedi said and nodded at him as he quickly removed a torch from the wall.

Edward held the torch aloft in one hand with Anastasia and Salah on either side of him. They started pacing in an ever-expanding circle around the spot where the bangle had been found.

After about a minute of walking and peering, Salah asked uncertainly, "What exactly are we looking for, Edward?"

Edward realized that he wasn't certain either. "I'm not sure, Salah, but I think we'll know if we find it."

Salah said, "Fair enough, my friend. You can never win a match if you sit on the sidelines. Let's see what we find."

"Wait!" Anastasia said suddenly. "Edward, can you take a step or two backward?"

Edward froze with one foot still in the air. He tried not to panic as he slowly took two steps backward. *Am I about to step on a clue that I missed?*

"Did you see that?" she asked him.

"See what?" Edward asked, not knowing where to look.

"I didn't see anything either," Salah said, looking at Edward and shrugging his shoulders.

"Look at the torch and take one step forward again," Anastasia directed Edward.

He took a slow step forward and saw the flame on the torch waver just slightly as if it were being blown by the breeze. He stepped backward to make sure he had actually seen what he thought he had. It wavered again. Edward slowly pivoted his head to the left, trying to identify the potential source of the wind, but all he could see was the wall about three yards away. Edward looked at Anastasia, who nodded her head toward the wall.

They slowly marched forward toward the wall when Salah suddenly put his arm out in front of Edward and said, "Stop!"

Edward froze again and looked at Salah. Salah pointed at the ground. Edward spotted footprints in the dust that led right to the wall and then disappeared. There was a secret passageway behind the wall.

Edward, Anastasia, and Salah shouted in unison, "General!"

The general located the lever to open the door hidden behind the torch bracket. It wasn't something that anyone would have found easily without knowing how to look for it. "We have no idea where this passage goes," the general warned Akhenaten. "It may not lead to the Great Temple and Nefertiti. Even if it does lead there, we don't know how long it will take to get there if we follow it. It could be a fatal waste of time. We only have thirty minutes left before Anubis arrives; I am not sure we can take this chance."

"I know there is a risk, my friend," Akhenaten replied. "But there is no guarantee that we will get to Nefertiti in time even if we walk through the front gates of the Great Temple of Aten. We will still need to find the passage to the chamber underneath the temple, and as you pointed out earlier, they are likely to be waiting for us to come in that way."

Edward felt in his gut that Akhenaten was right. He believed that following the secret passage was their best chance of success. He found himself talking out loud before he realized what was happening. "I think the pharaoh is right," Edward said. "Both options for trying to rescue Nefertiti have serious risks, and there could be traps either way. But if we can find our way through this secret passage in time, we may take them by surprise. It could be the advantage we need to rescue Nefertiti and make our retreat to the palace prior to Anubis's arrival."

Akhenaten's eyes burned with intensity as he nodded at Edward and then the general before growling, "Up to now, Anubis and his disciples have been a step ahead of us. Let's see if we can't turn the tables on them. We will take this passage and find our way to that chamber. We will rescue Nefertiti."

Chapter 31

They plunged into the tunnel, racing down the dimly lit passageway with the general in the lead. He held a torch in one hand and his sword in the other while traveling as fast as he could with the limited light. The others were constrained by the narrowness of the roughly cut passage and traveled in single file behind the general. While there was another torchbearer in the back half of the column, the team was engulfed in deep and quivering shadows.

Even with her good eyesight, Anastasia could feel more than see that the floor was slightly uneven. She took great care to make sure that she lifted her feet as she ran in order to ensure that she didn't catch her toe on an unexpected ledge. She ran with her staff in one hand and the other extended as it lightly traced the position of the wall with her fingertips. It kept her centered in the passage, which seemed to curve every twenty or thirty yards. The passageway gradually sloped farther underground, and for the first time since they had arrived in Akhetaten, the air actually felt damp.

A sharp cry to halt was passed back through the column, but it didn't prevent the companions traveling behind from running into those in front of them. Anastasia slowed as quickly as she could but still managed to collide with Akhenaten's back. Fortunately, she rebounded directly into the arms of Salah behind her.

"Thanks for saving me. I guess we're even now," she told Salah as she rebalanced herself on her feet.

"You are welcome, Anastasia, but the ledger is not even close to level," he replied evenly.

As the commotion from the unexpected halt died down, the general relayed a message back, "There is a giant crevice in the sandstone ahead of me."

"Can we just leap over the crevice?" Akhenaten queried.

Anastasia could hear the urgency in his voice.

"No. It's actually more of a chasm. I was very lucky that I was able to stop myself at the precipice instead of plummeting in head first," his voice echoed.

"There must be some way to cross the chasm?" Akhenaten called to him.

"There is a wheel mounted to the wall with a rope that runs around it and stretches into the darkness. I am not sure what it is or where it leads to. Who sees well in the dark?" the general responded.

Before she could even answer, Anastasia heard Edward call out from behind her, "Anastasia has great eyesight. She's got eyes like a hawk."

"I don't know about eyes like a hawk, but I see pretty well," Anastasia added, eager to help in any way that she could.

"Come then, Anastasia. Hurry, child," the general implored.

Anastasia scooted up the left side of the tunnel to reach the general. It was indeed a chasm. The general's torchlight illuminated what appeared to be a natural, vertical split in the sandstone. The light wasn't strong enough to see either a ceiling or a floor. Given how fast they had been running, it was a miracle that the general hadn't ended up testing the depth of the chasm.

"These are the ropes and wheel I was talking about," the general said, pointing to a wooden wheel about the diameter of a Vespa tire that was mounted on the wall.

The wheel itself was about three inches wide with a furrow or track carved in the middle. A sturdy-looking rope was looped around the wheel and nestled into the furrow. Anastasia's eyes followed both ends of the rope as they reached out across the chasm and into the gloom. She focused on the lines of the rope and could just make out what appeared to be an opening on the other side. As she strained the limits of her eyesight, she spotted a dark, rectangular shape resting in the opening. Her brain subconsciously connected the dots, and she had a eureka moment.

"The ropes are a pulley system. There's a basket to carry passengers across on the other side," Anastasia told the general.

"You can see all that?" the general asked in disbelief.

Anastasia shrugged and nodded at the same time, not really knowing what to say.

"To be young again," the general muttered to himself. He sheathed his sword and took hold of the bottom rope. He gave it a pull, but it only moved about six inches before it stopped. He gave it another pull, but it moved no farther.

"The basket must be secured on the other side. Probably to make sure no one can follow them," Anastasia added, trying to be helpful.

All she got back from the general was a grimace.

"Is everything alright, General? Have you figured out a way across?" Akhenaten called out with just a hint of impatience.

The soldier just behind Anastasia and the general sprang forward. "Please, General, allow me to cross the chasm and release the basket. I am a good climber, sir."

The general considered the soldier's proposition for a moment before nodding. "Alright, Mehmet. Go get it. There's no time to waste."

Mehmet strapped his shield to his back before reaching up to grab the rope with both hands. He nimbly pulled himself off the ground, hooked both ankles over the top of the rope, and quickly began to shimmy out over the chasm. He hadn't traveled more than two meters when a giant, reptilian head erupted from the darkness below. Its crocodile-like jaws were open as it surged toward where Mehmet dangled from the rope. Mehmet must have sensed the danger as he pulled himself upward and twisted toward one side. The six-foot-long jaws snapped shut where he had been only a split second before, missing his body but still capturing his right arm in its maw.

Anastasia screamed in terror as Mehmet's hands were ripped from the rope by the weight of the horrendous monster. Its crocodile head was fused to a lion's torso. Its arms were covered in short fur and ended in paws instead of hands. Its squat and powerful legs were like those of a hippopotamus. It was like a nightmare. The same nightmare that Edward had given her when describing Ammit, the demon who devoured those who failed to pass judgment and enter into the afterlife. *Why can't it have a different type of head?* She really hated crocodiles; they were like her kryptonite.

Mehmet howled in pain as his arm slipped free from the crocodile's jaws and the demon's long teeth shredded his flesh.

Ammit growled in frustration as he fell back into the darkness of the chasm. Mehmet's body swung gently back and forth as he dangled from his ankles. The general lunged forward, grabbed Mehmet's leather belt, and then hauled him back into the mouth of the passageway. Their momentum sent both the general and Mehmet crashing backward into Anastasia, and they all tumbled to the ground.

Anastasia scrambled into a sitting position and found Mehmet's injured arm lying across her lap. It was bleeding heavily from two deep gouges that ran from his bicep to his wrist. Every fiber of her being was telling her to flee, but she knew she had to stop the bleeding quickly or Mehmet would die. She ripped the sash from around her waist to use as a tourniquet. Mehmet's screaming fell silent and his eyes glazed over while Anastasia hurried to tie the tourniquet tightly just above his bicep.

Before she could check to see if the bleeding had stopped, a strong arm wrapped around her waist from behind and pulled her backward. Her eyes swung upward to see the general dragging Mehmet toward her as Ammit's ferocious jaws snapped shut just behind them. The demon tried to pull himself over the lip of the passageway but plummeted back into the chasm when he couldn't hold on with his paws.

"What is Ammit doing guarding this passage? No demon is allowed on this plane!" the general growled with dismay.

"Is that demon guarding the chasm? Blast Anubis! Our time is running out," Akhenaten's voice echoed up the passage from his place in the line behind them.

Anastasia could sense the frustration in the pharaoh's voice from not being able to see what was happening at the head of the narrow passageway. She was trying to understand what the general had meant when she felt something squirming against her waist. Her eyes darted toward her waist and she saw that her white gown was now red and completely covered in Mehmet's blood. She felt the movement again. A bolt of cold fear charged through Anastasia as she realized that something was moving inside the belt bag that she had strapped under her gown. The one that held the Quetzalcoatl statue she had taken from Edward for safekeeping when they'd first arrived in ancient Egypt.

"Oh my god!" Anastasia exclaimed as she quickly unclicked the belt bag and let the blood-soaked bag fall to the ground.

She watched in terrified fascination as something writhed inside it. Anastasia kicked the bag away and tried to step backward but ran into the soldier who had pulled her clear of Ammit's jaws. There was nowhere to go. The canvas bag ripped open and the golden dragon's head with glowing, green eyes and red pupils emerged. The statue was alive.

The miniature Quetzalcoatl rapidly expanded in front of her eyes until his head engulfed half of the passageway. The god's golden, serpent body was as thick as an oak tree and coiled behind him. His feathered wings were folded back as they scraped the ceiling. Quetzalcoatl was motionless as he stared directly at Anastasia with glowing, green orbs that were now the size of volleyballs.

She could vaguely hear the shouts from the soldiers directly behind her. Anastasia was completely frozen with fear.

"What in Aten's name is that?" the general said with a mixture of fear and awe as he slowly reached for his sword.

"It has been many centuries since I have been to this world," a deep and ancient voice rumbled inside her head.

Quetzalcoatl is inside my head. He's talking to me directly inside my head.

"You have paid the blood price and summoned me, child. What is your need?" the voice inside her head continued.

She had no idea how to talk to an ancient Aztec god. That kind of thing was much more up Edward's alley. Anastasia stammered before finding her voice. "Mighty Quetzalcoatl, it is I who have summoned you. There is a demon blocking our way."

The general stopped drawing his sword halfway when he realized that Anastasia was communicating with the beast.

Quetzalcoatl remained motionless. "What is your need? Ask quickly, child, before I grow weary of this, as I am forever hungry," the voice echoed with impatience.

Anastasia tried to swallow her rising fear. "Oh, mighty Quetzalcoatl, will you unleash the power of the hurricane upon our enemy? Will you banish him from our world?"

The god's head nodded almost imperceptibly as howling winds suddenly swept through the passage. Quetzalcoatl swiveled and dove into the chasm with a roar. Within a second, his roar was answered by an angry growl from within the chasm. The walls of the passageway shook and stones fell as the god and demon battled out of sight on the bottom of the chasm.

Anastasia was still shaking as she exhaled and looked at the general. He stared at her wide-eyed and nodded wordlessly toward the chasm. He was clearly waiting for an explanation.

"I'm sorry, General. I promise I'll explain everything if we make it through this alive, but right now there's no time. We have to go now while Quetzalcoatl has Ammit occupied," Anastasia pleaded.

The general pursed his lips as the sounds of battle raged on within the chasm. He seemed to realize that explanations would have to wait as he nodded and handed Anastasia his torch. "My pharaoh, I will retrieve the basket from the other side of the chasm. There is an otherworldly battle being waged on the chasm's floor. Hopefully this will keep Ammit occupied, but we must be ready to move quickly," he shouted down the passageway.

Without waiting for a reply, he reached above his head and grabbed ahold of the bottom rope with both hands. The thick muscles in his arms flexed as he swung his legs up off the ground and hooked his feet over the rope. Anastasia gulped in fear as he proceeded to reach hand over hand to pull the rest of his body along the rope and out over the abyss.

Anastasia heard him mutter "I am getting too old for this" as he inched his way across the darkness through the ferocious chorus of snapping jaws and tearing flesh.

Sixty seconds later, the ropes on the basket started to move again and the wheel began to turn. In another twenty seconds, the basket reached the torch's ring of illumination. It was suspended from the bottom rope, and she could see the general standing in the basket and pulling hand over hand on the top rope. There was an opening on each end and probably room for another three or four people in the basket. She could see the sweat on his brow as he propelled it forward. Two of his soldiers seemed to realize how hard the general was working and leaped forward to help pull the basket across at the same time. The speed of the basket accelerated. The basket crossed over the edge of the chasm, and the general hopped back down onto the floor.

He pointed at the first four of his soldiers and said, "Get to the other side and secure the entrance. It will take us three or four trips to get everyone across." He turned to the soldier holding Mehmet upright and said, "Theptha, you must take Mehmet and return to the palace."

Edward had climbed into the basket after it returned from depositing Anastasia and Salah on the other side. He was white-knuckled and shaky on his feet when he exited the basket on the far side of the chasm. "I'm so glad I didn't have to see whatever was down there."

"Yeah, I almost lost my flatbread just listening to them," Salah shivered and clutched his stomach, his normally brown face as white as Edward's.

"It was the most terrifying thing I have ever experienced. My brain won't even let me think about what happened back there," Anastasia admitted quietly. "I'm just glad we made it across."

Her twin wrapped his arms around her and gave her a giant hug.

"I suppose that bringing Quetzalcoatl to Egypt was a pretty smart idea after all," Edward said, smiling nervously as he let go of her.

Anastasia glared at her brother and his smile quickly disappeared.

Chapter 32

After the last group of soldiers was safely across the chasm, the group took off again, running faster than before. They had lost ten minutes they couldn't afford to lose so they were pushing the pace. The party heard a triumphant roar from Quetzalcoatl echo down the passage and then everything fell silent behind them. Anastasia silently prayed that she would never have to see either Ammit or Quetzalcoatl again. There was no talking other than the odd warning of uneven footing or a patch of sand on the floor as they ran through the twisting tunnel. Anastasia felt focused and determined. She knew they didn't have much time left if they were actually going to locate Nefertiti before Anubis arrived.

Another call to halt passed back down the column. Anastasia heard the general swear loudly and more than once.

"What is it, General Meketre?" Akhenaten called out from his place just in front of her.

"I have hit a crossroad. There are three other passageways to choose from here. With all the twists and turns we have taken, I just don't know which direction is the right direction," the general answered back to the pharaoh.

"We can't afford to get this decision wrong if we want any chance of recovering my wife prior to the jackal's arrival," Akhenaten said, verbalizing exactly what Anastasia was thinking herself.

If we make a wrong choice, who knows how long it will take for us to backtrack to the intersection. Plus we'd still be left with two other passageways and a 50 percent chance of getting it wrong again.

Edward tapped Anastasia on the shoulder. "Use your compass," he said.

"My what?" Anastasia asked.

"Your compass. You know, the one Dr. G. gave you," Edward said, looking at her like she had a big *L* on her forehead. "You can figure out which way is north. It's not perfect, but it's probably the best chance we have of guessing the right direction."

He's right. I can use the compass. The Great Temple was less than a mile directly north from the palace and they had already covered a lot of ground. *If we aren't completely off course, choosing a passageway that goes north is probably a good guess.* Anastasia found herself scooting up the left side of the passageway once again, saying "Excuse me, excuse me" to the soldiers as she went.

"You again?" the general said with raised eyebrows when she reached the intersection.

She pulled on the chain around her neck to remove the necklace from underneath her robes. "Could you please bring your torch a little closer?" Anastasia politely asked the general.

He nodded without saying anything and did as he was asked.

"That way is north. Like the star Thuban. I think the temple lies that way," she said, pointing to the passageway on their left. "I can't guarantee it's the right way, but I think it's a good guess."

The general regarded her and the small, golden device hanging from her neck for a moment before saying, "This isn't the same kind of surprise as the last one, is it?"

Anastasia quickly shook her head in response.

"Okay. We turn left here. Let's move." He turned left and ran off down the corridor as the soldiers fell in behind him. Akhenaten nodded his approval at Anastasia as he ran past.

She jumped back in line in front of Edward and Salah, who gave her a thumbs-up before they all sped down the corridor. They ran as fast as they could now. It was probably too fast to be completely safe, but they had passed that point of consideration. They were racing against the clock. The dimly lit walls of the passageway seemed to fly by in a blur. Anastasia was sweating now and she could hear Edward breathing hard behind her.

Then she heard a quiet call to stop come back down the column as the line of soldiers checked their speed and wound down to a complete stop. Their breathing slowed and soon the silence of the subterranean passageway engulfed them. A moment later, there was a quiet shuffling of feet as the soldiers pressed themselves up against the wall to make way for the general, who appeared in front of Akhenaten. He was radiating a quiet intensity.

"Young Anastasia chose the right direction. I believe we have arrived, my pharaoh. The passage turns slightly and a chamber opens up about seventy yards ahead," he said, gesturing for Akhenaten to follow him before turning and walking back toward the front of the column.

"Let us see what there is to be seen, my friend," Akhenaten said.

The torches were extinguished and the whole column crept silently forward behind the general and Akhenaten. Anastasia could see the light at the end of the passageway getting closer and closer. About twenty yards away from the end of the passage, the general turned around and signaled the group to wait.

"Akhenaten and I will scout ahead to see what is happening inside the chamber," he said. He paused as he looked back and added, "Anastasia, come with us. We may need your young eyes."

Anastasia gulped in a combination of excitement and fear. She wanted to help find Nefertiti, but part of her was frightened of what she might see. *What if Nefertiti is hurt or, even worse, what if Anubis has already arrived?* She looked at Edward and he reached out and gave her hand a quick squeeze of encouragement.

They shimmied forward on their elbows and stomachs in order to stay low and reduce the chance of being seen or heard. They stopped before leaving the last shadows of the passageway, just before reaching the southern end of the chamber. Anastasia's eyes took a moment to adjust to the light as she took in the sight in front of her.

The secret chamber was actually a cavern. It was shaped roughly like an oval that was close to fifty yards long and forty yards across. It must have been here even before the city was constructed. On the eastern side of the chamber was the opening of a passageway that disappeared in a direction that led underneath the gardens. There was also a stairway that was carved into the left side of the wall. Anastasia's instincts told her that the stairs had to lead to the Great Temple of Aten. Six large, metal braziers were laid out in a circle in the middle of the room. The glowing, hot coals that filled them were burning brightly and casting long and malicious shadows on the uneven surface of the cavern's smoke-filled ceiling.

In the middle of this burning circle were approximately two dozen figures clad in leopard skins and black, wooden, jackal masks. Priests of Anubis, his disciples. Anastasia gasped involuntarily at the sight. They each held a papyrus and chanted around what appeared to be a dead body laid out on a flat stone table. The chant was slow and deep as it reverberated powerfully through the chamber. The priests' masks gleamed frighteningly in the firelight of the braziers.

One priest stood out from the others. He wore an elaborate and snarling jackal mask that was edged in gold. He was bare-chested and his body was tattooed in the likeness of a jackal. His wiry and muscular frame was the picture of menace. He stood next to the body with a long, curved knife that was covered in blood in one hand and a canopic jar in the other. It was like a scene from a horror movie, but she knew it was real. Anastasia was momentarily gripped by despair. She thought, *There are so many priests. How are we ever going to get past them?*

Then she saw her. Directly above and behind this priest was Nefertiti. She was imprisoned in a metal cage. She looked disheveled, her once beautiful gown dirty and torn, but she still stood tall and defiant. She didn't appear to be seriously injured. The cage was suspended by a rope above a canal at the north end of the chamber.

The water underneath roiled and seethed with large, reptilian bodies. Even from across the chamber, Anastasia could tell that these were enormous Nile crocodiles. *Really? After just dealing with the crocodile-headed demon, Ammit, does it have to be crocodiles again?* She'd been brave this whole time, fighting off people with knives and swords, but crocodiles were what truly terrified her. They were like living dinosaurs, and she had seen enough wildlife specials to know what those prehistoric jaws could do. *Facing those jaws for the second time in less than fifteen minutes is totally unfair!* She didn't really believe in reincarnation, but she was starting to get the feeling that she must have done something really bad in a prior life.

"Nimlot, the jackal's high priest and right hand," growled Akhenaten under his breath. "I expected nothing less. He has always hated Nefertiti. He could never stand the thought of a woman capable of thinking for herself. Kidnapping and caging her is a vile act of pure cowardice!"

"They have killed an innocent. They are perverting the book of the dead and the act of embalming to make their summoning of Anubis stronger. This must end," the general whispered and shook his head in disgust. The general asked Anastasia, "Do you see anyone else? Have we missed anything?"

She was still in her own little world and so focused on the crocodiles that the general's question caught her by surprise. She peered around the cavern, again looking for what she hadn't seen before. She spotted two more priests positioned at the bottom of the staircase that she'd missed the first time. They were partially covered in the shadows and appeared to be watching or guarding a trap door at the top of the stairs.

"There are two guards at the bottom of the staircase," she relayed as she continued scanning the room. Then her breath caught in her throat. There was a man dressed in black with white hair and a matching beard. He was just outside the direct circle of light cast by the braziers. "Oh my god, it's him. It has to be Dr. Augustino!" Anastasia said as she quietly pointed in his direction.

The leader of the Corsairs was reclining on a small bench observing the events unfolding around him in a detached fashion. Almost as if he were bored with the proceedings.

"It stacks the odds further against us, but that is no matter. We must move quickly," Akhenaten whispered to the general.

The general nodded in agreement before executing the same shimmy maneuver in reverse to return deeper into the shadows and back to the rest of the group. Akhenaten and Anastasia followed suit. The general and Akhenaten didn't betray any emotion as they motioned for the group to follow them as they retreated further up the passageway. Anastasia felt just a touch claustrophobic as they clustered together tightly in the narrow corridor. She somehow ended up crammed right in between Edward and Salah. Strangely, it reminded her of playing the game sardines, and she was incredibly certain that she didn't want to be found by that high priest right now.

The general convened his troops and relayed in hushed tones what they'd found. "We don't have much time, so listen closely," he said. "We will split into three units. The first unit will be led by the pharaoh and Djedi. This unit will attack the main body of the disciples and create a wedge between their position and Nefertiti," the general said, motioning to the first ten soldiers, who nodded as one in affirmation. The general paused and looked at Akhenaten as he said, "My pharaoh, I will need to ask you to draw on Aten's power to negate their advantage in numbers."

Akhenaten confidently replied, "I can assure you that Nimlot and his pack will feel Aten's wrath in full this night."

"Horbaef and Mesen will come with me in the second unit," the general said, nodding to the remaining two men. "We will be responsible for rescuing Nefertiti from her prison and getting her back to this entrance." The general paused as he looked at Anastasia, Edward, and Salah. "You three will comprise the third unit. You will remain here and secure the exit. Once we have retreated to this narrow passage, we will be able to hold them at bay while the pharaoh and Nefertiti return to the palace with Djedi." He turned toward Anastasia and the boys as he said, "You will also return to the palace with Akhenaten and Nefertiti."

Anastasia wanted to object but knew that she, Edward, and Salah had no real business engaging in the ensuing battle. They were just kids who weren't trained to fight with swords. They were likely to just get in the way or, even worse, get killed. They had already done so much and come so far. Maybe they had already played their part. Edward and Salah didn't seem to want to argue about it either.

"We do this to rescue Nefertiti, our Queen. We do this to end the tyranny of Anubis and to ensure that all Egyptians have access to the afterlife. We do this for Aten," Akhenaten said in a quiet but commanding voice.

The gem of his scepter started to glow like the sun, banishing the darkness from the passageway.

Chapter 33

Edward watched nervously from the passageway as Djedi and his men quietly stepped into the chamber and formed a shield wall in front of Akhenaten. They raised their weapons and silently charged toward Nimlot and the other priests of Anubis.

Akhenaten's scepter shone a brilliant yellow as he called on Aten and cast a bolt of pure energy into their midst. It missed Nimlot by less than a meter. One of the priests behind Nimlot was completely consumed, leaving only a cloud of fine ash. Another was tossed like a rag doll across the chamber when the bolt exploded against the floor. Nimlot dove behind the stone table and disappeared from sight. Akhenaten cast another bolt from his scepter, which incinerated the priest closest to Nefertiti and the canal. The explosion scorched the floor black as the priest's sword clattered to the ground.

While Akhenaten claimed an initial advantage through surprise, it only took a moment for the priests to cast aside their papyruses and draw their own swords. Djedi and his men finished closing the distance between the edge of the chamber and the circle of braziers burning brightly in the center. They formed a shield wall that curled around the edge of Anubis's disciples to seal off the canal and Nefertiti as the sound of metal clashing with metal rang throughout the chamber.

The general, Horbaef, and Mesen were only seconds behind the initial charge as they raced toward the canal full of crocodiles and Nefertiti's prison. The general stopped about five yards short of the canal while Horbaef and Mesen kept going until they reached the very edge. They stopped and faced one another as they bent their knees and locked their hands together at waist height to form a platform. The general shouted something to Nefertiti that Edward couldn't hear before he took four running steps and planted his right foot on Horbaef and Mesen's locked hands as they heaved upward. The general was flung more than ten feet into the air above the surface of the canal and the pack of long, dark bodies circling and thrashing underneath Nefertiti. As he soared, he grasped the metal bars of Nefertiti's hanging prison with both hands and held tightly. The impact of the collision set the metal cage swinging violently, but the general did not let go. More than one of the crocodiles used their powerful tails to propel themselves out of the water toward the cage before falling harmlessly back into the water.

Edward watched as Nefertiti braced herself before the impact. Thankfully, she wasn't hurt. The general pulled his feet up to the floor of the cage and withdrew a knife from his belt. He hacked through the series of leather bonds that held the door to the cage closed. The general removed a coil of rope from his belt and tied one end to a metal bar before casting the other back to Horbaef and Mesen. They caught the rope and began to pull it taut, drawing the cage out of the center of the canal and toward the bank. Edward could see that the general and Nefertiti would only be left with a yard or two to jump to reach the safety of the shore when the plan came unraveled.

An arrow suddenly appeared embedded in Horbaef's neck. He went slack as he let go of the rope and collapsed to the ground. Mesen struggled to hold the rope and keep the cage in place when another arrow pierced his side below his armpit. Mesen refused to let go as he struggled to keep his feet. His strength faded quickly and he was dragged by the collective weight of the general, Nefertiti, and the cage into the canal. The water foamed and roiled as prehistoric jaws snapped ferociously, and Mesen disappeared beneath the water's dark and bloodied surface.

The moment the second arrow struck Mesen, time seemed to slow down. Edward surprisingly found himself running in what felt like slow motion toward Akhenaten and the raging battle. Although he was horrified by what had happened to Horbaef and Mesen, he knew that he had to help stop those archers before they targeted the general as well. At that point, at least eight of Anubis's priests lay dead on the ground, but the battle had become more even. In close combat, Akhenaten did not have as many clear shots at the priests of Anubis. In most instances, he risked striking one of his own soldiers so he had to pick his spots. It was now down to more traditional fighting.

To Edward, it seemed so long ago that he had seen Djedi practicing in the training yard. On the battlefield, Djedi was a whirling blend of power and precision. He engaged with two priests who tried to use their numerical advantage to surround or flank him, but they could not penetrate his defenses. As the disciple in front slashed at Djedi's head with his sword, Djedi caught it on his shield and stepped in close to deliver a ferocious blow with the pommel of his sword to the man's head. The man's mask and his head underneath split as he crumpled to the ground.

The second disciple lunged from behind in an attempt to remove Djedi's head with a sweeping blow of his blade while he was distracted. He hadn't anticipated that Djedi would gracefully reverse his blade and drop to one knee, causing the disciple's blade to cut through the air inches above his head. Even through the jackal mask, Edward could see the surprise in the man's eyes as his momentum impaled him through the stomach on Djedi's blade. He staggered backward, holding his stomach before slumping to the ground.

Despite this personal victory, Edward realized that Djedi had lost three of his own men, which took their numbers down to nine, including Akhenaten. The priests still outnumbered them by close to two to one. Those numbers were making it hard for even these elite soldiers to hold their ground. Edward continued to dash toward Akhenaten, vaguely aware of Anastasia and Salah, whom he had left at the entrance, calling his name.

Nimlot hadn't stayed hidden for long either. He had risen from behind the stone table wielding a black flail and shield that appeared to be made of the blackest shadows. He was responsible for the death of at least one of the soldiers as Edward had seen the evil black flail do its work. While the blow hadn't appeared to be a killing blow, the soldier's body had seemed to shrivel to a husk as though the weapon's touch had actually destroyed the soldier's soul.

Edward began shouting Akhenaten's name at the top of his lungs, paying no mind to the danger he was running toward. When he had almost reached him, Akhenaten finally heard Edward's call over the din of the battle and pivoted his head to look in his direction.

"The archer on the stairs! You have to stop the archer on the stairs!" Edward shouted, pointing toward the staircase on the far side of the room.

Akhenaten turned his gaze toward the stairs. Edward saw the archer taking aim for the swinging cage that contained Nefertiti and the general when Akhenaten cast Aten's rays across the chamber and exploded the stairway from beneath the archer's feet. Edward felt a wave of relief and he turned to find that both Anastasia and Salah had left the entrance and were now by his side.

"That was amazing!" Salah exclaimed.

"It was more than amazing. It was courageous!" Anastasia said with pride in her eyes.

"I don't even know where that came from," Edward said honestly as he looked at his sister. "It just happened."

"It's always been in you," Anastasia said sincerely.

The general and Nefertiti stood at the door of the now motionless cage. It suddenly struck Edward that although they were safe from the archer, he didn't have any idea how they were going to get back to the safety of the canal shore.

Then the strangest thing happened. Nefertiti climbed onto the general's back the same way Edward did when his dad used to give him a piggyback ride when he was little. The general opened the cage door and squatted down as he grabbed the bar at the base of the cage with both hands. He slowly turned so that he was facing the center of the cage before he lowered himself and Nefertiti until they were both dangling from the bottom of the cage facing the shore. They were dangerously close to the surface of the canal.

"What are they doing?" Edward asked.

"I was hoping you were going to tell me. I hate to think the general has chosen now to go crazy," Salah said as the crocodiles once again worked themselves into a frenzy, not sated despite their meal from just a few minutes earlier.

Then, with Nefertiti still on his back, the general began to swing his legs back and forth. The momentum soon had the cage swinging like a pendulum in an ever-expanding arc. It dawned on Edward that the general was planning to build enough momentum to launch Nefertiti and himself to the shore. Even from a distance, Edward could see that the general was straining to hold both his and Nefertiti's weight. His jaw was clenched, his face was flushed, and pretty much all of his enormous muscles were bulging. The general was doing the most extreme obstacle course that could ever be imagined with metal cages, evil priests, and crocodiles. Edward, in comparison, had failed to complete a single pull-up in the sixth-grade presidential fitness test.

With only three or four swings left to achieve the necessary momentum, trouble arrived. Two jackal-masked disciples appeared on the bank of the canal, where the general was planning on landing, with swords in hand. They beckoned toward the general and Nefertiti. Edward couldn't believe it. *It's not fair.*

"We have to save them," Edward found his new, courageous self shouting.

Edward, Anastasia, and Salah all sprang into action, running as fast as they could and shouting warnings to the general and Nefertiti. Edward was stunned that the general hadn't stopped swinging. *He has to see Anubis's disciples on the shore.* He kept swinging his legs forward and then backward as the crocodiles propelled themselves out of the water in vain attempts to grab his and Nefertiti's legs. Edward was afraid that they weren't going to get there in time to help.

At the end of his last backswing, the general let go of the bottom bar of the cage with his right hand. As he swung forward, bearing all the weight on his left hand, he withdrew the dagger from his belt and flung it at one of the priests in one fluid motion. The dagger went right through the eye of one of the disciple's masks and embedded itself to the hilt with a wet thunk. His head snapped backward and he dropped like a stone.

The other disciple was so surprised by the general's attack that he was still watching his fallen brother when the general's heel struck him flush in the nose, smashing bone and cartilage. His masked head bounced off the floor with a thud. The general landed heavily on his feet before his and Nefertiti's momentum caused him to topple face forward into the dust. Edward and the others arrived as Nefertiti was dusting herself off and the red-faced general was grimacing and slowly rising to his feet.

"You're both safe!" Salah shouted.

"I can't believe it!" Anastasia grinned.

"That was so amazing!" Edward shouted euphorically.

"I must admit, I can't quite believe we made it either. I wasn't sure how much longer I could hold on," the general said, smiling through labored breaths.

"I will never be able to thank you enough for rescuing me, General. However, if you will excuse me, now it's time to return the favor to Anubis's followers!" Nefertiti said with fire flashing in her eyes before marching determinedly toward the fray.

The tide was turning against Nimlot and his underlings. Only ten of the original twenty-six disciples were left. Djedi had lost two more men, leaving only seven, including both the general and Akhenaten. For the first time, the numbers were much more even.

Edward saw that Akhenaten was engaged in direct combat with the high priest, wielding his glowing scepter as an otherworldly mace. Akhenaten pressed forward, whirling the scepter with speed and precision as he rained blows at his jackal-masked nemesis. Nimlot was on the defensive, barely managing to deflect the blows with his shadowy shield. Each blow sounded like a deafening clap of thunder within the chamber. Holding the end of his scepter in both hands like a baseball bat, Akhenaten whirled in a 360-degree turn as he aimed a tremendous blow at Nimlot's chest. The high priest continued to retreat and raised his shield to block the blow. However, when the scepter struck the shield, the shield exploded into a thousand fragments of black smoke. Nimlot was thrown ten yards across the room and lay motionless.

Akhenaten let out a roar of triumph and the soldiers responded with their own battle cries. He looked back and saw that his wife Nefertiti was now freed and racing toward him. Edward saw that the pharaoh paused as his eyes connected with Nefertiti's.

They shared the briefest of moments, as if alone within the eye of a hurricane, before he turned his head and charged back at the remaining disciples.

Just as they looked to press their advantage and finish off the disciples, the light in the room took on a purple hue. Edward looked around for the source of the light. He spotted a familiar, purple orb glowing at the edge of the canal near the metal cage where Nefertiti had been imprisoned. As its intensity grew to a blinding level, the room fell silent except for an electrical humming that Edward recognized with fear. All around him, the Egyptians stared at the three-meter-high glowing, purple sphere in awe and wonder. A thin, black crack appeared in the center of the floating sphere. As Edward expected, the black crack soon spread wider and wider. In moments, the fissure became a black mouth of a cave in the middle of the pulsing, purple glow. The portal was open.

Edward and Anastasia turned to one another as they both cried, "Anubis is coming!"

Chapter 34

Anastasia stood frozen as she watched an enormous, black hand with claw like nails reach out of the dark opening of the portal. It was followed by a long, muscled arm and then a shoulder. The skin was smooth like stone and the color of obsidian. Then a canine head with red eyes emerged from the blackness. The head craned slowly from side to side, taking in everything within the chamber. The large jaws were partially open, revealing a mouthful of long, pointed teeth. Then the rest of the god's imposing body appeared as he stepped through the opening of the portal in a crouch before standing fully upright on the edge of the canal.

Anubis was over ten feet tall from the tip of his ears to his human feet. He bordered on lean, but his wiry muscles were incredibly defined and looked ready to spring. He wore a traditional linen wraparound over his waist and carried a sinister, black flail on his belt. It was a lot like the one that Nimlot had wielded, except that it was twice as long. He clutched two thick, golden chains in his left hand. As he stepped forward, he pulled two long, golden objects through the portal. They were sarcophagi, just like the ones from the story that Edward had told her.

It immediately registered with Anastasia that Anubis was much bigger and more wolflike than the images she had seen in Edward's books on Egyptology. Those books made him look docile, almost like a man with a pet doberman pinscher's head. This god radiated immense power and pure evil. Then Anubis lifted his head toward the ceiling of the cavern and let loose a bone-chilling howl that reverberated over and over. It could only mean one thing: death.

Anastasia, numb with shock from witnessing Anubis's arrival, was shaken free from her trancelike state when the general called for the party to immediately fall back to the passageway entrance. With Nefertiti's rescue accomplished, it was time to run for the palace. Fear kicked in and Anastasia felt no signs of weariness. She, Edward, and Salah ran as if the God of the Underworld was after them, which in fact, he was. Akhenaten placed himself between Nefertiti and the howling god as they sprinted directly behind them. The soldiers formed a shield wall with the general and Djedi at the center as they retreated across the chamber.

Their flight to safety was short-lived. Ten yards before they reached the opening, Anubis raised his clawed hand and summoned a spear-shaped bolt of blackness from the underworld. He hurled it at the stone just above the passageway, which shattered from the impact and caused the entire roof of the passageway to collapse. It was completely blocked. Retreat was no longer an option.

Anastasia's shoulders slumped in despair as she turned back toward the center of the chamber. It was eerily silent. There was nowhere left to run. Anubis's remaining disciples gathered around him like a pack to their leader. She got the sense that they were preparing to charge. The general and his men tightened their wall of shields, preparing for whatever came next.

Akhenaten's face hardened with defiance and he seemed to grow in stature as he commanded, "May Aten banish you and your kind back to the underworld." He released two bolts of sunlight from his scepter in quick succession.

The first seared through the air right at Anubis's canine head, but he was too fast to be caught by surprise. Anubis raised his obsidian hand and blocked the bolt, which exploded on contact. He howled in pain and rage but didn't seem seriously hurt. The second bolt landed directly amid his remaining disciples with the ensuing blast twisting three of their bodies into unnatural shapes.

Despite the chaos and death raging all around her, Anastasia felt a glimmer of hope starting to growing inside her. They now outnumbered the disciples. *Maybe, just maybe, we have a chance to win this fight.*

Anubis shook his head and wagged his finger at the pharaoh the way Principal Eckersly admonished students at the Blake Academy. Anubis reached his hand out palm up toward the nearest fallen disciple. He curled his long and sinister fingers and lifted his hand. The body rose as if it were a puppet on a string, and its eyes snapped open. Its wounds had not healed, but the disciple was alive. Anubis repeated the gesture another half a dozen times as the souls of his fallen disciples returned to the land of the living to reanimate their bodies. Anastasia refused to believe that it was possible, but it was happening right before her eyes. *It's completely unfair!* The glimmer of hope she had felt just moments ago was ruthlessly snuffed out. With the wave of darkness came fear.

Anastasia could see the shoulders of some of the soldiers droop as the enemies they had just worked so hard to kill instantly came back to life. Anubis's shoulders shook as he laughed a wicked and inhuman laugh and continued to raise the rest of his fallen disciples.

The general spoke quietly over his shoulder, "I say we make a run for the stairs or the passageway on the other side of the chamber. It's our only chance. Even his disciples will eventually grind us into the sand if he can keep raising them from the dead."

"Aten and I will protect the party from his foulness. You and your men should focus on the disciples," Akhenaten replied. His jaw was set and his eyes shone with righteousness and more confidence than Anastasia felt was justified.

"All of you must stay within Aten's light," Nefertiti shouted. She turned toward Anastasia, Edward, and Salah and ordered them, "Do not leave the light, whatever you do! Do you understand me?"

"Yes, Your Highness!" they replied as one.

Anastasia watched in fascination as Akhenaten closed his eyes and his face became a mask of concentration. He raised his glowing scepter in the air with both hands before swinging downward to strike the butt of the scepter on the ground. The golden light from the gem radiated outward to a radius of about five yards. It just managed to cover all of them. It was like they were enveloped in a golden halo of love and life. It was beautiful.

Akhenaten was perspiring as he opened his eyes and calmly said, "You may proceed, General. I must recommend that we move as quickly as possible."

The general and his soldiers had just begun their advance as Anubis finished raising his army. All twenty-six of the disciples stood before them, including Nimlot, who appeared to have lost his flail. Anubis dropped the golden chains from the sarcophagi and left them lying on the ground. He replaced them with the black flail from his belt. Anubis summoned another black bolt from the underworld to his right hand and hurled it at Akhenaten as he howled his order to charge. The bolt struck the edge of the glowing, golden light and shattered into smoke.

The six soldiers in the shield wall met the charge of the disciples head-on and rebuffed the first wave. All of the soldiers in this company were elite, but the general and Djedi were extraordinary swordsmen. With their flanks protected, they each slew two disciples in the blink of an eye. Seven bodies lay on the ground as Anubis's disciples fell back and looked uncertainly at their god.

The party continued to advance, eating up several precious yards and reaching the center of the braziers. Anubis howled in rage and bounded forward more than six yards in a single leap, swinging his flail directly at the general's head. The flail struck the golden light like a clap of thunder, but could not penetrate the perimeter. Anubis swung his clawed right hand at the general only to be blown backward off his feet.

The soldier next to Djedi spied the opening and darted forward, slashing his blade across the back of the fallen god's knee in an attempt to sever his hamstring. Nefertiti cried out "No!" as the soldier's blade clanged against the god as if he were a statue made of granite. Before the soldier could retreat back to his position, the wicked flail whipped forward to catch him on his sword arm. Upon contact, the soldier withered and shriveled before Anastasia's eyes. The shield wall closed the gap silently and now there were only five soldiers.

The battle with the disciples raged on. While Anubis had been frustrated that he couldn't destroy them directly, he was now fighting a war of attrition through his disciples. While the general and his men continued to cut down the enemy, Anubis simply brought them back to life almost as quickly. The general hadn't lost any more soldiers, but several of his men had small wounds, and Anastasia could tell that they were tiring. She knew that they only needed to gain another ten or fifteen yards to the east to make a break for the open passageway. If they were lucky, Aten's shield might protect them and the passageway from Anubis's black bolts of death.

Anastasia gasped in surprise when she saw a black-clothed figure emerge from behind the stone table. She had completely forgotten about Dr. Augustino during the melee. *He must have hidden there in an attempt to avoid the fighting.*

"It's Dr. Augustino!" she shouted to Edward while pointing at the Corsair, who was now running across their field of vision for the portal.

Edward's eyes bulged as he saw him running. "He's going to get away!" he shouted with outrage.

Without thinking, Anastasia shifted her staff to her right hand like a javelin and took two steps before launching it on a vector that intersected with the Corsair's route to the portal. Its flight over the twenty yards was true. Anastasia watched as the metal end of the staff struck Dr. Augustino directly between the shoulder blades. The force caused him to face-plant onto the stone floor.

Anastasia couldn't keep herself from shouting across the chamber, "It serves you right, you coward!"

Dr. Augustino slowly raised himself from the floor and looked directly at Anastasia. He had blood dripping from both his nose and his mouth. Despite looking like a candidate for cosmetic dental surgery, Dr. Augustino shook his head and laughed. "Has the Order gotten so desperate that they are now relying on children to fight their battles?"

"That's not what your second-in-command said!" Edward shot back at the Corsair.

Dr. Augustino's eyes narrowed. "If you two manage to live through this ordeal, which I seriously doubt, I will make it my personal business to find you." He dusted himself off and straightened his clothes. "Now I am afraid I must go. No point in dying before I become immortal." He took the last two steps and disappeared into the portal.

Anastasia realized that they had just made an enemy for life. She turned her attention back to the events unfolding around her.

She could see that Akhenaten was breathing raggedly now. It must be taking an extraordinary effort to maintain the protective shield around their party.

"General, I will not be able to sustain this for too much longer. We must make our move soon or we will never make it," Akhenaten said evenly while trying to maintain his concentration.

"There are just too many, my pharaoh. We cannot break through their line," the general called back while dispatching yet another disciple.

At that moment, the light emanating from the gem on the scepter began to falter. It started to dim and a few moments later became intermittent. Not long after that, the light ceased. The halo of sunshine that had protected them from the God of the Underworld disappeared altogether. The pharaoh was left doubled over with one knee resting on the ground. Nefertiti wrapped her arms around him, supporting his weight.

Anubis, who had been observing the battlefield while raising his dead, howled in delight. All of the disciples that were still standing answered his howl with a chorus of their own howls. Anubis bounded back to the sarcophagi and reached down and snatched the golden chains in his hands. He strode purposefully toward Akhenaten and Nefertiti, dragging the golden sarcophagi along the ground behind him. His disciples parted to let him through.

"I have to warn them," Edward said as he darted over to Akhenaten and Nefertiti. "You cannot let Anubis get ahold of you. If he can put you in those sarcophagi, you won't be able to get out."

They stared back at him blankly. "I am afraid I don't understand what you mean, Edward," Nefertiti said with a genuine look of confusion on her face.

"They're magical. Once there are living souls trapped inside, Anubis and the sarcophagi will get recalled to the underworld and we won't be able to stop him," he told them.

Akhenaten grimaced ruefully as he said, "I can assure you I will do everything in my power to avoid falling into his clutches."

He climbed back to his feet and steadied himself with his scepter before adding, "However, that may be difficult."

While the other three soldiers attempted to deal with the disciples, the general and Djedi formed a human barrier between Anubis and the pharaoh with their shields and swords at the ready. Anubis bounded forward and swung his flail overhead at them, cracking the stone floor as they dove and rolled to either side of the evil god to evade the blow. Djedi slashed at Anubis's exposed right side with his sword as he finished his roll and sprang to his feet. The sword's blade broke clean in half as it struck the impenetrable surface of Anubis's skin. Anubis growled angrily at Djedi as his flail cut through the air with a hiss. Djedi's shield was smashed into a pile of broken kindling by the wicked flail, and he was knocked senseless to the ground.

As Anubis prepared to finish Djedi with a final blow, the general struck. He had come out of his roll with his forward momentum carrying him two steps past the stone table. The general turned and leaped onto the table, avoiding the deceased victim of Nimlot's unfinished embalming, and used it as a springboard. He vaulted high in the air, aiming a powerful backhand slash at Anubis's canine neck. The god sensed the attack at the last moment and ducked so that the general's whistling blade only lopped off the top of Anubis's ear. Anubis dropped both flail and chains as he howled in pain and rage, clutching what remained of his bloody ear. Anubis didn't bother to pick up his flail. He simply lashed out and delivered a vicious backhand that sent the general flying.

With the pathway to the pharaoh now clear, Anubis snapped his fingers and the lids of the sarcophagi slid open. Anastasia found herself stepping backward as Anubis stalked toward the pharaoh and his queen. Every instinct within her told her to run. There was no way to defeat this god. With his staff gripped in both hands, she watched Akhenaten step forward to meet the God of the Underworld. The fur on Anubis's neck stood on end as a low, guttural growl escaped his throat. He leaped the last ten feet and attempted to seize Akhenaten in his clawed hands. Akhenaten swung the scepter with both hands and used the residual power to bat Anubis's hands aside in a flash of light. Anubis lunged again and was rebuffed by another golden blast. On the third attempt, the remaining power in the scepter began to falter. While the pharaoh was able to block the blow with the scepter extended in both hands above his head, Anubis's black hands also closed around the scepter. Ever so slowly, he forced Akhenaten to his knees.

Anastasia felt tears come to her eyes. She knew it was almost over. Anastasia felt someone tug at her hand. She thought it was Edward but turned to find that it was Salah. He looked at her serenely, like he was in a very different place from the subterranean cavern filled with death and destruction in which he stood.

"I must go now. My destiny awaits," he said calmly. "I will never forget you nor be able to thank you for everything you have done. I wish that we'd had more time." He gently raised himself on his tiptoes and placed a delicate kiss upon her lips.

Anastasia's lips tingled lightly as her voice completely left her.

An instant later, he was gone, sprinting through the chaos of the chamber and holding only his small shield for protection. She didn't understand what he was doing. Salah stopped where the general was just regaining his feet and said something in his ear. The general nodded in response and patted Salah affectionately on the shoulder. Then it hit her as they both turned and ran the last three strides to the open sarcophagi lying on the floor.

"No!" she screamed from the depths of her soul as she fell to her knees.

It was too late. They each leaped into one of the open sarcophagi. Their faces were at peace as her eyes briefly met first Salah's and then the general's. An invisible force then pulled them backward and the lids of the sarcophagi snapped shut.

Anubis wrestled the scepter from Akhenaten's hands and cast it aside as the lids of the sarcophagi closed. The sarcophagi slid across the floor of the chamber toward the open portal. Anubis's red, canine eyes registered shock and disbelief as the invisible magic of the golden sarcophagi exerted its will. He growled in frustration and reached vainly for Akhenaten, who was just beyond his claws. Though Anubis struggled mightily and clawed at the ground, leaving deep furrows in the stone, the tether of the magic was not to be denied.

The sarcophagi were now floating a meter off the ground and gaining speed as they traveled toward the maw of the portal and back to the underworld. In moments, the golden coffins disappeared into the blackness and were followed immediately by Anubis, still howling in rage and frustration. The blackness of the portal began to collapse upon itself and was soon only a thin, black line. Then there was only the purple light that remained. That light slowly faded and the portal was closed.

Chapter 35

Edward sat with Anastasia in the gardens of the Royal Residence that served as the actual home for Akhenaten and his family.

The walled gardens were elaborate and lush. Figs and pomegranate trees abounded as well as colorful flower beds. There were ponds stocked with fish and lined with willow trees. It was a dramatic contrast to the surrounding desert.

Despite the beauty, Edward found it hard to keep his eyes dry. He had never really known anyone who had died before. His grandparents on both sides of the family were still alive as were all of his aunts and uncles. The closest he had ever come to seeing death firsthand was when his pet hamster had died when he was seven. He had been quite attached to the hamster at the time, but it certainly hadn't prepared him for this.

To be fair, nothing could have prepared him for what had happened. Salah's and General Meketre's deaths had left his emotions battered and raw. While he hadn't known either of them for long, he felt that they had been kindred spirits. With his kindness and sense of adventure, Salah would have been his friend whether they'd met in ancient Egypt or at the Blake Academy. He knew intellectually that it was possible for someone to die at the age of twelve; however, it was incredibly unlikely in the world he came from.

General Meketre's death also cut him deeply. In many ways, the general represented the type of man that Edward someday hoped to become: smart, kind, brave, and universally respected. Edward thought he would do okay with the first two attributes, but he still worried that the latter two might not be in the cards for him. Too often he was the opposite of those things.

It had all ended so quickly the night before. They had been on the verge of defeat and certain death before Salah and the general had made the ultimate sacrifice to save Akhenaten, Nefertiti, and the rest of them. When Anubis had been dragged back with Salah and the general to the underworld and the portal had closed, it had also broken the spell that his resurrected disciples had been under.

No longer under Anubis's control, all except for Nimlot had thrown down their weapons.

Nimlot had tried to use the confusion to sneak up behind Nefertiti and kill her. The gravity of the situation had not prevented Djedi from spotting and ending the danger. He had quickly snatched one of the discarded swords and thrown it the ten yards he could not cover quickly enough on his feet. Nimlot had never gotten a chance to lay a hand on Nefertiti as he had been killed for a second and final time. Akhenaten, Nefertiti, Djedi, Anastasia, Edward, and the final two soldiers had been all that had remained of their party.

As they had walked toward the remnants of the shattered stairway, Edward had jumped sideways over something black lying on the ground and shouted, "Snake! Snake! I almost stepped on one of those asps."

Anastasia had looked closely and saw that it hadn't been a snake at all. It had been one of the tendrils from a flail. Nimlot must have dropped it here when Akhenaten had blasted his shield to smithereens and blown him across the room.

"It's not a snake. It's Nimlot's flail," Anastasia had said as she'd bent down to pick it up by its black handle.

But Akhenaten had gently laid his hand upon her shoulder. "Please allow me, Anastasia. This is a most foul and wicked weapon," he had said as he'd carefully grasped the flail. "It leeches men's souls and does not belong here in our world. I will need to find a safe place to dispose of this so it does not trouble my kingdom again."

"I know exactly what you mean," Edward had said, nodding his head in agreement. "Dr. G.'s got a whole vault back home where he keeps things just like that locked up."

"A whole vault, you say?" Akhenaten had said rhetorically while arching his eyebrows in thought.

They had left that dreadful chamber by scaling the broken stairs to the Great Temple of Aten before returning to the palace. As it had turned out, many of the resurrected disciples had not survived the night. They had perished from the grievous wounds they had already suffered. A few of them would survive, although their names would never be found in any history books.

Edward felt particularly shattered about his friends' deaths because he had never really gotten to say goodbye. Although Salah had told Edward that he'd needed to go and that he had been pleased that they had become friends, Edward hadn't really understood what he'd meant until it had been too late. All he had managed to say was, "Huh?"

He had done even less with regard to saying goodbye to the general. Now there would be no bodies to say goodbye to or photos to keep. Salah and the general had sacrificed so much. He hoped that he wouldn't forget them.

He could see that Anastasia was taking it very hard as well. She was no more experienced with death than he was. Edward had the feeling that the kiss that Salah and Anastasia had shared made this even more confusing for her. He thought that she might feel responsible. That somehow Salah had made the sacrifice because of her. Not that he understood anything about kissing. As far as he could tell, you had to be able to talk to a girl before you could kiss her.

The pharaoh and Nefertiti found Edward and Anastasia in the gardens of the Royal Residence together in their melancholy.

"Saying goodbye to friends is always very hard," Akhenaten said compassionately. "Normally, our burial process gives us structure and time to come to grips with our grief."

Edward scratched his head. "Is that why it takes so long?" Edward asked, trying to reconcile what he remembered reading about ancient Egyptian burials with what the pharaoh had just told him.

"No, Edward. The process is that long because it is very involved. It is important that the body is preserved perfectly for what is to come in the afterlife. The organs have to be removed and placed in canopic jars. The body has to be fully dried with a special salt to avoid decay. It must be wrapped in linen many times and the proper spells must be cast. Aten's rays will often shine upon us more than seventy times before the body is ready for burial."

Nefertiti cut in on her husband as she said, "I see the timing of this process as a fortunate coincidence. There is a final chance to say goodbye after we have resolved our own inner turmoil and when there are no longer any clouds lingering above our heads."

Edward felt the tears return to eyes. "I'm just not sure why it had to be them. Why did they have to go? Why wasn't it me?" he found himself asking, without having been aware that it was how he felt.

Then he heard Anastasia crying softly and realized that was how she must have felt as well. He put his arms around his sister and held her.

"I think our friends Salah and General Meketre were cut from the same cloth. I am going to tell you a story about how I met the general that may help to explain why it had to be them," Akhenaten said, reaching and gently lifting each of their chins so he could look them in the eye.

"I was only a boy when I first met Meketre. Actually, if I were to be totally honest, I was a young and pompous princeling," Akhenaten said with a wan smile. "I wasn't a particularly nice boy. I spent far too much time telling everyone in Thebes who I was and how important I was. I used my position as prince to get what I wanted. I was the worst kind of bully."

Nefertiti put her arm gently around her husband. "You have come a very long way, my husband," she said softly.

"While that may be true, my queen, I was insufferable at the time," Akhenaten replied, laughing quietly. "I was seven years old. On this day, like many others that had come before it, I was ordering the boys in the palace around for sport. I had demanded that one of the younger boys give me his pomegranate. He was probably five and he started to cry because the pomegranate was a special treat from his mother.

"Just as I was preparing to berate the boy further, a new boy stepped in between me and the boy with the pomegranate. I had not met him before. He was the son of an officer from the Upper Nile who had just returned to the capital. He said to me, 'My apologies, my prince, but why would you take the pomegranate from this young boy? Have you not eaten, my prince? Are you weak with hunger?'

"'No!' I said, annoyed. 'I simply want it. Who are you to ask questions of me anyway?' I shouted as I attempted to intimidate this new boy.

"'My apologies, my prince, but that is not good enough. This is a special gift of love from his mother. You can see what it means to him. It is not good enough that you should simply want it,' the officer's son said calmly and firmly.

"The room became very quiet and I could feel the color rising in my cheeks. I was outraged that anyone should speak that way to me. That anyone should deny me. I attempted to slap this boy across his insolent face. When my hand met nothing but air, I almost fell over. I lashed out at him with my closed fist, but he had shifted just outside of my range. He was very fast. This was repeated many times as I worked myself into a rage. The officer's son did not gloat, but I cursed him all the same.

"Then some of the other boys laughed. I had ruled them with fear. Now someone was standing up to me, and I proved myself incompetent in dealing with it. Instead of laughing along with these other boys, the officer's son lambasted them. 'You must never laugh at our prince! One day he will be our pharaoh,' he said with a quiet anger. The other boys became afraid of the officer's son and left us.

"I was both exhausted and humiliated when I asked him, 'Why have you defended me?'

"He bowed his head as he replied, 'I am your servant, my prince. It gives me no pleasure to tell you when you have done the wrong thing.'

"I tried to process what he had told me, but I was still angry. 'I will have you beaten for your insolence,' I said harshly.

"The officer's son raised his eyes to meet mine. 'That is your choice, my prince. However, my belief is that your role as our leader is to protect and inspire us. You must act like a god if you expect us to treat you like a god and to follow you to the ends of the world no matter what the consequences. My duty as your servant is to tell you this even if it means I get beaten,' he said.

"I am ashamed to say that I did have him beaten. It was only as I watched him bear his punishment with strength, dignity, and only a few lonely tears did I realize that he was actually trying to help me. He was the only one who cared enough to tell me what everyone else already knew. I was a little monster and not a prince. Egypt did not need a little monster and he knew that. He knew the personal risk of standing up to me, but that did not stop him from doing what he believed was the right thing," Akhenaten said with tears now in his own eyes. "He soon became my closest friend and my most trusted advisor. That was almost thirty years ago."

Edward found himself crying even harder than before after hearing Akhenaten's story. Anastasia was practically sobbing in his arms. If it was supposed to make them feel better, the pharaoh had definitely missed the mark.

"I did not tell you this to upset you further. I was trying to explain who the general was and what he meant to me," Akhenaten smiled affectionately at Edward and Anastasia. "As I said before, I think Salah was very similar to the general. He was very brave and selfless. They made their choices consciously. They both did what they thought was best for their country and those they love."

Edward felt Anastasia's crying stop. She looked up slowly at Akhenaten and said, "Thank you, Pharaoh. I think I understand now. I will try not to feel so guilty."

Edward still felt confused. There must have been a point to the story that he had completely missed.

"They did what they thought was right," Anastasia told her brother. "They chose their time. There isn't anything for us to feel guilty about."

"She is right, Edward," the pharaoh said. "We should remember their courage and their sacrifice. We should keep that in our hearts and allow it to guide us. They would not want us to feel guilty. They made their choice so that we might live and that Egypt might thrive."

Edward nodded. He understood now. "It's just hard."

"What you have both been through is more than anyone so young should ever have to endure," Nefertiti told him before turning to Akhenaten. "Though we were victorious, the memories will be a heavy burden."

Akhenaten nodded back at his wife in understanding. Edward saw him close his eyes for a moment and then the gem on his scepter started to glow.

"There is something I can do to lighten this burden," Akhenaten said. "Aten's rays are the source of life. They will not cause you to forget what happened, but they will suffuse your thoughts with love and amplify your positive memories."

The light grew brighter and Edward and Anastasia felt the sun shine again

Chapter 36

Anastasia woke to a beautiful, sunny morning in Akhetaten. She felt a sense of happiness and excitement at the prospect of returning home.

She and Edward had been successful in their mission and had thwarted the efforts of the Corsairs and Anubis. Akhenaten had shared the tremendous news with them the night before at dinner with Nefertiti and his family. It had turned into an impromptu celebration.

He had waited until they had all been seated on cushions at the low table before telling them, "I have communed with Aten this afternoon and have good news."

Conversation around the table had stopped as everyone had looked at the pharaoh expectantly.

Akhenaten had smiled as he said, "Anubis's power has been broken. While we did not defeat him in our battle, he expended an enormous amount of his remaining power. He will not be able to manifest on earth again, nor will he regain the power he has lost after our successful changes to our religion. Aten and the other gods are now in a position to keep Anubis in check. He can no longer hold access to the afterlife hostage. We have vanquished the shadow over our land. We are free!"

The table had erupted with applause. Anastasia had turned to Edward, who had held out his fist for a fist bump. She had shaken her head, laughing, and had pushed his fist aside and hugged him fiercely. *We did it!*

The evening had been full of high spirits and great conversation. In some ways, Anastasia had been disappointed that they hadn't had a chance to meet Akhenaten and Nefertiti's family before. She still wasn't impressed by the fact that he had five wives. However, after getting to know him, she had realized that you shouldn't judge a book by its cover.

She had found herself and Edward talking to Nefertiti at one point in the evening and had asked her, "Now that Anubis has been defeated, will things go back to the way they were before? Will you worship all the old gods, or will Egypt always worship only Aten?"

Nefertiti had smiled at her. "What a luxury to be able to ponder such a question. I don't know. We instituted the change in our religion to try to stop Anubis. It was an enormous change for our people, and a number of our gods have suffered mightily. While it's no longer necessary, it would be very hard to ask our people to make another major change so soon. Reverting to the old religion is likely inevitable as old habits die hard. However, I think it may be best for that to occur on its own timeline without royal assistance." Nefertiti had regarded them both with a very serious look. "You have made such a difference to our country in such a short time. Selfishly, I wish nothing more than for the two of you to stay in Egypt. I think we could accomplish many great things together."

Anastasia had been at a loss for words. *The Queen of Egypt, perhaps the greatest woman of her time, is talking to us like we're something special.*

Edward had been the first to find his words. "It's really hard to leave, Your Highness. It's been the most amazing adventure, and you and Akhenaten have been completely awesome. It's just that we miss our parents, and I think they would miss us too."

Nefertiti had nodded. "I said it was a selfish desire. You are right to go home. No parent should be separated from their child. We will miss you. I will have to write down all that has happened so that Akhenaten and I may never forget you and your deeds."

Anastasia had gulped. "I'm sorry, Your Highness, but I don't think anyone should know what actually happened. Otherwise, the Corsairs might discover how we foiled their plot and stopped Anubis. What if they try to come back again?"

"I can assure you that Akhenaten and I will never share the story with anyone else. We will take that secret to our graves," Nefertiti had assured her honestly.

Anastasia had still felt worried. *It's pretty hard to encrypt papyrus.*

"I've got an idea that could solve this problem," her brother had piped up with a glint in his eye that worried Anastasia.

She had known that look. It had told her that he'd thought he was being really clever.

"Could I please have a papyrus and a pen and ink?" he had asked one of the royal servants on hand.

The servant had returned within moments with the requested items.

Anastasia and Nefertiti had watched Edward dip the pen in the ink. He had written a brief message and had drawn some sort of diagram on which he'd marked an X. Then he had rolled and tied the papyrus closed with string made from reeds. Finally, he had dipped the pen again and had written another message on the outside of the papyrus. He had given it a moment to dry before handing it to Nefertiti, clearly pleased with himself.

"Do not open this for fifteen years," Nefertiti had said, reading aloud what Edward had written on the outside of the sealed papyrus. She had looked at Edward questioningly.

"You'll be able to write the story down without any repercussions if you follow the instructions in the papyrus when you open it," her brother had said, nodding his head repeatedly like a bobblehead. He had turned toward Anastasia and had given her a big smile and a wink that had clearly been supposed to mean "Trust me."

"I am intrigued, young Edward, by your mysterious note, but you have a deal. I will follow your instructions in fifteen years," Nefertiti had laughed.

After the celebration had ended late in the evening, Anastasia had slept soundly. She and Edward were now finalizing preparations for their departure. Anastasia checked to make sure that she still had her silver ring with the fragment of Refractium Crystal so they could reactivate the portal and return home.

"Do you still have yours as well?" she asked Edward, holding her ring.

A look of surprise crossed his face, and he started patting himself down nervously until he looked down at his hand and saw that it was still on his finger. He smiled and gave her a thumbs-up. "Of course I have it," he said as if it had never been in question.

"So what exactly did you write in that note that you gave to Nefertiti?" she asked now that they were completely on their own.

Edward's face lit up with a giant grin. "She already said she would literally take the story to the grave with her. I just specified where the grave should be so that no one would ever find her."

He was super pleased with himself, which made Anastasia slightly worried. "Where exactly would that be?" she asked him.

"In a secret chamber behind King Tut's tomb. I drew a diagram of the actual tomb and marked the wall to build the secret chamber behind. No one has ever been able to find anything there. It's the perfect spot!" Edward said, putting his hand up for a fist bump.

Anastasia just looked at him in disbelief.

"Don't leave me hanging, sis," Edward said, still smiling and holding his fist out.

"What happens if technology improves in the next twenty years and someone finds it? Did you think about that, bro?" Anastasia asked with her hands planted firmly on her hips.

Edward's smile seemed to evaporate as he realized that he had been slightly less clever than he had intended.

"I suppose we'll have to tell Dr. G. when we get back and see what he can do," Anastasia said, shaking her head.

Edward's bluster completely deserted him as his shoulders drooped and he hung his head.

She was just about to resume the preparations for their departure by filling their waterskins when it occurred to her that there was something she still didn't understand. "I almost forgot. Why did you ask Nefertiti to wait fifteen years to open the papyrus?"

"Well, Akhenaten doesn't die for another ten years and Tutankhamun hasn't been born yet and doesn't become pharaoh for at least another thirteen years. I just thought it wouldn't be right for her to have to know those things before they actually happen."

He has such a good heart, she thought. "Well, you definitely got that part right, bro," Anastasia said, holding her fist out for a belated bump, which Edward's fist gladly answered.

Anastasia and Edward said their goodbyes to the royal couple in the gardens of the Royal Residence while the sun was still early on its ascent into the Egyptian sky. Akhenaten had given Anastasia a thick leather case containing Nimlot's flail. He had asked if they could take it with them for safekeeping in Dr. G.'s vault. They couldn't blame him for wanting to find a safe place for it well outside of his kingdom. It was difficult to leave after everything they had gone through and the bond they now shared, but the pull of home was too strong.

They walked along the Royal Road in a peaceful silence. Anastasia's breath caught as they neared the temple and she spotted Bilji and two of his gang walking in the opposite direction, directly toward her and Edward. She instantly clutched the leather case more tightly. Bilji was one of the last people she wanted to get their hands on a soul-leeching otherworldly flail. She could see both the recognition and surprise written on their faces as they spotted her and Edward in the same moment.

"I've got this," Edward said confidently as he stepped in front of her before she could react. His fists were raised and his feet spread in a fighting stance.

Bilji and his two companions froze. Without speaking, they slowly raised their hands in surrender. They kept their hands up as they shuffled to the other side of the road, giving them a wide berth as they passed. Edward pivoted, keeping himself between Bilji and Anastasia before they faded into the foot traffic further down the Royal Road.

"All clear, sis," Edward said nonchalantly as he winked at her. "Are you ready?"

Anastasia shook her head in wonder as she looked at her brother. She wasn't sure if he was standing straighter or if he had somehow grown taller in the last few days. Whatever it was, he was different. *When you get plunged into the fire of the forge, you only have two options: melt or come out stronger,* she thought to herself as they resumed their journey. *Maybe we're both a little different now.*

Anastasia was far less worried passing the guards at the northern gates of Akhetaten on the way out than she was on the way in. The soldiers and their weapons weren't as menacing after spending six eventful days in the city.

They had walked along the road, which was already filling with other travelers, for about a mile prior to veering off across the desert to return to the location where they had first come through the portal into ancient Egypt.

Anastasia and Edward stopped to take long drinks from the waterskins they had been given for their short journey. She watched Edward as he stared at the walled city in the distance as if he were trying to lock it in his memory.

"In little more than a decade, Akhetaten will be abandoned and the capital moved back to Thebes," Edward said with a trace of sadness in his voice. "I guess we'll always have these medallions to remind us." Edward held the sun medallion that he had been given by Akhenaten and Nefertiti in between his thumb and forefinger.

Anastasia slid her hand inside his other hand, and they stood there silently for more than a minute. "Come on, Edward. Let's go home." She gave his hand a squeeze before they turned and resumed their journey across the yellow desert sand.

"I think this is the spot," Edward told her, pointing to an outcropping of rock that rose about ten feet above the sand of the desert floor.

"Are you sure?" she asked him while looking at the yellow sand that stretched in all directions.

"Definitely," he answered confidently.

Anastasia looked over at her brother to see if he was ready, and he nodded that he was. Anastasia turned the face of her ring counterclockwise and then raised her hand to the sun as Edward did the same. The fragments of the crystal slowly began to glow purple. They each emitted a thin beam of purple light that crackled through the air to a point about five yards away and formed a purple spot of light the size of a quarter. The fragments on the rings stopped glowing and the thin beam of light disappeared. However, the spot of light remained in the air about a meter off the ground. A loud humming noise like the sound of a power generator being turned on thrummed through the air and the spot of light started to grow. Soon there was a purple ball of light more than seven feet tall with a pitch-black opening in the middle. The portal back to the Smithsonian, to Washington, DC, to home was open. They held hands as they walked into the beckoning blackness and didn't look back.

Chapter 37

Edward fell through the blackness, holding Anastasia's hand, for what seemed like a very long time. There was no sense of time in the portal. He wondered if the journey was longer or shorter depending upon how far in time you were traveling. He also wasn't sure if he was screaming, because the portal was completely void of sound. The contrast between the heat of the Egyptian desert and the subzero temperatures of the journey through the portal made the cold even more biting.

Edward came through the absolute darkness and bone-freezing chill of the portal with one thought firmly in his mind: *Don't face-plant again.* While it sucked to have a mouthful of sand the first time he'd gone through the portal, it really wouldn't do to knock his teeth out on the floor of the Refractium Crystal room.

He held on to Anastasia's hand tightly and kept his knees slightly bent as he completed the journey and emerged into the light. He stumbled slightly but quickly righted himself.

"Yes! I so rock!" Edward exclaimed, pumping the fist of his free hand after keeping his teeth intact.

"Dr. G.!" Anastasia shouted.

He looked up quickly and spotted Dr. G. standing beside the levers that controlled the Refractium Crystal. He had a very confused look on his face. He was wearing the same clothes that he'd had on when they had left, but he was no longer leaning on a walking stick.

"I must admit that seeing you two emerge from the portal is one of the last things that I would have expected," Dr. G. said, raising his eyebrows. "I am guessing that the two of you will have quite a story to tell me."

They both rushed across the room and wrapped their arms around him. Edward looked up and smiled back. "Maybe we should go to your office, Dr. G. You might need to sit down for this one."

"That's so cool. It's still 5:37 p.m.," Anastasia said. "It's like we never left."

Edward and Anastasia settled in the wingback chairs in Dr. G.'s office with cups of peppermint tea. It wasn't exactly a normal drink for twelve-year-olds, but it was a habit that Dr. G. had gotten them hooked on over the years. Dr. G. sat in his usual spot on the chaise lounge with his English breakfast tea.

It was incredibly difficult to summarize the events of their time in Egypt in thirty minutes, but they did it. The words flowed as Edward and Anastasia took turns taking the lead in telling the story and, at times, finishing each other's sentences. Dr. G. listened intently and asked questions along the way to clarify their excited stream of dialogue and to connect the dots fully.

"Well, well, well," Dr. G. beamed at them when they finished relaying the highlights of their time in Akhetaten. "That is an extraordinary tale. I cannot tell you how proud I am of you both. You have thwarted the Corsairs, including Augustino himself, and have preserved the order of time and the world as we know it. In doing so, you have conducted yourselves with intelligence, courage, and integrity. I am not sure a fully-fledged member of the Order could have done any better."

Edward and Anastasia looked at each other and couldn't help but smile. *It's pretty impressive when you say it that way.*

"I had always thought that you two were ideal candidates for the Order from the first time we met. I just thought your introduction would be another ten years from now when you were adults," Dr. G. said with regret in his voice.

"We made the choice to make that trip through the portal, Dr. G. Not you," Anastasia said, making it clear that she wasn't upset about what had happened.

"Plus there really weren't a lot of other options at the time. Someone needed to save the world, and Superman was busy, so you got us instead. Look how well it turned out," Edward added, throwing in a few muscle poses for good measure.

"You are both very brave, but I am terribly sorry that I put you in such danger. Especially as it has resulted in creating an enemy of Dr. Augustino," Dr. G. said gravely and then paused for a moment. "Dr. Augustino has already sent his nefarious agents after you once. I'm afraid it is unlikely to be the last time as well. It may not be simple for you to step away from this life now, even if you chose to do so," Dr. G. said with a pained expression on his face.

Edward felt a shudder of fear. He had almost forgotten Dr. Augustino's parting words about making it his personal business to find them. He hadn't connected it to the freaky pirate dude in the rotunda either. Apparently, the boost of courage that he'd felt when they had been battling Anubis under the Great Temple of Aten had already deserted him. *Oh well, things are back to normal.*

"Well, I suppose it's time for us to lock this away," Dr. G. said as he picked up the leather case that held Nimlot's flail. "We most certainly can't have this evil thing devouring people's souls on the streets of Washington, DC," Dr. G. said, then stopped after walking past his antique French desk. He looked back over his shoulder as he asked, "Are you two coming?"

Edward jumped up, eager to see Dr. G.'s vault again. He turned toward Anastasia's chair and was startled to find it already empty. By the time he looked back toward Dr. G., Anastasia was already standing next to him. She motioned impatiently with her hand for him to hurry up. *How did she do that?* Edward scrambled across the room to catch up. Dr. G. stopped directly in front of the large painting of George Washington on a rearing stallion.

"Um, Dr. G., I thought you were going to show us the secret vault," Anastasia said questioningly, still looking from side to side.

"It wouldn't be a secret vault if it was in plain sight, would it?" Dr. G. chuckled. He reached behind the edge of the painting and it suddenly swung away from the wall, opening like a door.

While Edward had already known where the vault was located, Anastasia gasped. It revealed a large, dark, metal door with a silver handle and a matching silver rectangle with a black, circular window in its center. Dr. G. winked at them after he removed his glasses and then proceeded to put his face in front of the black, circular window. The outside edge of the circle emitted a blue, electronic light before it beeped and the light changed to green.

"Is that a retinal scanner? I've never seen one of those outside of movies," Anastasia asked excitedly.

"There is no such thing as being too careful with these items," Dr. G. said somewhat ominously.

The lock disengaged with a thunk as Dr. G. finished speaking, and the thick door opened to reveal a metal room twenty feet long by ten feet wide. Just as Edward remembered, the shelves that lined the walls from floor to ceiling held all manner of crates and cases. They followed Dr. G. inside as he found an open space among the shelves where he placed the leather case containing the flail.

"Dr. G., is that the crate that held the Quetzalcoatl statue?" Anastasia asked as she pointed at the familiar crate.

Dr. G. cleared his throat self-consciously. "Yes, I had put it here for safekeeping. I didn't want to frighten the two of you at the time. I had a suspicion that the statue came directly from the Temple of the Feathered Serpent and, with enough blood sacrifice, it might actually summon Quetzalcoatl. It turns out I was right, but I apologize for having been dishonest."

Anastasia's face softened and she giggled, "Yeah, I think you made the right call, Dr. G. It probably would have been a bit too much at the time. It's actually hilarious how a blood-craving statue doesn't even faze me now."

"Yeah, who knew that phrases like 'enough blood sacrifice' and 'summon Quetzalcoatl' would seem so natural," Edward chuckled in agreement.

They were all still laughing as they exited the vault and Dr. G. swung the painting of George Washington back in place. Just then the office phone on Dr. G.'s antique French desk rang. Dr. G. looked at the phone as if wondering if he should answer it.

"Pardon me, Edward and Anastasia. I won't be a moment," he said and crossed the room to his desk. His eyes appeared to light up in recognition as he looked at the digital readout on the phone. He quickly snatched the phone up and said, "Hello, Sem Sem. It's very late in Cairo right now. Is everything okay?"

Edward couldn't believe his ears. *Sem Sem is alive!* He looked at Anastasia, who looked just as surprised as he was, as she sat with her mouth literally wide open.

Dr. G. nodded his head as he said, "Yes, that is very exciting news indeed. It is quite an honor to be selected for such an endeavor, Sem Sem. I will definitely need to discuss this with you in much further detail when we have a moment. However, I am just in the middle of a meeting. Can I call you back in my morning?" Dr. G. nodded as he listened to Sem Sem's voice on the other end of the receiver. "I will talk to you tomorrow, my friend. Have a good night," Dr. G. said as he hung up the phone.

Dr. G. saw the looks of shock on Edward's and Anastasia's faces as he walked back to where they sat. "Yes, Sem Sem is alive. His death was a result of the ripples wrought by the Corsairs in ancient Egypt. Your work in preventing those changes has prevented Sem Sem's death the same way you prevented the broken leg you indicated that I would have suffered," Dr. G. explained logically.

"I guess I just hadn't fully thought it through, but that's wonderful news. I know he's a close friend of yours," Anastasia said to Dr. G. with a big smile.

Edward found himself smiling as well. *We really did do good work.*

"He was just calling to let me know that he has been selected to lead an archeological survey of King Tutankhamun's tomb by the Egyptian government. The survey will search for a potential secret chamber," Dr. G. said and raised his eyebrows at the twins.

Edward felt the color drain from his face as he thought about the implications of Nefertiti's secret tomb being discovered.

"Don't worry, Edward. I will let him know in the morning that the survey cannot be allowed to be successful. He may be disappointed by the news, but that is a small matter in the grand scheme of things."

Edward looked at the clock and saw that it was almost six thirty. They were going to need to move quickly if they were going to make it home in time for dinner. They made plans to see Dr. G.

again the next day and hugged him goodbye before visiting the costumes department to have a shower and change back into their own clothes. Edward's skin bore only minor traces of the fake tan, and he was able to wash out the colored hair spray after three shampoos. It actually felt weird to put pants on again after six days of wearing something that was a lot closer to a dress. Thankfully, the details on the fake tan and dress were not something that he would ever have to share with any of his friends at school.

"Let's have a quick peek at *Eternal Life in Ancient Egypt* before we catch the bus. I can't wait to see it again after having actually been there," Anastasia said to him excitedly.

"I just can't wait to see it in one piece after the last time we saw it," Edward said, thinking of the disastrous state it was in after the attack on Dr. G.

They walked quickly through the *Live Insect Zoo*. The insects still creeped him out. There were far too many legs and far too many exoskeletons in the *Live Insect Zoo* for his liking. His squeamish feelings completely vanished as they entered *Eternal Life in Ancient Egypt*.

The hall was immaculate. There was none of the broken glass or rubble that he remembered from his last visit there. The sarcophagi that had been toppled across the floor now sat upright as part of the display of artifacts from ancient Egypt. He gazed in renewed wonder around the room. While he had always loved this hall, all of these things seemed so much more beautiful and meaningful to Edward now.

Edward's reverie was shattered when he heard Anastasia gasp loudly. She was staring across the room as if she had seen a ghost. Edward followed her line of sight and gasped himself at what he saw.

There was the bust of Nefertiti, just as they had seen in Thutmose's studio only a few days ago. Its beauty was not dimmed by the more than three millennia that had passed. Next to it, though, sat an equally stunning bust of Salah, their friend. His youthful face was lit with his ever-present smile and framed by his curly hair.

Anastasia had seen a ghost—one that brought tears to both of their eyes. They read the plaque under the exhibit when they had recovered enough from their shock. It cited these two sculptures as the seminal works of Thutmose, the Royal Sculptor of Akhenaten: *Queen Nefertiti* and an *Unnamed Boy*. While they had prevented the Corsairs from corrupting the past, Edward realized wistfully that it might be impossible not to change the past at all.

They burst through their front door at a sprint and dropped their Blake Academy backpacks in the hallway. Edward was breathing hard after running full speed from the bus stop on P Street while carrying his heavy backpack. His nose detected a rich and savory aroma permeating the air that could only mean one thing. *Lamb shanks!* He punched the air with excitement.

"I'll race you to the—" Edward started to say only to realize that Anastasia had already taken off down the hallway toward the kitchen ahead of him.

By the time he got there, Anastasia was already standing in the middle of the kitchen with her left arm around their mother and her right arm around their father. Their parents looked both bemused and confused at the same time.

Edward shouted "Family hug!" as he joined in wrapping his arms around everyone.

"We love you so much, Mom and Dad!" Anastasia told them through the crush of the family hug.

"I knew you two loved lamb shanks, but I didn't know they meant that much to you," their father said, laughing.

"Be quiet, darling. It's been a very long time since we've gotten this kind of unsolicited affection from our children. I say we just enjoy it," their mother said, hugging them back.

Later that night, Edward sat on the end of Anastasia's bed feeling happy, full, clean, and sleepy. He had to admit that the electric toothbrush and an exfoliating body scrub had him feeling like a new man.

"It almost doesn't seem real," Anastasia said, propped up on her pillows and wearing her pajamas and dressing gown.

"I know," Edward said, stifling a yawn. "Dad's never gotten the mashed potatoes right before. I don't know where that came from either."

"I was talking about how we traveled to ancient Egypt, saved the pharaoh, stopped the Corsairs, and battled a god—not the lamb shanks, Edward," Anastasia laughed.

"Yeah, that was definitely unreal too," Edward smiled sheepishly back at his sister.

Her mirth disappeared and she got serious. "You know it's not over. Dr. Augustino and the Corsairs are going to try to find us," Anastasia said, pulling her dressing gown tighter.

"I know. I don't think he's going to take the whole not-becoming-immortal thing very well," Edward agreed, nodding his head.

It made him worried too. Then he paused as he thought about what Anastasia had said before. About everything they had accomplished on their adventure. He truly wouldn't have believed it possible if they hadn't done it. He smiled at her as he said with real confidence, "We'll be ready, though. We've stopped them once. We can do it again. Plus Dr. G. and the Order will be there to help. Maybe they're sitting around the Corsairs' headquarters wondering what they're going to do about Anastasia and Edward?"

Anastasia laughed again. "I'm not sure I'd go that far, but we are a pretty awesome team. I don't know what the future or, for that matter, the past may hold for us. Whatever's in store, I know we'll do it together," she told him, smiling now, her fist extended toward him.

"Anywhere and anywhen," Edward said, bumping his fist with hers before they said good night.

The sky was unusually bright that night in Georgetown. Almost as if the sun were getting ready to rise unexpectedly early and surprise the stars. Some people thought it must have been the result of a supermoon. Others thought it might have been aliens. Regardless, peace descended on the Upstons' house, and its inhabitants slept peacefully. All was right in the world. For now.

About The Author

Scott Southall is an American author and banking executive. He grew up in the suburbs of Washington D.C. playing sports, exploring the woods behind his house, and stretching his imagination by reading any book he could get his hands on. He attended Georgetown University where he earned a degree in business.

Scott spent the first fifteen years of his career as a management consultant working with Fortune 500 companies around the world. In 2006 he changed careers and became a banker. While he loves to bank, telling stories is his true passion. The Order of Time is his debut novel.

Scott and his Australian wife Kylie live with their family in the paradise which is also known as Sydney Australia.

CPSIA information can be obtained
at www.ICGtesting.com
Printed in the USA
LVHW050030151220
674148LV00015B/2362

9 780648 695400